APPRENTICE Lord of Darkness

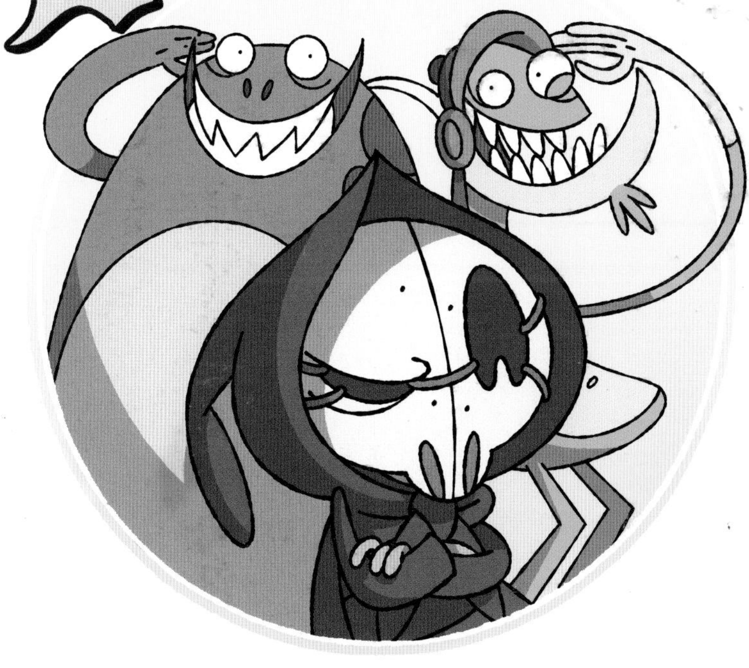

Thanks to Jean-Philippe, Alexandre, and Terry

-CED

To my three gorgeous ones, Adelia, Maeva, and Tanaquil. Thanks to Maeva, my oldest of six years, for her lovely frame illustrations. Thanks to Ced for the continued confidence in this amazing project. Thanks to Shopains, Djief, Mikaël, and Richard, for their friendship and crazy and contagious genius. Thanks to André and Damien for their invaluable help during the crazy period prior to printing. Thanks to Phoebe for her daily assistance. Thanks to Charlotte, Xavier, and Frédéric for their follow-up and extraordinary commitment to this collection. A big shout-out to Lucas, my godson, who loves "the mean guys."

-JPM

YELLOW JACKET

an imprint of Little Bee Books

yellowjacketreads.com

ISBN 978-1-4998-1274-9 (pb) 10 9 8 7 6 5 4 3 2 1 | ISBN 978-1-4998-1275-6 (hc) 10 9 8 7 6 5 4 3 2 1 | ISBN 978-1-4998-1276-3 (eb)

New York, NY | Text copyright © 2022 by Little Bee Books | Original edition © Sarbacane, Paris 2014, 2015, 2016, 2017, 2018
English language translation by Zachary R. Townsend
All rights reserved, including the right of reproduction in whole or in part in any form. | Yellow Jacket and associated colophon
are trademarks of Little Bee Books. | Library of Congress Cataloging-in-Publication Data is available upon request.
First Edition | Manufactured in China RRD 0322
This is a work of fiction. Any references to historical events, real people, or real places are used fictitiously. Other names, characters, places, and
events are products of the author's imagination, and any resemblance to actual events or places or persons, living or dead, is entirely coincidental.

For information about special discounts on bulk purchases, please contact Little Bee Books at sales@littlebeebooks.com.

APPRENTICE
Lord of Darkness

CED   MORIN

 YELLOW JACKET

Chapter 1

APPRENTICE, LORD OF DARKNESS

200 YEARS AGO, THE LAND OF ALKYLL WAS PLUNGED INTO FEAR AND DARKNESS.

BOURGVILLE, THE ONCE SPLENDID CAPITOL, WAS RUINED BY THE CONSTRUCTION OF THE TERRIBLE TOWER.

MWAHAHAHA HAHAHAHAHA!

STEARAS, THE MASTER OF ABSOLUTE EVIL, CAUSED CHAOS AND DESTRUCTION...

MWHAHA HAHAHA!

MASTER, YOU ARE LAUGHING FOR NO REASON—THAT FRIGHTENS OUR MEN!

BUT A PROPHECY CONFIRMED THAT EVIL WOULD BE DRIVEN OUT BY A HERO POSSESSING A MAGIC SWORD.

HM... I'M NOT SURE! IT'S EITHER: "HERO WITH A MAGIC SWORD"

OR: "ROSE WITH A MAGGOT'S WART!"

AND INDEED, A HERO DROVE STEARAS OUT OF THE KINGDOM!

AND DON'T COME BACK!

CENTURIES PASSED AND THINGS IMPROVED IN THE KINGDOM. SHOPS OPENED AND NEW HANDICRAFTS DEVELOPED.

COSTUMES OF ALL KINDS

IN SHORT, EVERYTHING WAS GOOD IN THE LAND OF ALKYLL. UNTIL ONE DAY...

AND WHAT ARE YOU GOING TO DO WITH THIS LOVELY MASK?

CONQUER THE WORLD! MWAHAHA!

CED-MORIN

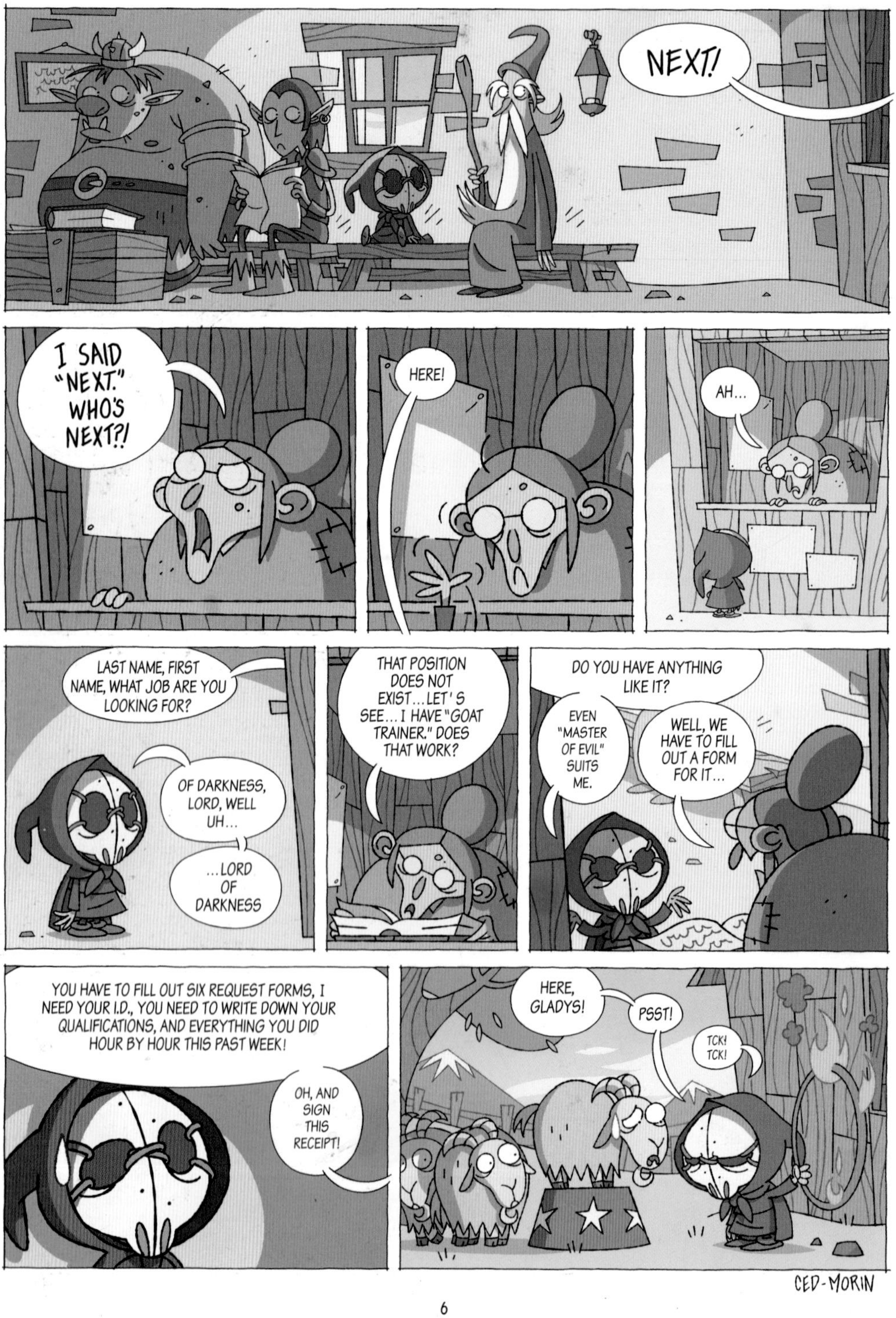
NEXT!
I SAID "NEXT." WHO'S NEXT?!
HERE!
AH...
LAST NAME, FIRST NAME, WHAT JOB ARE YOU LOOKING FOR?
OF DARKNESS, LORD, WELL UH...
...LORD OF DARKNESS
THAT POSITION DOES NOT EXIST... LET'S SEE... I HAVE "GOAT TRAINER." DOES THAT WORK?
DO YOU HAVE ANYTHING LIKE IT?
EVEN "MASTER OF EVIL" SUITS ME.
WELL, WE HAVE TO FILL OUT A FORM FOR IT...
YOU HAVE TO FILL OUT SIX REQUEST FORMS, I NEED YOUR I.D., YOU NEED TO WRITE DOWN YOUR QUALIFICATIONS, AND EVERYTHING YOU DID HOUR BY HOUR THIS PAST WEEK!
OH, AND SIGN THIS RECEIPT!
HERE, GLADYS!
PSST!
TCK! TCK!

CED-MORIN

IF YOU WANT TO BE A LORD OF DARKNESS... YOU MUST HAVE A MYSTERIOUS AND GLOOMY LAIR!

PROPERTIES FOR RENT OR PURCHASE

THIS LUXURY CASTLE HAS JUST BECOME AVAILABLE!

FOR SALE

PERFECT! I WILL CALL IT *THE CASTLE OF CHAOS!!*

AND HERE'S THE PRICE!

OH...

UH...WOULD YOU HAVE SOMETHING MORE... AFFORDABLE?

WELL, WE HAVE THIS!

MY MANOR OF MAYHEM!

RENT $10000

MAYBE SOMETHING ELSE...

THE ESTATE OF HATE?

HMM...

$

THE CABIN OF CONFLICT?

T-T-T!

FOR RENT $1500

BOX OF BADNESS

CED-MORIN

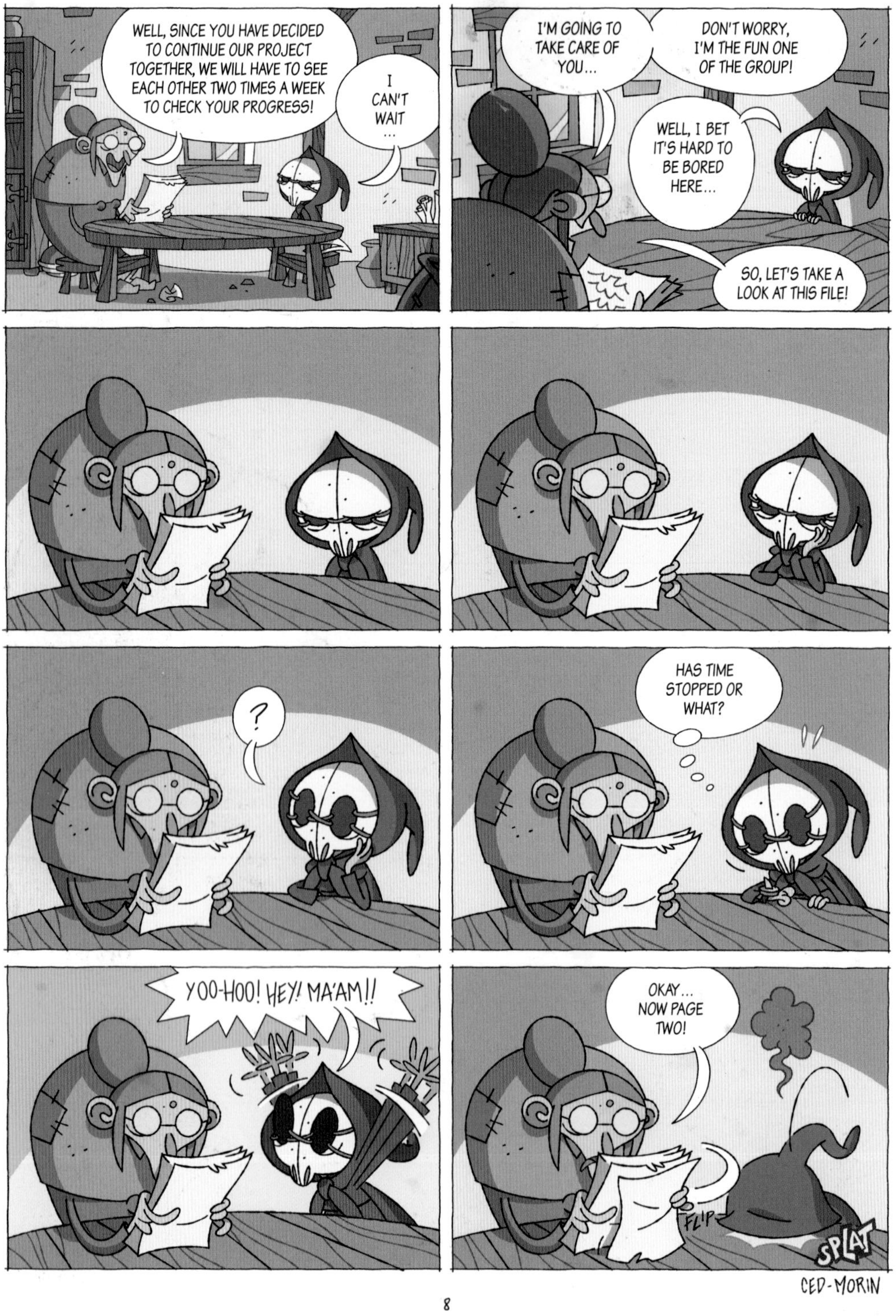
WELL, SINCE YOU HAVE DECIDED TO CONTINUE OUR PROJECT TOGETHER, WE WILL HAVE TO SEE EACH OTHER TWO TIMES A WEEK TO CHECK YOUR PROGRESS!
I CAN'T WAIT ...
I'M GOING TO TAKE CARE OF YOU...
DON'T WORRY, I'M THE FUN ONE OF THE GROUP!
WELL, I BET IT'S HARD TO BE BORED HERE...
SO, LET'S TAKE A LOOK AT THIS FILE!
?
HAS TIME STOPPED OR WHAT?
YOO-HOO! HEY! MA'AM!!
OKAY... NOW PAGE TWO!
FLIP
SPLAT
CED-MORIN

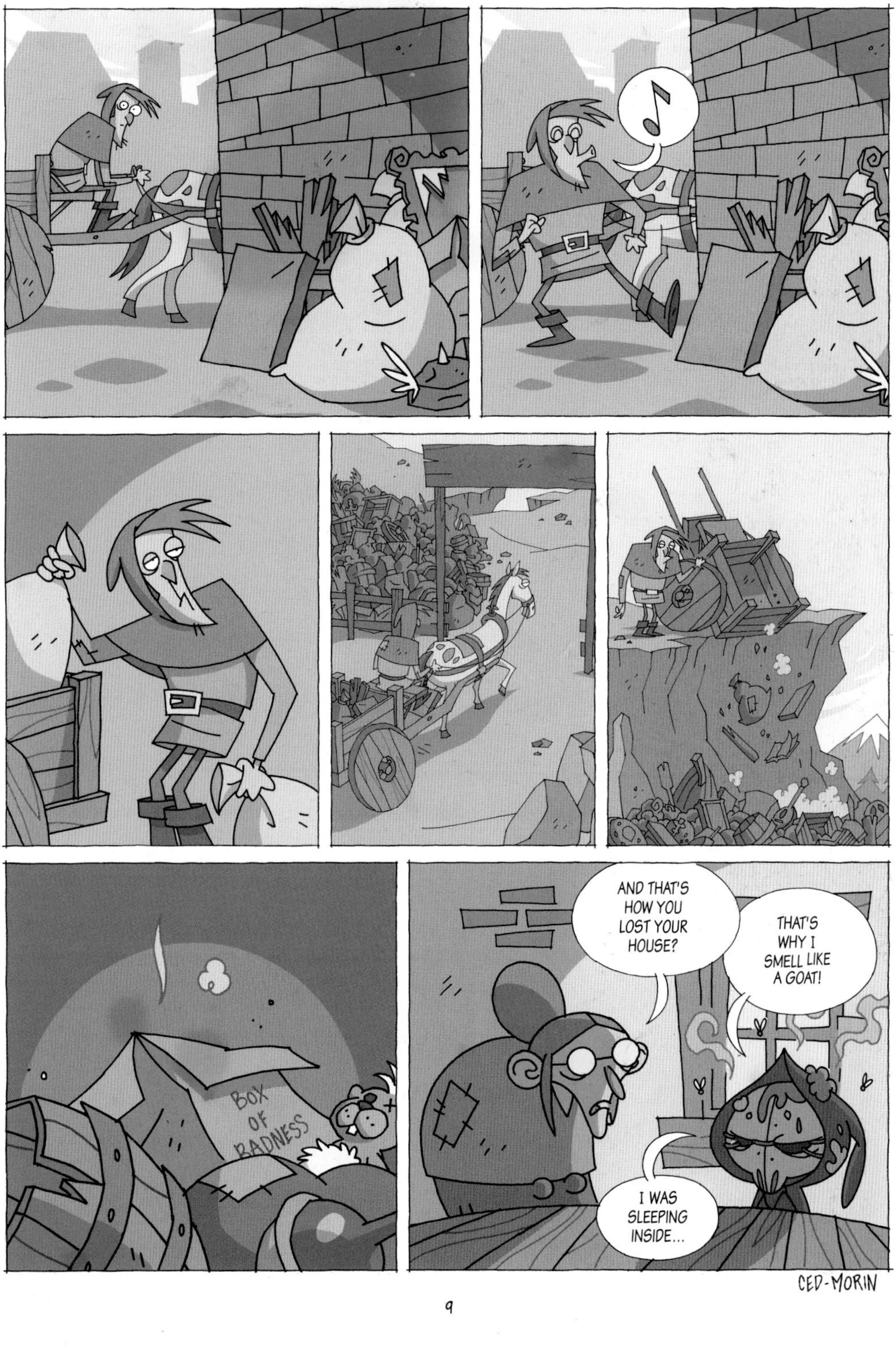
AND THAT'S HOW YOU LOST YOUR HOUSE?
THAT'S WHY I SMELL LIKE A GOAT!
I WAS SLEEPING INSIDE...
BOX OF BADNESS
CED-MORIN

OFFICE OF ORGANIZATIONS

HELLO, I'M HERE BECAUSE I SAW ON YOUR...

WELL, HELLO THERE, ARE YOU FAMILIAR WITH OUR OPERATION?

NO, BUT HONESTLY, I...

WE OFFER SPACE FOR DIFFERENT CLUBS TO MEET.

ON MONDAY IT'S MACRAME, ON TUESDAY IT'S BINGO, ON WEDNESDAY WE MAKE LITTLE HATS IN THE SHAPE OF ANIMALS...

TAP TAP

YES-YES, OKAY...

ON FRIDAY IT'S THE MATCHBOX-MAKING WORKSHOP, ON SATURDAY...

I JUST WANT TO KNOW WHAT DAY MY GROUP CAN MEET!!!

OH... THURSDAY! ON THURSDAY, IT'S AVAILABLE!

WELL, THERE YOU GO! THAT WASN'T SO HARD! SEE YOU ON THURSDAY THEN!

THE FOLLOWING THURSDAY...

I DON'T KNOW IF I TOLD YOU, BUT THE SCHEDULE CAN BE SUBJECT TO CHANGE!

NO KIDDING...

CED-MORIN

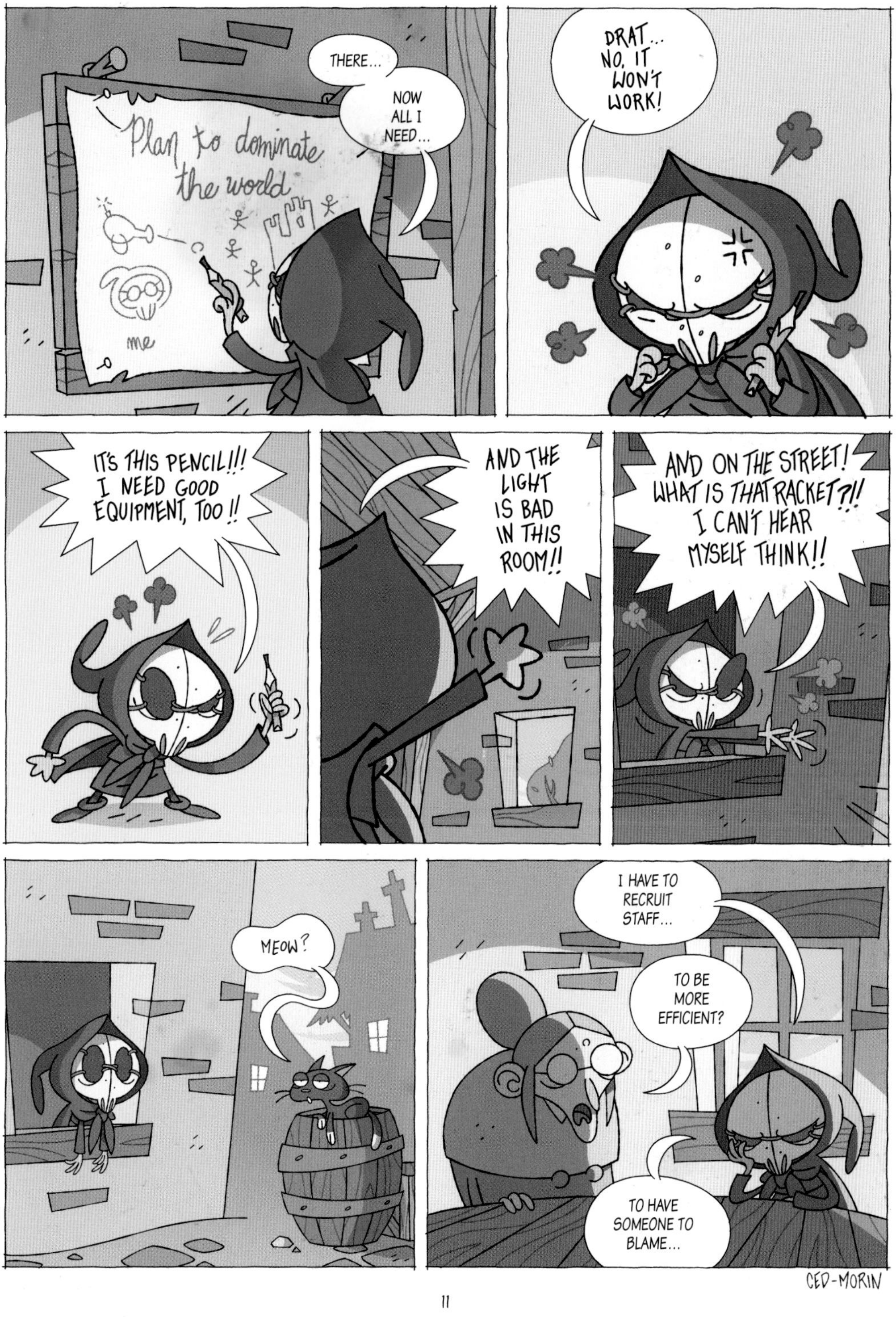
THERE...
NOW ALL I NEED...
Plan to dominate the world
me
DRAT... NO, IT WON'T WORK!
IT'S THIS PENCIL!!! I NEED GOOD EQUIPMENT, TOO!!
AND THE LIGHT IS BAD IN THIS ROOM!!
AND ON THE STREET! WHAT IS THAT RACKET?!! I CAN'T HEAR MYSELF THINK!!
MEOW?
I HAVE TO RECRUIT STAFF...
TO BE MORE EFFICIENT?
TO HAVE SOMEONE TO BLAME...
CED-MORIN

I HAVE THE PLEASURE OF INFORMING YOU THAT YOU HAVE PASSED YOUR INTERVIEW WITH FLYING COLORS.

boss's office

WAIT FOR ME IN THE HALL! I'LL CHECK YOUR QUESTIONNAIRES.

YES, SIR!

THANK YOU, SIR!

DID YOU PASS, TOO?

YES!

HOW DID IT GO FOR YOU?

IT WAS HOR-RI-BLE!

I SPILLED HIS COFFEE, I TRIED TO CLEAN IT UP, THEN I MADE HIM ANOTHER COFFEE, I TURNED IT OVER AGAIN, I CLEANED IT UP AGAIN, AND WHEN I WIPED IT UP, I SPILLED THE SOAP BUCKET ON HIM...

AND YOU?

IT WAS WORSE!

I CALLED THE BOSS "MAMA," I KNOCKED DOWN HIS DOOR WHEN I OPENED IT, AND WHEN I WAS FILLING OUT THE QUESTIONNAIRE, I MANAGED TO SET IT ON FIRE!

...

SLURP!

GONZAG!

BUT THEN, I WONDER... OF ALL THE CANDIDATES, WHY DID HE KEEP US BEHIND?

HERE WE ARE! SO I UNDERSTAND THE TWO OF YOU DON'T KNOW WHAT THE WORD "SALARY" MEANS?

CED-MORIN

AS YOU KNOW, WE SHARE THIS PLACE WITH OTHER GROUPS! OUR FIRST MISSION WILL BE TO GET RID OF THEM AND TO HAVE THE SPACE JUST FOR OURSELVES!

THIS WILL CREATE ENEMIES FOR ME, SO I NEED A BODYGUARD!

IT WILL BE YOU, GONZAG! YOU ARE A GOBLIN, A FEROCIOUS AND MOST INTELLIGENT CREATURE!

I'M A GOBLIN, AM I?

I CAN EASILY IMAGINE WHAT BATTLES AND OTHER BRAWLS YOU MUST HAVE CAUSED IN THE PAST!

ONCE, I TRIED TO SMASH A SPIDER!

BUT IT GOT THE UPPER HAND!

YOU WILL TRAIN! I ASKED SLURP TO MAKE A DUMMY THAT WILL REPRESENT MY ATTACKER...

I'VE NAMED HER MIRANDA!

WHY DID YOU DRESS HER UP LIKE A LITTLE GIRL?

I FOUND THE OUTFIT IN THE SEWING GROUP'S STUFF!

IT'S NICER!

BUT WHY WOULD A LITTLE GIRL ATTACK ME?!!

DON'T WORRY, I THOUGHT OF A SITUATION!

YOU STOLE HER SISTER'S DOLL.

CARMINA!

BY THE WAY, I CREATED HER DUMMY TO LOOK BELIEVABLE!

WH...WHAT?

AND HERE, HER MOM AND DAD, TOO!

I'M GOING TO BUY A DOLL AND WE CAN REENACT THE SCENE!

MY DOMINATION OF THE WORLD IS GOING TO BE HARDER THAN I THOUGHT...

CED - MORIN

13

AND HERE WE ARE!

WE HAVE BANNED TROLL HUNTING BY DECREE OF THE KING!

GONZAG HAS HIDDEN ALL THE BINGO CLUB PRIZES IN THE FORBIDDEN FOREST!

I INVENTED A VIRUS THAT SIMULATES ALLERGIES TO CATS! ALL THE "CAT LOVERS" HAVE FLED.

AND ABOVE ALL, WE BURNED ALL THE WOOL IN THE VILLAGE!

TO GET RID OF ALL THESE CURSED ITCHY BONNET MAKERS!

SO NOW IT'S JUST US!

NOT QUITE! ACCORDING TO MY INFORMATION, A NEW CLUB CALLED THE "TALL PLATE LOVERS" HAS JUST BEEN FORMED!

WHAT, A PLATE LOVERS CLUB?

THEY ARE MEETING IN THE NEXT ROOM!

COME WITH ME, YOU TWO!

LET'S GO YOU WRETCHED PLATE LOVERS! WE'RE TAKING YOUR PLATES AND TAKING OVER!

"TROLL WEIGHT LIFTERS"!

I VOTE WE LET THEM STAY...

CED-MORIN

14

FOR MY DIABOLICAL PLAN, I WILL NEED MONEY!

THIS IS WHY I RENTED YOU A BOOTH AT THE FLEA MARKET!

SLURP, YOU WILL BUY MERCHANDISE AND GONZAG, YOU WILL RESELL IT!

JUST LIKE THAT, WE'LL MAKE MONEY.

HERE IS SOME MONEY TO GET STARTED!

HMPH...

SO, I SELL AND YOU BUY, IS THAT IT?

OH, I KNOW! IF I SELL TO YOU THAT WILL BE FASTER!

BUT... YOU HAVE NOTHING TO SELL ME!

BUT YES I DO!

THE MONEY!

LOOK! I'LL SELL YOU THESE FIFTEEN BUCKS.

OH, UHH... SO HOW MUCH WILL I OWE YOU?

WELL, UMM... FIFTEEN BUCKS!

THIRTEEN, FOURTEEN, AND FIFTEEN!

AND THERE YOU GO, MISSION ACCOMPLISHED!

WE ARE GENIUSES!

YOU SAID IT!

CED-MORIN

DID YOU FIND SOMETHING INTERESTING?

JUST THIS BOOTH THAT SELLS CELERY ICE CREAM! EVEN I THINK THAT SOUNDS A LITTLE GROSS!

HEY! IT REALLY QUENCHES YOUR THIRST IN HOT WEATHER!

AN ICE-CREAM STAND, HUH? I SEE IT WAS A GOOD IDEA FOR ME TO BRING YOU TO THE MARKET WITH ME...AT LEAST YOU AREN'T HANGING AROUND THE USED MOP BUCKET BOOTH ANYMORE!

AS FOR ME, I FOUND A BOOK OF MAGIC SPELLS!

WITH THIS, I CAN CREATE CHAOS!

CAN I SEE?

EH, DON'T TOUCH!

HERE! "SPELL TO UNLEASH TERROR ON EARTH"! PERFECT!

KLAATU BARADA NIKTO!!

?

NOTHING!

LET'S GO BACK HOME! I HAVE TO LEARN HOW TO USE THIS SPELL BOOK...

WHO KNOWS WHAT WILL BE POSSIBLE WHEN I CAN CAST AN EVIL SPELL!

OR IF YOU READ A SPELL BACKWARD...

CELERY ICE CREAM?

IT'S DELICIOUS WHEN IT'S HOT OUT...

CED-MORIN

16

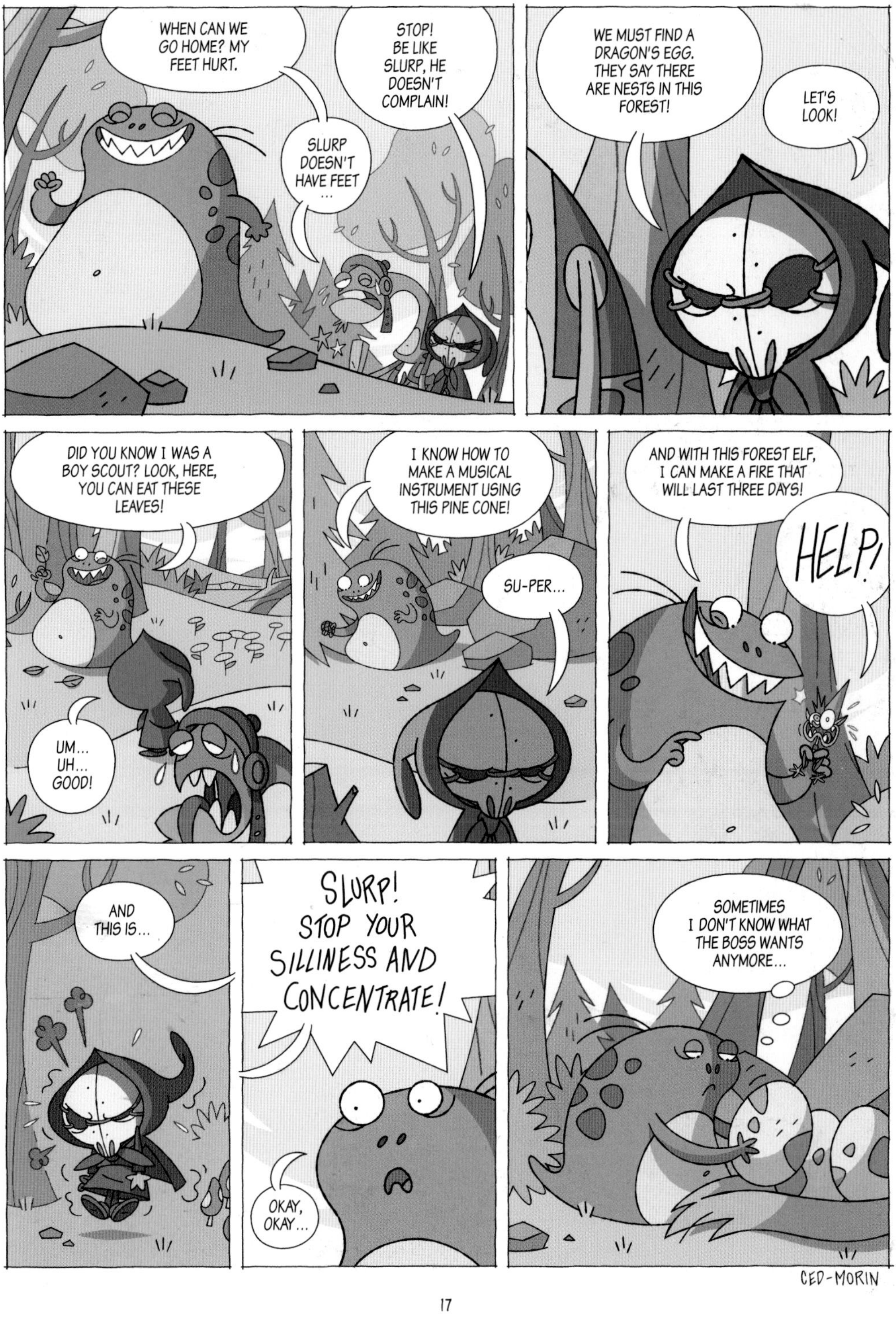
WHEN CAN WE GO HOME? MY FEET HURT.
SLURP DOESN'T HAVE FEET ...
STOP! BE LIKE SLURP, HE DOESN'T COMPLAIN!
WE MUST FIND A DRAGON'S EGG. THEY SAY THERE ARE NESTS IN THIS FOREST!
LET'S LOOK!
DID YOU KNOW I WAS A BOY SCOUT? LOOK, HERE, YOU CAN EAT THESE LEAVES!
UM... UH... GOOD!
I KNOW HOW TO MAKE A MUSICAL INSTRUMENT USING THIS PINE CONE!
SU-PER...
AND WITH THIS FOREST ELF, I CAN MAKE A FIRE THAT WILL LAST THREE DAYS!
HELP!
AND THIS IS...
SLURP! STOP YOUR SILLINESS AND CONCENTRATE!
OKAY, OKAY...
SOMETIMES I DON'T KNOW WHAT THE BOSS WANTS ANYMORE...
CED-MORIN

WHAT?! YOU FOUND A DRAGON'S EGG AND YOU DIDN'T TELL ME?!!

BUT YOU SAID...

I... I'LL SHOW YOU!

SO, THE FIRST THING WE HAVE TO DO IS DISINFECT THE EGG TO GET RID OF ALL THE SMELLS!

THIS IS HOW THE MOTHER DRAGON FINDS HER EGGS!

NEXT, I'LL WASH MY HANDS TO NOT LEAVE ANY TRACE! TAKE A TOWEL AND DO THE SAME, SLURP!

AND NOW...

LET'S SCRAM!!

THIS IS GOOD. WE ARE FAR AWAY NOW...

SAY, SLURP...

IS THAT STRAW FROM THE DRAGON'S NEST STUCK TO YOUR TAIL?

OH, LOOK, YES

HAHA! THAT'S FUNNY!

CED-MORIN

18

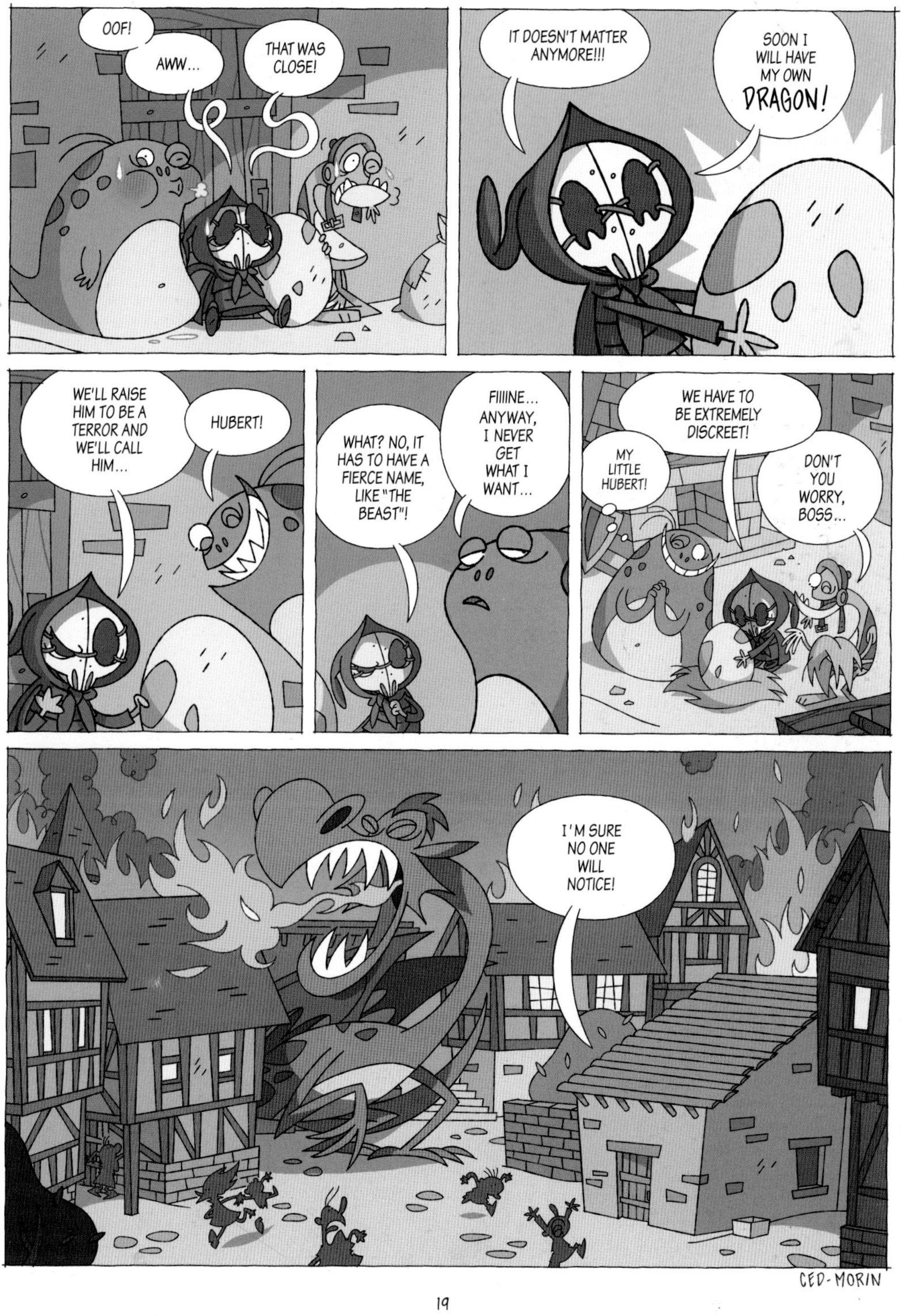
OOF!
AWW...
THAT WAS CLOSE!
IT DOESN'T MATTER ANYMORE!!!
SOON I WILL HAVE MY OWN DRAGON!
WE'LL RAISE HIM TO BE A TERROR AND WE'LL CALL HIM...
HUBERT!
WHAT? NO, IT HAS TO HAVE A FIERCE NAME, LIKE "THE BEAST"!
FIIINE... ANYWAY, I NEVER GET WHAT I WANT...
WE HAVE TO BE EXTREMELY DISCREET!
MY LITTLE HUBERT!
DON'T YOU WORRY, BOSS...
I'M SURE NO ONE WILL NOTICE!

CED-MORIN

DO I HAVE TO STAY HERE?

WE HAVE TO TAKE TURNS INCUBATING THE EGG! TODAY IS YOUR TURN!

BOSS, YOU'LL BE PROUD OF ME!!!

IT'S STRANGE, WHEN YOU SAY THAT, I FEAR THE WORST...

I FOUND A POWERFUL WIZARD WHO CAN TRAIN YOU. HE CAN MAYBE HELP YOU WITH THE SPELL BOOK!

REALLY?! WHERE IS HE?

LET'S GO RIGHT AWAY!

I BROUGHT HIM WITH ME! HE'S WAITING FOR YOU IN THE NEXT ROOM!

I KNEW HIRING YOU WAS A GOOD IDEA!

BRAVO, SLURP!

WHERE DID YOU FIND THIS WIZARD?

IN A NEWSPAPER AD!

IT SAID HE'S THE MASTER OF MAGIC!

TA-DA...

THE HANDKERCHIEF WAS IN YOUR EAR!

CED-MORIN

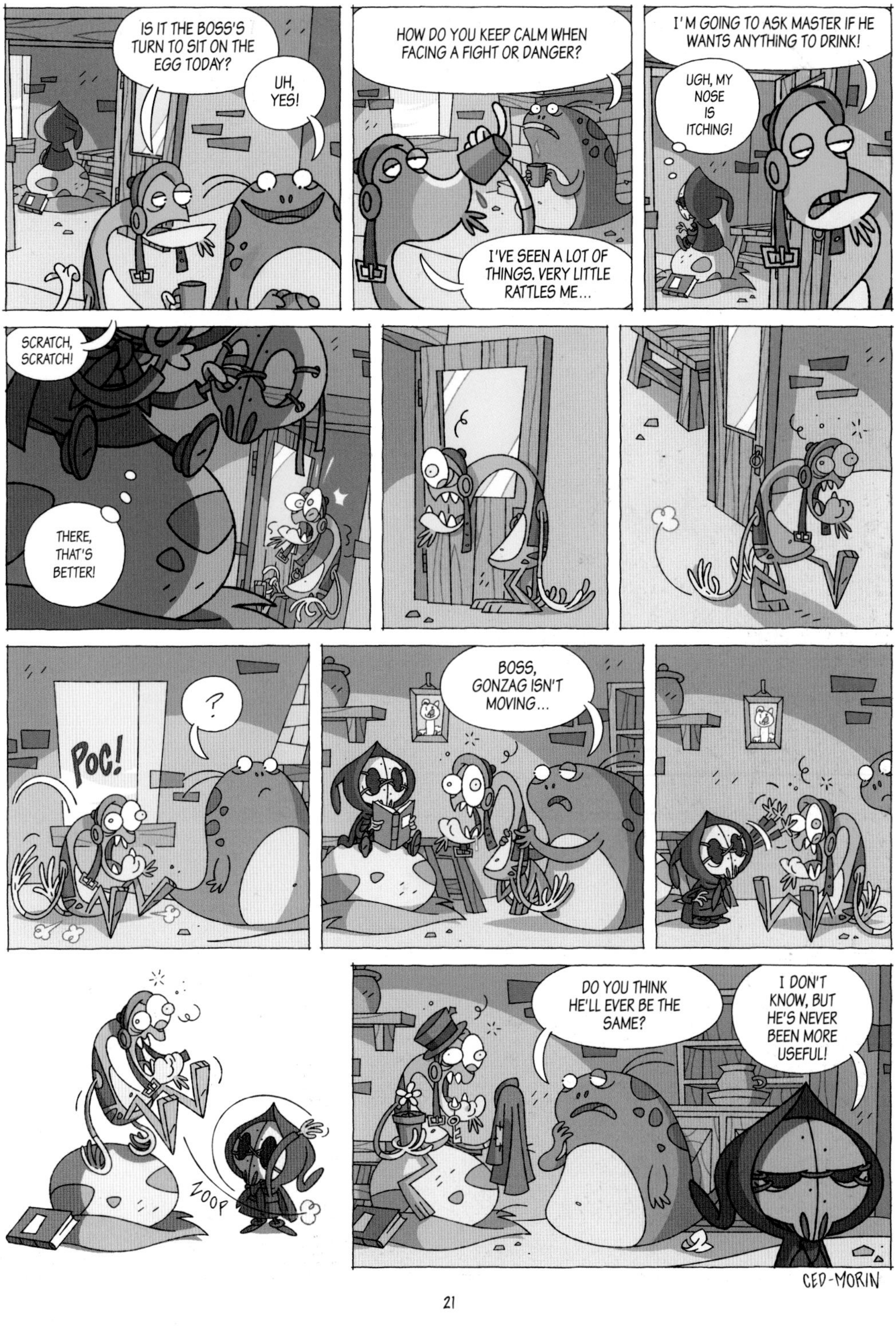
IS IT THE BOSS'S TURN TO SIT ON THE EGG TODAY?
UH, YES!
HOW DO YOU KEEP CALM WHEN FACING A FIGHT OR DANGER?
I'VE SEEN A LOT OF THINGS. VERY LITTLE RATTLES ME...
I'M GOING TO ASK MASTER IF HE WANTS ANYTHING TO DRINK!
UGH, MY NOSE IS ITCHING!
SCRATCH, SCRATCH!
THERE, THAT'S BETTER!
POC!
?
BOSS, GONZAG ISN'T MOVING...
ZOOP
DO YOU THINK HE'LL EVER BE THE SAME?
I DON'T KNOW, BUT HE'S NEVER BEEN MORE USEFUL!
CED-MORIN

GONZAG, WE'LL BE BACK IN AN HOUR! I'M COUNTING ON YOU TO KEEP THE EGG WARM!

YES, BOSS! FINE, BOSS!

I'M WARNING YOU, I DON'T WANT YOU TO LEAVE THIS SPOT! DON'T BUDGE AN INCH!

NOT EVEN A TINY BIT!

I'M WARNING YOU, GONZAG!

BLAM!

DON'T BUDGE AN INCH, DON'T BUDGE AN INCH...

OH GEEZ, I'M SO HUNGRY.

GROWL

AND THE REFRIGERATOR IS JUST A FEW STEPS AWAY...

NO, DON'T FORGET, NOT EVEN AN INCH...

BUT I'M STAAAARVING...

GRUMBLE

LET'S SEE... WHAT IS CLOSE BY THAT I CAN EAT?

...

GONZAG!!! WHAT HAVE YOU DONE TO THE EGG?!!

RELAX! YOUR BEAST ALREADY HATCHED!

I WAS JUST USING THE EGG TO EAT CEREAL OUT OF!

LOOK! HE'S RIGHT THERE.

ZZZ

CED - MORIN

22

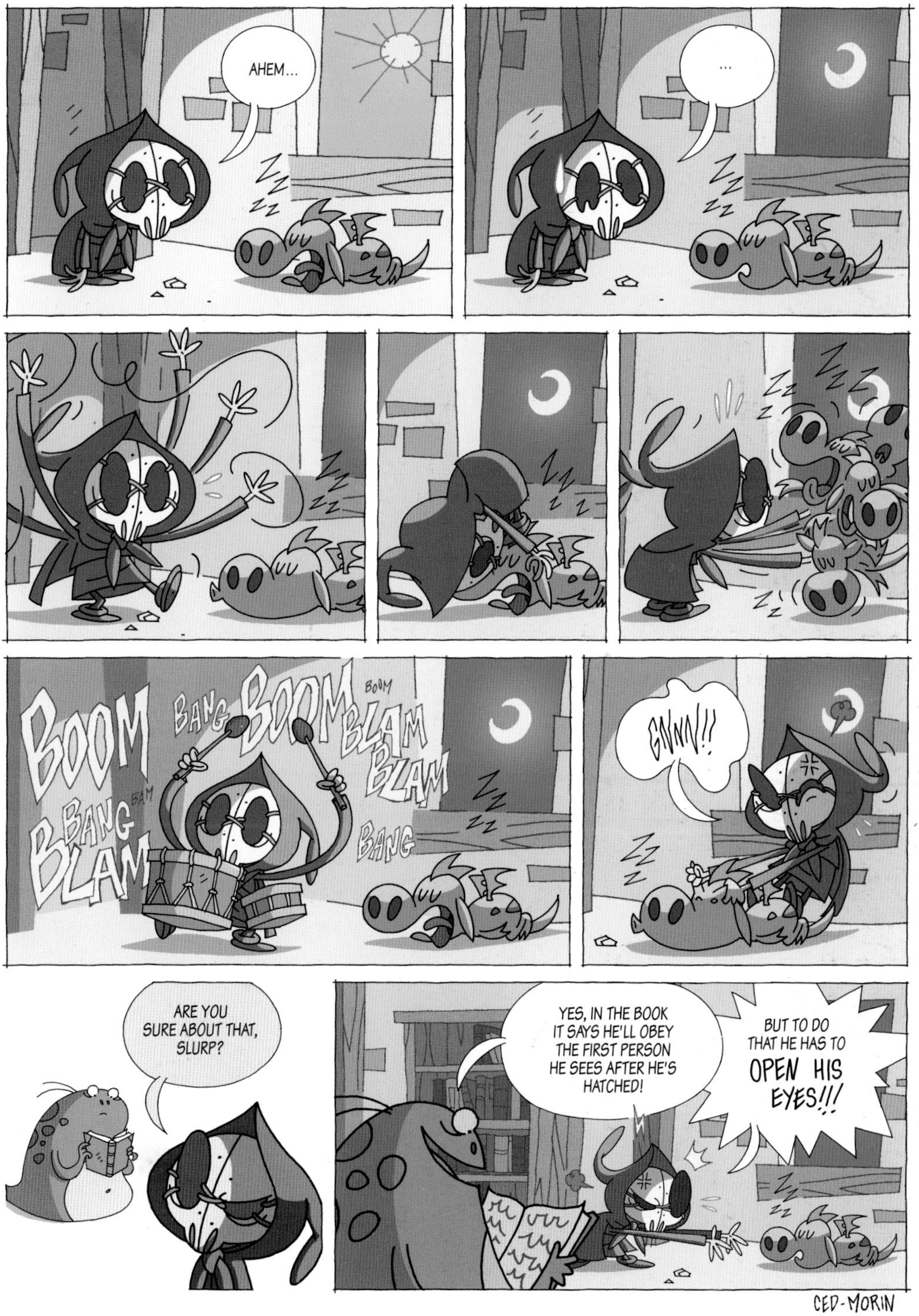
AHEM...
Z Z Z
...
BOOM
BANG
BOOM
BOOM
BLAM
BLAM
BANG
BAM
BLAM
BANG
GNNN!!
ARE YOU SURE ABOUT THAT, SLURP?
YES, IN THE BOOK IT SAYS HE'LL OBEY THE FIRST PERSON HE SEES AFTER HE'S HATCHED!
BUT TO DO THAT HE HAS TO OPEN HIS EYES!!!
CED-MORIN

DO YOU KNOW WHERE THE MASTER IS?

HE SPENT THE NIGHT TRYING TO PERFECT HIS DEATH RAY, BUT HE SAID THERE ISN'T A BUDGET TO FINISH IT...

BUT, WHAT IS THIS? ...

GAGA?

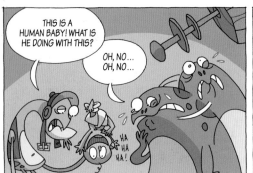

THIS IS A HUMAN BABY! WHAT IS HE DOING WITH THIS?

OH, NO... OH, NO...

HA HA HA!

IT'S THE MASTER!!!

THE DEATH RAY MALFUNCTIONED. HE TURNED BACK INTO A BABY!!

WHAT ARE WE GOING TO DO?!!

WE NEED TO REVERSE THE UH...POLARITY!

PUT THE MASTER IN FRONT OF THE MACHINE. I'M GOING TO FIND THE RIGHT SETTING!

IT MUST BE THIS ONE...

DEATH RAY | SUPER DEATH RAY | STOP!

EXCELLENT!!! GONZAG, SLURP! YOU'LL NEVER GUESS WHAT JOB I GOT TO EARN SOME MONEY!

BABYSITTING!

READY, ONE, TWO, THREE...

CED-MORIN

GOOD, NOW LET'S BEGIN OUR MEETING! IT'S TIME TO REVIEW OUR OBJECTIVES!

LET'S REMIND OURSELVES OF OUR PRIMARY MISSION: TO MAKE ME A GREAT LORD OF DARKNESS!

ANYTHING WILL DO TO ACHIEVE THIS, ESPECIALLY ANYTHING EVIL!

I CAN'T PROMISE YOU THIS WILL BE EASY! WE'LL SUFFER A LITTLE, BUT WE'LL ESPECIALLY MAKE OTHERS SUFFER!

AND FINALLY ONE DAY I'LL BE AN EVIL GENIUS FEARED BY ALL!

THERE'S JUST ONE QUESTION I HAVE BEFORE WE...

PRRR

BLBLBL

AND FOR THE LAST TIME...

STOP WATCHING THE BABY AND CONCENTRATE!!!

HAHA! HE JUST MADE A BUBBLE WITH HIS NOSE!

CED-MORIN

MASTER! COME LOOK, SLURP HAS DISCOVERED SOMETHING!

LOOK, BOSS

I GAVE HUB ...UH, THE "BEAST" THE REST OF MY CHILI FROM LAST NIGHT!

YOU MEAN THE ONE THAT WAS TOO SPICY?

IT WAS JUST RIGHT! I PUSH LIGHTLY ON HIS BELLY AND...

BURP!!

HE'S BELCHING FIRE! FINALLY!!

WE HAVE TO GIVE HIM MORE! A LOT MORE!

BOSS, BE CAREFUL!

I KNOW WHAT I'M DOING! THEN I PRESS ON HIS BELLY AND...

OKAY...

MAYBE IT WAS A LITTLE TOO SPICY...

CED-MORIN

EXCUSE ME, BUT...

DO YOU HAVE AN IDEA WHERE WE'RE GOING?

NO, NOT A SINGLE IDEA! I HAVE NO IDEA WHERE TO GO, THANKS TO BOTH OF YOU!!

WHAT? BUT IT WAS YOU WHO...

SHHHHH! HAHAHA! WHY DON'T WE GO TO YOUR PLACE, GONZAG?

WHAT, YOU WANT ME TO TAKE YOU TO MEET MY WIFE?

WELL, THEN YOU'LL KNOW WHAT A REAL LORD OF DARKNESS IS!

ALL WE NEED IS A SPACE THAT'S GOT LOTS OF ROOM, IS QUIET, AND CHEAP!

THANK YOU, SLURP, YOU'RE REALLY HELPING THINGS!

AND WHAT DO YOU THINK? A PLACE LIKE THAT REALLY EXISTS JUST UNDER OUR NOSE?

CED-MORIN

27

CREEAKk

THE TERRIBLE TOWER...

THE LAST HOME OF STEARAS, THE MASTER OF EVIL!

WHY DIDN'T I THINK OF THIS BEFORE?

IT'S DREARY, DON'T YOU THINK? DO YOU THINK IT'S HAUNTED?

NO, THE GHOSTS LEFT. THEY WERE TOO SCARED!

WH...

WHAT?!

DON'T ACT LIKE A SCAREDY CAT...

NORMALLY I'M LOYAL TO YOU! BUT I'M NOT GOING TO TAKE ANOTHER STEP AND NOTHING'S GOING TO CHANGE MY MIND!

OH? AND WHAT ABOUT THAT?

OH...

ZZZ

THANK YOU! THANK YOU!

SLURP, YOU'RE SMOTHERING ME!

HOW DID YOU CONVINCE HIM?

A CASTLE THAT HASN'T BEEN OCCUPIED FOR 200 YEARS!

FOR SLURP, IT'S LIKE HAVING A BIRTHDAY EVERY DAY!

OH, IT'S SO DISGUSTING!

CED-MORIN

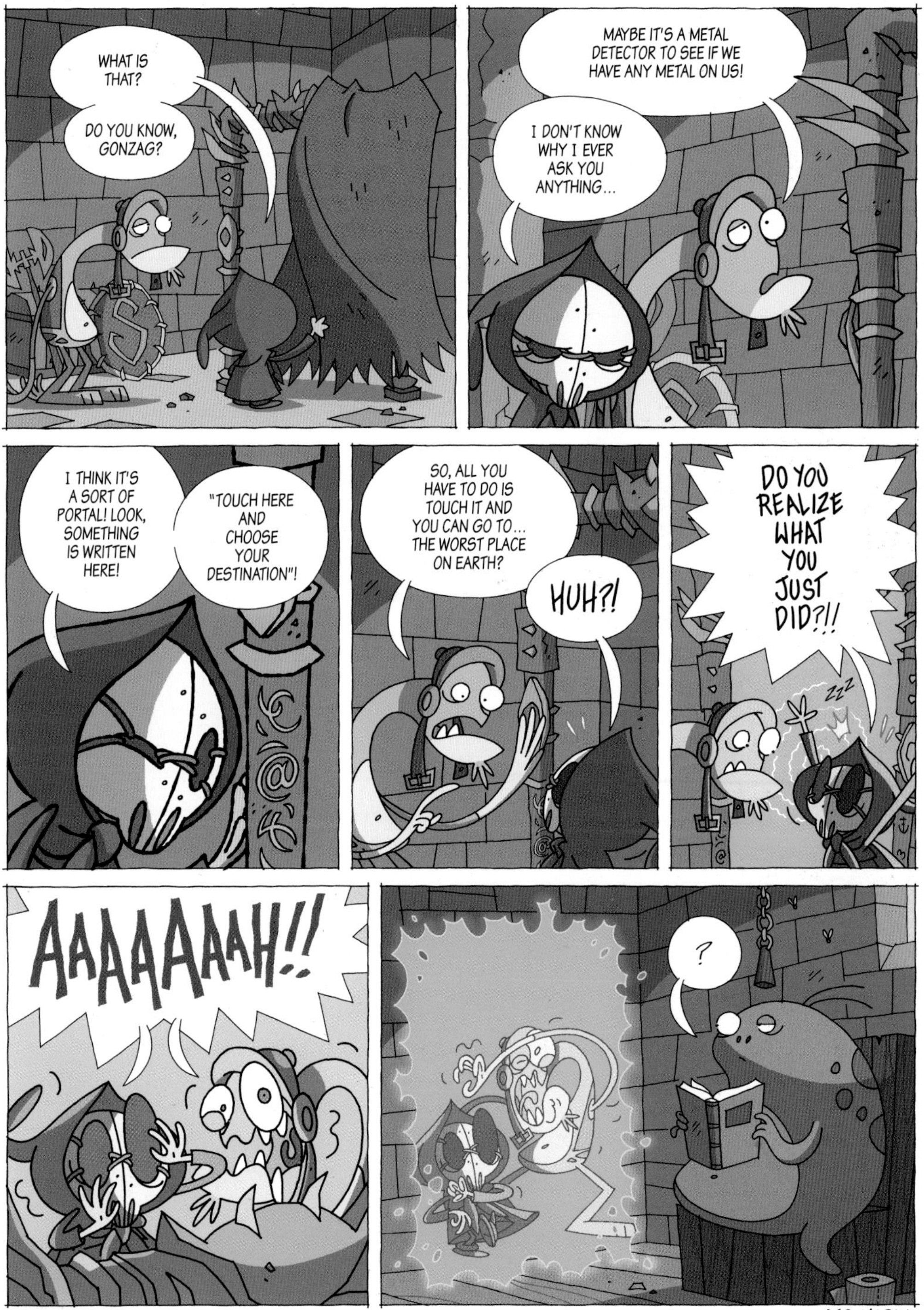
WHAT IS THAT?
DO YOU KNOW, GONZAG?
MAYBE IT'S A METAL DETECTOR TO SEE IF WE HAVE ANY METAL ON US!
I DON'T KNOW WHY I EVER ASK YOU ANYTHING...
I THINK IT'S A SORT OF PORTAL! LOOK, SOMETHING IS WRITTEN HERE!
"TOUCH HERE AND CHOOSE YOUR DESTINATION"!
SO, ALL YOU HAVE TO DO IS TOUCH IT AND YOU CAN GO TO... THE WORST PLACE ON EARTH?
HUH?!
DO YOU REALIZE WHAT YOU JUST DID?!!
ZZZ
AAAAAAAH!!
?
CED-MORIN

SO BOSS, ARE YOU HAPPY WITH YOUR NEW PLACE?

YAH, WELL...

THIS CASTLE IS SO NICE! LOTS OF ROOMS TO SCRUB! EVERY DAY THERE IS A NEW DUSTY DUNGEON!

IT'S JUST THAT... NO ONE KNOWS WE'RE HERE...

WE NEED A BIG EVENT THAT EVERYONE WILL TALK ABOUT!

WELL NOW, I THOUGHT ABOUT THAT AND...

OH! I THINK I HAVE A GREAT IDEA!

I'M SURE WE HAVE THE SAME ONE!

WE'RE GOING TO

KIDNAP THE KING'S DAUGHTER!

ORGANIZE A PAELLA PARTY!

WHAT DID YOU SAY?

"KIDNAP THE KING'S DAUGHTER!"

I SAID, "KIDNAP THE KING'S DAUGHTER!"

PSSST!

CANCEL THE GIANT PAELLA!

OH NOOOO...

CED-MORIN

DID YOU UNDERSTAND? THE MOMENT WHEN THE PRINCESS IS OUTSIDE AND NOT BEING WATCHED IS VERY SHORT!

YOU MUST BE VERY ORGANIZED!

BE QUICK AND DON'T LET ME DOWN!

LATER...

BOSS, WE'RE BACK!

BUT... IT'S THE PRINCESS!!

BUT WHAT WERE YOU EXPECTING?

YES, BUT...UH... I DIDN'T THINK YOU WOULD SUCCEED!

I DON'T KNOW... I'M WAITING FOR ANOTHER DISASTER, OR SOMETHING.

AH, NOT THIS TIME, NO!

I JUST REMEMBERED... I PULLED OUT THIS BEAM THAT WAS BLOCKING THE PATH! IT WAS AGAINST THE LARGE WALL!

CRAAASHH!

YOU KNOW WHAT? IN ONE WAY I'M RELIEVED.

HA HA! IT'S FUN HERE!

CED-MORIN

?

GENTLEMAN, I WOULD LIKE TO CONGRATULATE YOU!

I ASKED YOU TO KEEP YOUR EYES ON OUR PRISONER AND I NOTICED YOU FOLLOWED MY INSTRUCTIONS TO THE LETTER!

YOU SEE, PRINCESS! DON'T EXPECT TO BE ABLE TO ESCAPE WITH SUCH A MEAN SET OF GUARDS WATCHING YOU!

KEEP IT UP, GENTLEMEN!

OKAY, LET'S START AGAIN.

NOBODY HAS MOVED, RIGHT?

ONE, TWO, THREE, RED LIGHT!

CED-MORIN

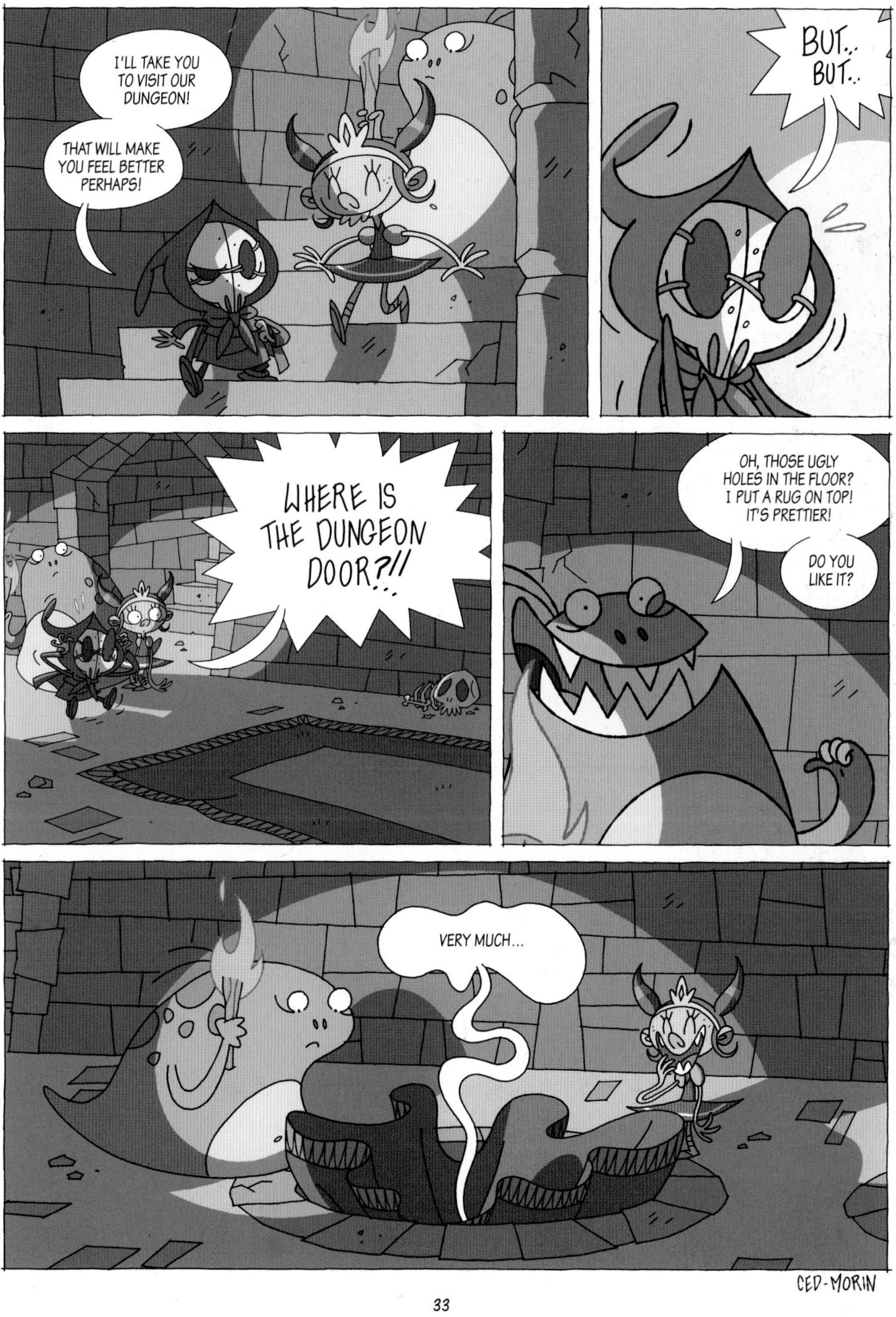
I'LL TAKE YOU TO VISIT OUR DUNGEON!
THAT WILL MAKE YOU FEEL BETTER PERHAPS!
BUT... BUT...
WHERE IS THE DUNGEON DOOR?!!...
OH, THOSE UGLY HOLES IN THE FLOOR? I PUT A RUG ON TOP! IT'S PRETTIER!
DO YOU LIKE IT?
VERY MUCH...
CED-MORIN

SHE'S BEEN OUR PRISONER FOR THREE DAYS AND NO ONE SEEMS TO HAVE NOTICED...

NOT EVEN HER!

YEEPEE!!

BOING BOING

NO CONTACT FROM THE KING...WE CAN'T EVEN ASK FOR A RANSOM...WHAT DO KIDNAPPERS NORMALLY DO?

MAYBE THEY HANG POSTERS?

YEAH...

I'M GOING TO ASK SLURP TO WATCH AFTER HER!

HE'S SICK. WHEN HE BLOWS HIS NOSE, PART OF HIM COMES OUT, SO HE WENT BACK HOME!

YOU THEN...

UH, NO, IT'S THE END OF THE DAY. I'M GOING HOME.

WH... WHAT?!

YOU'RE THE ONE WHO MADE ALL THE RULES! AND I RESPECT YOU TOO MUCH TO ARGUE WITH YOU!

GONZAG, GET BACK HERE NOW!!!

SEE YOU MONDAY, BOSS!

SLAM!

...

SO...THAT WAS POINTLESS...YOU CAN GO BACK HOME!

HUH?!

NO, NO WAY.

I'VE NEVER HAD THIS MUCH FUN!

I'M STAYING HERE!

FINE...

BUT ON ONE CONDITION!

KIDNAPPED $8000

KIDNAPPED $8000

?

KIDNAPPED

KIDNAPPED $8000

COLLE

KIDNAPPED $8000

CED-MORIN

FOLLOW US, CITIZENS! LET'S TAKE BACK THE PRINCESS!

DOWN WITH THE DEMON!!

GET RID OF THIS ABOMINATION!

AAAH... WHAT A SWEET MELODY...

KIDNAPPER!!!

THERE ARE SO MANY OF THEM. SHOULDN'T WE RUN AWAY?

BAH, THIS FORT IS IMPENETRABLE! AND BESIDES, WE HAVE OUR BOILING OIL!

FOR THE MOMENT, I'M GOING TO BASK IN MY TRIUMPH!

BOO, YOU'RE THE WORST!!

THE PEOPLE WILL HAVE YOUR HIDE!!

BUT... BUT... GONZAG?!

SLURP, GET THE OIL!

BUT WHAT ARE YOU DOING THERE, YOU BLOCKHEAD?!

OH, BOSS! I FOLLOWED THE CROWD! THEY SAID THERE WAS AN EVIL MENACE HERE!

BUT I'M THE MENACE!! YOU DIDN'T RECOGNIZE THE CASTLE?

UH, IT'S SO BIG. I THOUGHT MAYBE THERE WAS ANOTHER EVIL MENACE INSIDE!

WHAT SHOULD I DO WITH THE BOILING OIL?

STAY CALM! HIS BRAIN IS JUST SO SLOW, HE DOESN'T EVEN KNOW IT...

CED-MORIN

35

AH, SO THERE YOU ARE!

SORRY FOR THE CONFUSION, EH!

YEAH, SLURP, WHERE ARE YOU WITH THE BOILING OIL?

EVERYTHING IS GOING AS PLANNED...

BUT I CAN'T HEAR THEIR CRIES.

WELL, BOILING OIL IS REALLY BAD FOR YOUR HEALTH!

SO, I ONLY WARMED IT!

YOU MEAN YOU POURED WARM OIL ON THEM?

WELL... THAT WOULD BE VERY DIRTY... SO I PUT IN SOME WATER!

SO TO SUM UP, YOU ATTACKED THE VILLAGE BY POURING WARM WATER OVER THEM...

YES...

FLAVORED WITH A LITTLE VANILLA...

SLURP...

THAT'S NOT REALLY WHAT I WAS HOPING FOR...

DON'T WORRY, MASTER! I PUT IN SOME SOAP TO BURN THEIR EYES!

YOU'LL SEE, IT WILL REALLY BE IRRITATING!

CED-MORIN

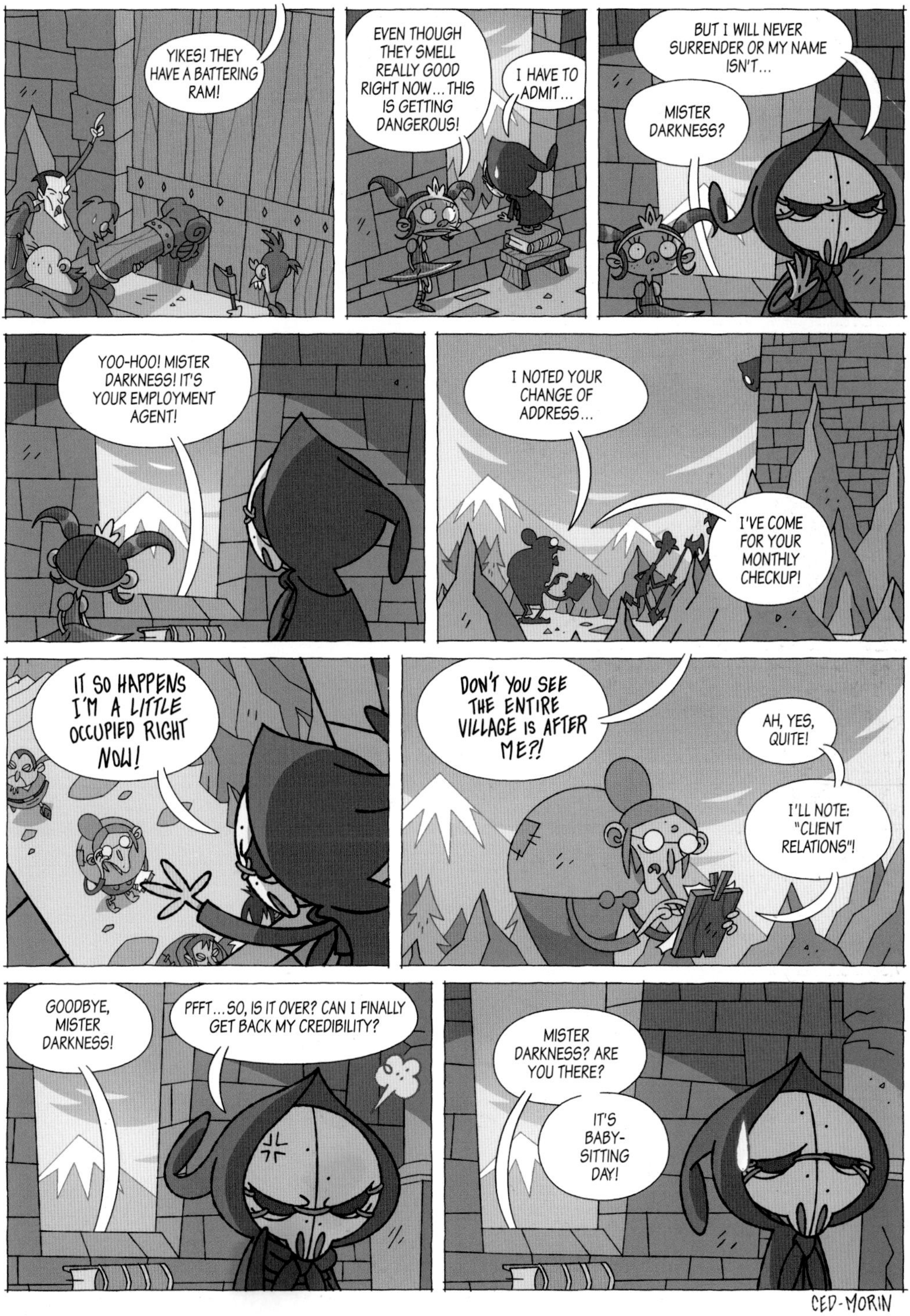
YIKES! THEY HAVE A BATTERING RAM!
EVEN THOUGH THEY SMELL REALLY GOOD RIGHT NOW... THIS IS GETTING DANGEROUS!
I HAVE TO ADMIT...
BUT I WILL NEVER SURRENDER OR MY NAME ISN'T...
MISTER DARKNESS?
YOO-HOO! MISTER DARKNESS! IT'S YOUR EMPLOYMENT AGENT!
I NOTED YOUR CHANGE OF ADDRESS...
I'VE COME FOR YOUR MONTHLY CHECKUP!
IT SO HAPPENS I'M A LITTLE OCCUPIED RIGHT NOW!
DON'T YOU SEE THE ENTIRE VILLAGE IS AFTER ME?!
AH, YES, QUITE!
I'LL NOTE: "CLIENT RELATIONS"!
GOODBYE, MISTER DARKNESS!
PFFT... SO, IS IT OVER? CAN I FINALLY GET BACK MY CREDIBILITY?
MISTER DARKNESS? ARE YOU THERE?
IT'S BABY-SITTING DAY!
CED-MORIN

I KNOW THIS IS WHAT YOU WANTED, BUT I THINK WE'RE FINISHED, BOSS...

MAYBE I WENT A LITTLE TOO FAR ...

FINE, LET'S HAND HER OVER. AT LEAST WE HAD OUR MOMENT...

STOP EVERYTHING! STOP THE SIEGE!

?!

IT'S THE PRINCESS! SHE'S SAFE AND SOUND!

WAVE GOODBYE TO THE PRINCESS!

WAVE GOODBYE, BABY!

HE'S KIDNAPPED A BABY! GET HIM!!

SLURP ...

SAY HELLO TO THE CRYING MASTER!

SAY HELLO!

CED-MORIN

BOOM BOOM

THE DOOR WON'T HOLD MUCH LONGER!

MASTER, I HAVE A FUNNY FEELING IN MY HEAD...

OH!

IT'S AN IDEA!!!

GONZAG! WHERE ARE YOU GOING?

LET'S GO, MAGIC PORTAL!

HELP US GET OUT OF HERE! ANYWHERE!

DRAT!

WHY DOESN'T IT WORK?!!

GONZAG! I NEED YOU HERE!

I'M COMING!

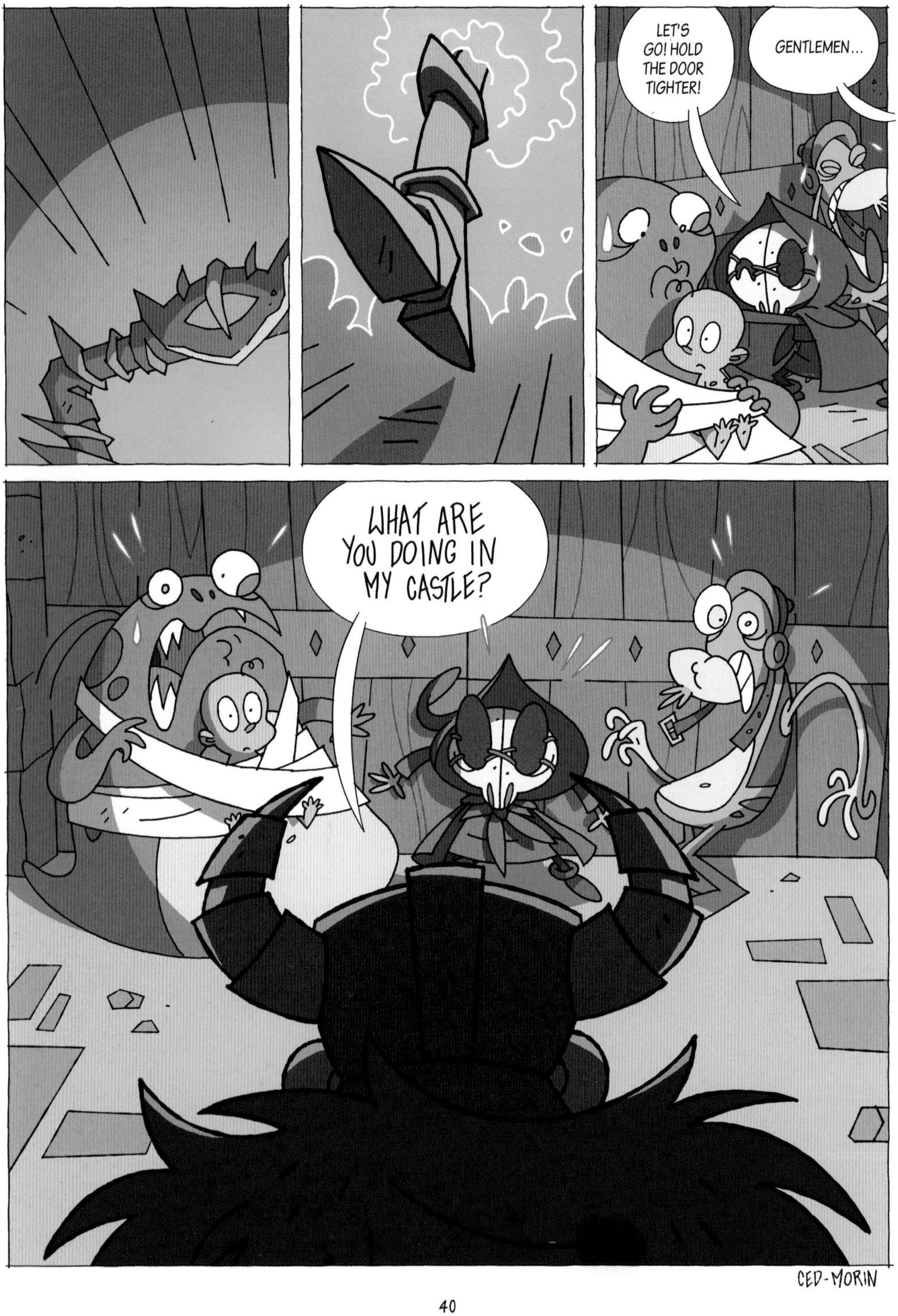
LET'S GO! HOLD THE DOOR TIGHTER!
GENTLEMEN...
WHAT ARE YOU DOING IN MY CASTLE?
CED-MORIN

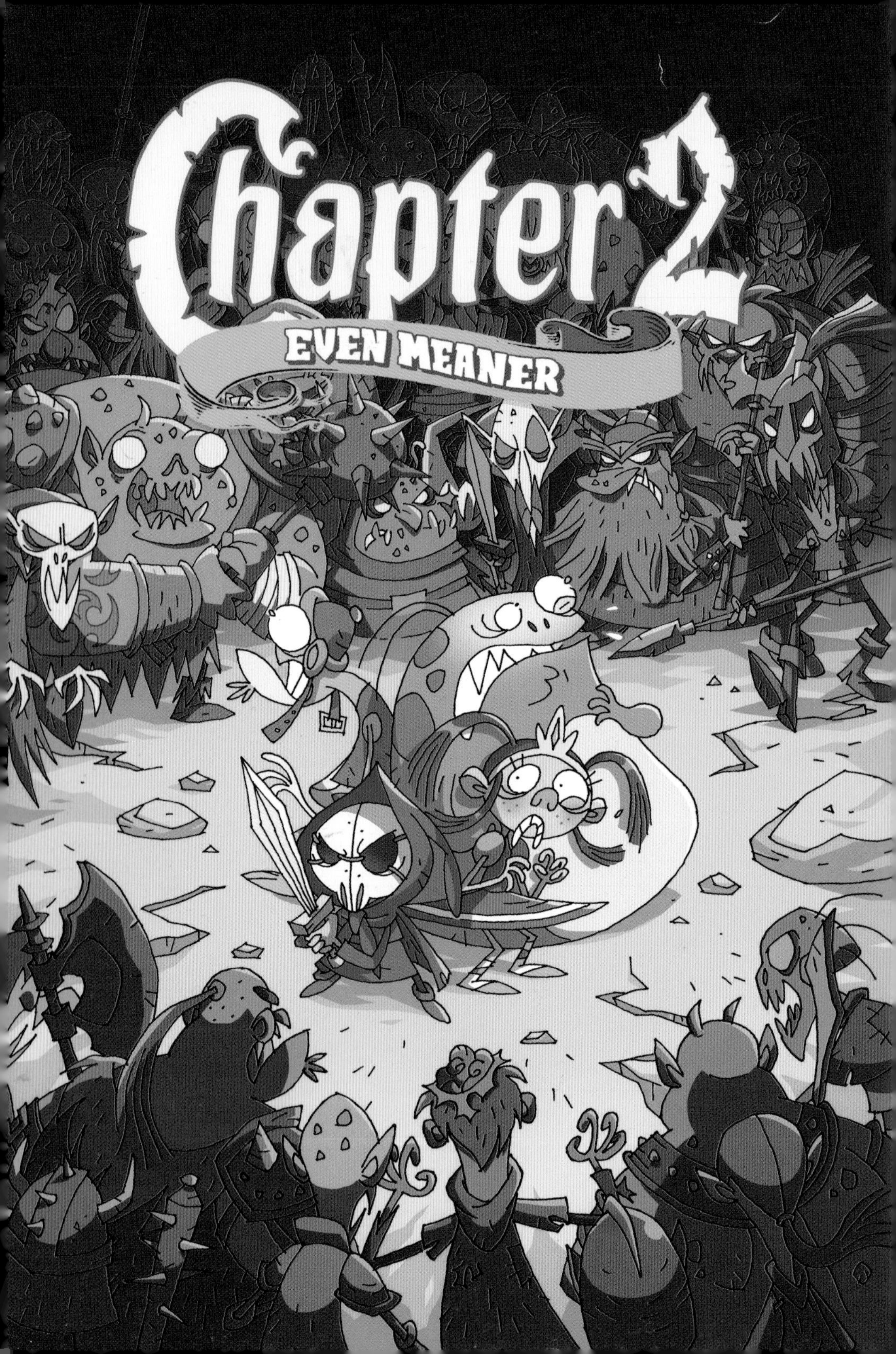
Chapter 2
EVEN MEANER

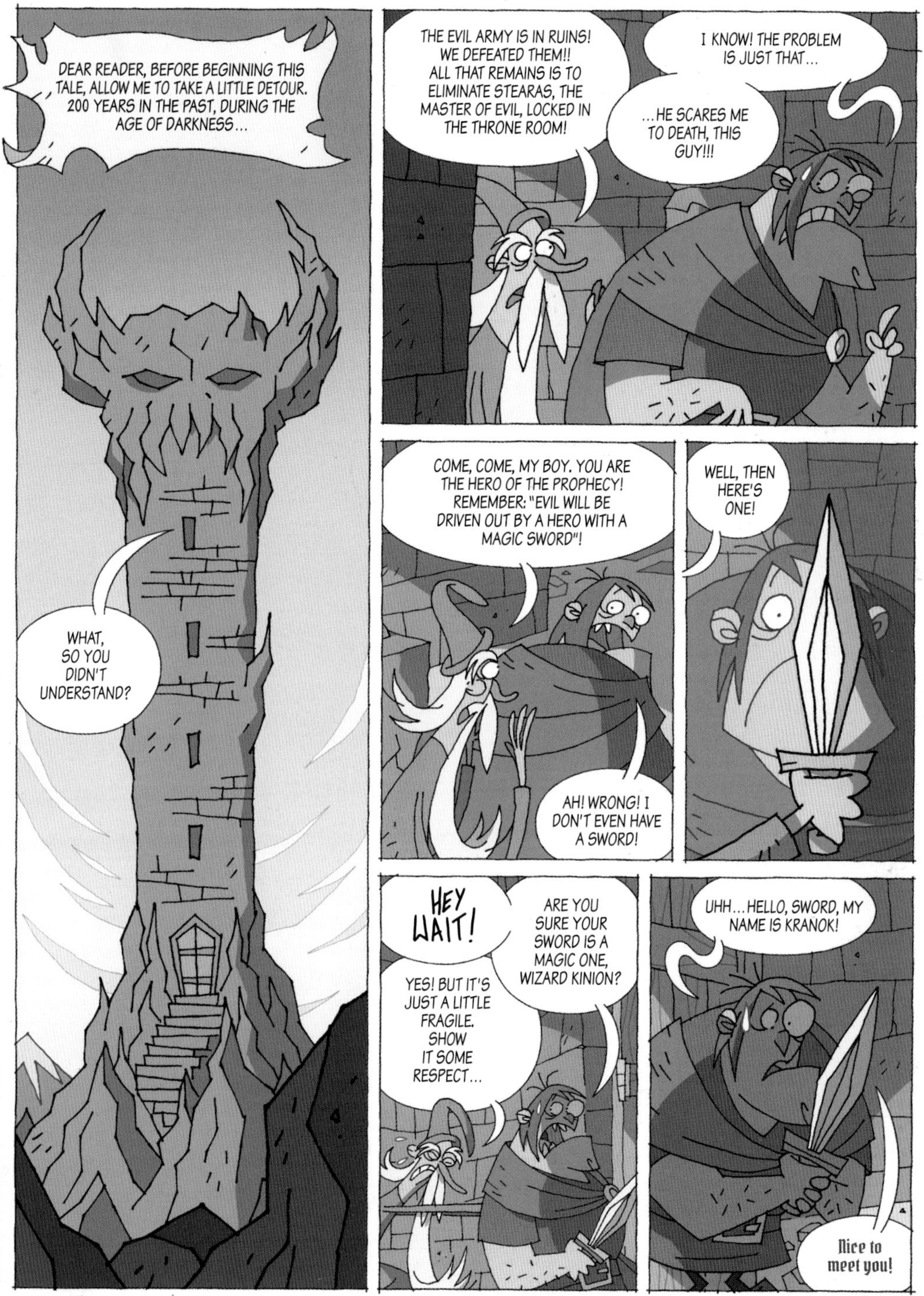

DEAR READER, BEFORE BEGINNING THIS TALE, ALLOW ME TO TAKE A LITTLE DETOUR. 200 YEARS IN THE PAST, DURING THE AGE OF DARKNESS…
WHAT, SO YOU DIDN'T UNDERSTAND?
THE EVIL ARMY IS IN RUINS! WE DEFEATED THEM!! ALL THAT REMAINS IS TO ELIMINATE STEARAS, THE MASTER OF EVIL, LOCKED IN THE THRONE ROOM!
I KNOW! THE PROBLEM IS JUST THAT…
…HE SCARES ME TO DEATH, THIS GUY!!!
COME, COME, MY BOY. YOU ARE THE HERO OF THE PROPHECY! REMEMBER: "EVIL WILL BE DRIVEN OUT BY A HERO WITH A MAGIC SWORD"!
AH! WRONG! I DON'T EVEN HAVE A SWORD!
WELL, THEN HERE'S ONE!
HEY WAIT!
ARE YOU SURE YOUR SWORD IS A MAGIC ONE, WIZARD KINION?
YES! BUT IT'S JUST A LITTLE FRAGILE. SHOW IT SOME RESPECT…
UHH… HELLO, SWORD, MY NAME IS KRANOK!
Nice to meet you!
CED-MORIN

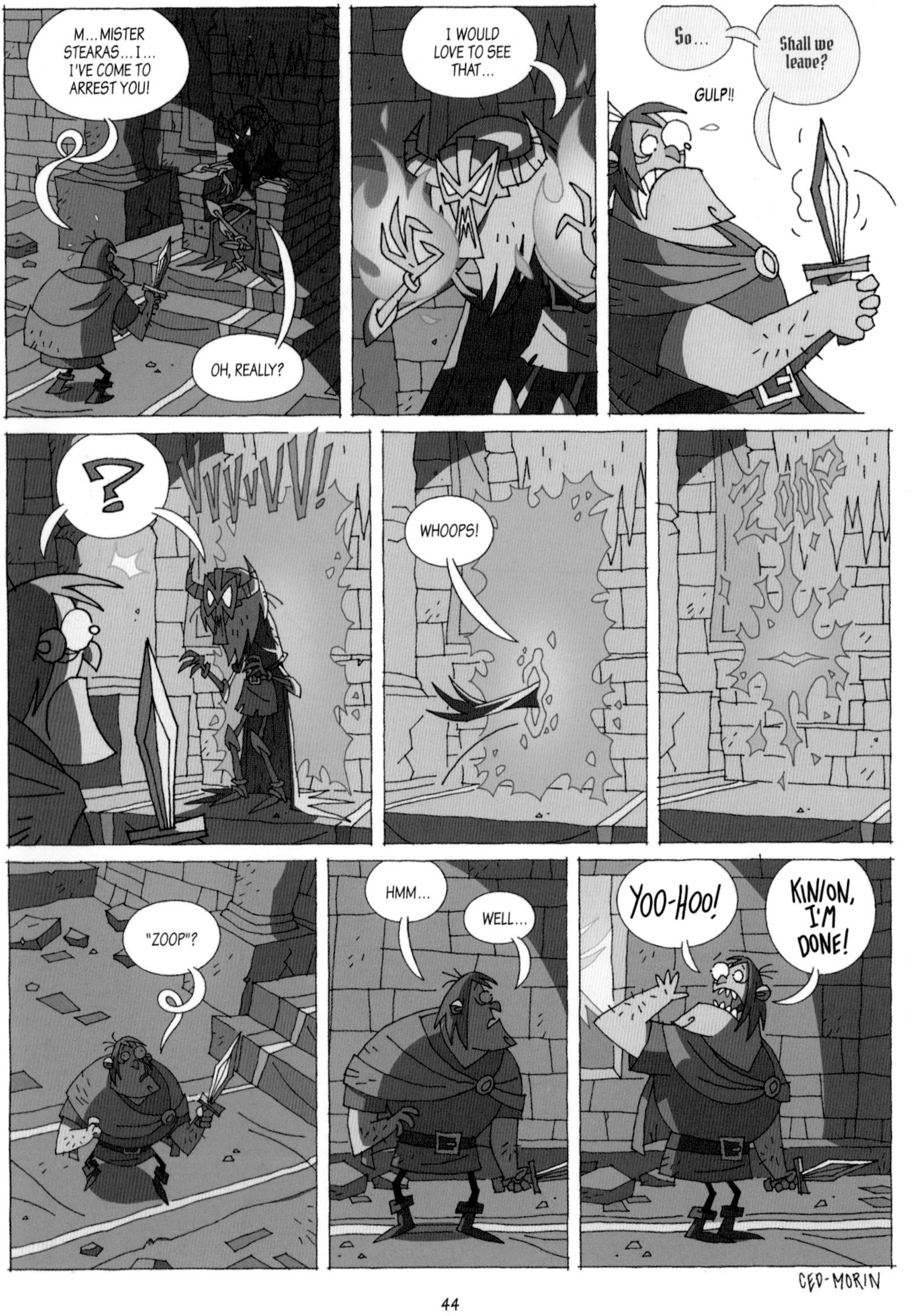
M... MISTER STEARAS... I... I'VE COME TO ARREST YOU!
WAAAAM
OH, REALLY?
I WOULD LOVE TO SEE THAT...
So...
Shall we leave?
GULP!!
?
VvvvvvV!
WHOOPS!
ZOOP
"ZOOP"?
HMM...
WELL...
YOO-HOO!
KIN/ON, I'M DONE!
CED-MORIN

BOSS, THE ANGRY CROWD IS AFTER US!

THE DOOR WON'T HOLD LONG!

BOOM BOOM

THERE ARE TOO MANY OF THEM...

GENTLEMEN, WHAT ARE YOU DOING IN MY CASTLE?

STEARAS?!

BUT HOW CAN YOU BE HERE?

MASTER, IT'S GOING TO GIVE WAY! IT'S THE END...

THE TIMING IS PROBABLY WRONG, BUT...

CAN I ASK YOU FOR AN AUTOGRAPH?

CED-MORIN

BOOM

WE'RE THROUGH!!

BY THE GODS!!

IT'S STEARAS!!

HE'S COME BACK!!!

RUN!!

FORGET THE PIPSQUEAK!

HEY!

I AM ENTITLED TO RESPECT!

COME BACK HERE AND FACE ME! THAT'S AN ORDER!!

CED-MORIN

HEY, YOU!

THE SHORTY, THERE!

HEEE! HE'S TALKING TO ME!

WHAT YEAR IS THIS?

UH...200 YEARS AFTER YOU DIED!

I SEE, EVERYONE THOUGHT I WAS DEAD ALL THIS TIME!

SAY, SLURP! WHO IS THIS?

HE IS OUR MASTER! HE HIRED US AS HENCHMEN, WE HAVE BEEN WORKING FOR HIM FOR MONTHS!

NO—NOT HIM, THE OTHER ONE!

STEARAS! HE WAS THE LORD OF EVIL HERE FOR CENTURIES! THE BOSS IS HIS BIGGEST FAN!

HMMM... I MUST BUILD AN ARMY!

OH, I BEG YOU! TAKE ME! I WON'T LET YOU DOWN!!!

I AM LIKE YOU! EVERYONE FEARS AND HATES ME!

AH, MISTER DARKNESS, I'VE COME TO GET MY SON. THANKS FOR LOOKING AFTER HIM!

HERE IS A LITTLE SOMETHING FOR BABY-SITTING!

...

IS THERE ANY CHANCE WE CAN PRETEND THAT DIDN'T HAPPEN?

SLAM!

I GUESS NOT...

CED-MORIN

WOW...

YOUR IDOL JUST SLAMMED THE DOOR IN YOUR FACE!

SO, DOES THAT MEAN THAT WE ARE EXPELLED FROM THE CASTLE?

YES...BACK ON THE STREET AND WITHOUT A PLAN!

BUT IT'S NOT A BIG DEAL, BECAUSE THE MASTER ALWAYS HAS AN IDEA!! RIGHT?!

YOU WILL FIND A NEW HIDEOUT, AND WE WILL START MAKING SECRET PLANS TO DOMINATE THE WORLD!!

AND THEN, WE'LL WAKE UP HUB...UH...THE BEAST, AND HE'LL BECOME A REAL MONSTROUS DRAGON AND EVERYTHING, RIGHT?

AND THEN, YOU CAN EVEN SEND US ON A MISSION!

WHAT DO YOU WANT US TO DO FOR YOU, MASTER?

WHAT ARE YOUR ORDERS?!

I WILL NOT GIVE YOU ANY MORE ORDERS!

I GIVE UP!

UGGH...

GO HOME!

YES, MASTER!

AS YOU SAY, MASTER!

CED·MORIN

EMPLOY-MENT AGENCY

SO, MISTER... LORD OF DARKNESS!

WHERE ARE YOU LIVING NOW?

NOWHERE! I GIVE UP!

COME NOW, WHAT HAPPENED?

THE LAST TIME WE SAW EACH OTHER IT WASN'T GOING TOO BADLY FOR YOUR BUSINESS OF...UH...

...ABSOLUTE EVIL!

THINGS HAVE CHANGED! ANOTHER MUCH MORE POWERFUL MASTER OF EVIL RETURNED AND TOOK MY PLACE!

AND HE'S SO...FIENDISH! I'M NOTHING COMPARED TO HIM...

PERSONALLY, I FIND A LITTLE COMPETITION NEVER HURTS! IT CHALLENGES YOU TO DO EVEN BETTER!

?

WAIT!...YOU'RE RIGHT, HE'S JUST A COMPETITOR!

A COMPETITOR WHO IS 200 YEARS BEHIND! AND I AM MODERN!

I WILL BE BETTER THAN HIM! AN EVEN GREATER LORD OF DARKNESS!

AND ALL WILL BOW TO ME! MWAHAHA!

THANK YOU! THANK YOU VERY MUCH!

THINK NOTHING OF IT...

IT FEELS GOOD WHEN YOU MANAGE TO MOTIVATE A YOUNG PERSON!

CED-MORIN

LET'S GO, CHILDREN. IT'S BEEN FUN, BUT I HAVE TO GO!

OOOH...

A LITTLE LONGER, PAPA!

I WOULD LIKE TO, KIDS, BUT DADDY HAS TO GO TO WORK!

SO, THE VACATION IS OVER, GONZAG?

UH, YES, PRISCILLA! THE MASTER HAS RETURNED TO WORK. HE NEEDS US!

TOO BAD... IT'S TRUE THAT YOU ANNOY ME A LITTLE SOMETIMES... BUT I LIKE HAVING YOU AT HOME WITH US...

DON'T FORGET YOUR LUNCH!

GOOD LUCK!

THANK YOU!

BIZ

HEY, WHAT'S THAT?

the master

BURP!

GONZAG...

YOU LEFT SOME "WORK" AT HOME...

?

CED-MORIN

50

LOOKS LIKE STEARAS IS RECRUITING...

MMM...

DID YOU SEE THIS? THERE'S STILL ONE POSTER FROM WHEN WE KIDNAPPED THE KING'S DAUGHTER!

WE WERE PRETTY FED UP WITH HER, HUH?!

AND RIGHTLY SO! OUR NEXT STEP IS TO FIND A NEW HIDEOUT, AND I KNOW WHO IS GOING TO HELP US!

WHO'S THAT?

KIDNAPPED

THE POSTER PRINTER?

...

WAIT, IT'S A KIND OF RIDDLE! THE POSTERS ARE MADE OF PAPER, THE PAPER COMES FROM THE TREES... SO, UH...

THE ARBORIST?

THE PRINCESS! THE PRINCESS WILL HELP US !!!

AAAH... OKAY, YOU SHOULD HAVE SAID SO!

YES, YOU ARE RIGHT! I SHOULDN'T JOKE WITH THE TWO OF YOU ANYMORE!

I HAD FORGOTTEN HOW YOU SAP MY ENERGY!

OH, I KNOW!

THE PRINCESS!

OED-MORIN

51

HERE !S THE ROYAL CASTLE!

AND AT THE TOP, THE PRINCESS'S ROOM!

FROM NOW ON, THERE'S JUST ONE IMPORTANT WORD: SUB-TLE-TY!

WE MUSTN'T BE SPOTTED! LET'S THROW SMALL PEBBLES!

EASY...

TINK

TINK
TINK
TINK

"The man with the axe spotted George at the end of the street. It was dark."

TINK

SHE DOESN'T SEEM TO NOTICE!

LET'S THROW SOMETHING BIGGER!

"George then made the connection: all those people who had their heads recently cut off ... But it was too late, the man with an axe slowly approached and ..."

AAAAAH!

WHAT ARE YOU DOING?!!

PRINCESS, COULD I TALK TO YOU?

WITHOUT DRAWING ATTENTION FROM THE GUARDS?

YES, CLIMB UP. I'LL THROW YOU A ROPE...

CED-MORIN

DO YOU WANT ME TO FIND YOU A ROOM IN THE CASTLE?

I GUESS I CAN HIDE YOU IN MY ROOM! IT WILL BE FUN!

PRINCESS, I...

BONK!

BUT I WANT SOMETHING IN RETURN!

WHAT?

PRINCESS?

BONK!

I WANT TO OFFICIALLY BE PART OF YOUR GROUP! AND IT'S NOT NEGOTIABLE...

PRINCESS, WE...

BONK!

YOU UNDERSTAND THAT I WANT TO BECOME THE MASTER OF THIS KINGDOM...DESPITE YOUR FATHER!

OH, YES, I KNOW! TOO BAD FOR HIM. HE SHOULDN'T HAVE LOCKED ME IN HERE!

PRIN... BONK!

EXCELLENT! PRINCESS, YOU ARE NOW IN THE GROUP!

SORRY PRINCESS, ARE YOU OKAY? I THOUGHT I HEARD A NOISE?!

BONK!

WELL NOW, WE'RE GOING TO HAVE TO FIGURE OUT WHAT TO DO WITH ALL THESE GUARDS...

CED-MORIN

SO, DO YOU UNDERSTAND? YOU CAN STAY HERE, AS LONG AS NO ONE SEES YOU!

EVEN IF STEARAS IS MY FATHER'S ENEMY, HE HAS NOT FORGOTTEN THAT YOU KIDNAPPED ME!

GONZAG, I WILL SHOW YOU A SECRET PASSAGE TO REACH THE VILLAGE WHEN YOU LEAVE TO GO HOME!

GREAT! I LOVE SECRET STUFF!

DON'T WORRY, PRINCESS, WE WILL BE AS DISCREET AS...

WAIT! WHERE DID THE DRAGON GO?

HE NEVER MOVES, AND HE CHOOSES THIS MOMENT TO LEAVE?!!

YOU TWO, YOU TAKE CARE OF HIM ALL THE TIME! WHERE COULD HE HAVE GONE?

TO THE STABLES? HE LIKES ANIMALS...

OR TO THE KITCHEN?

AH? TODAY WE WERE SERVED STUFFED HOT PEPPERS!

HOT PEPPERS?! DO YOU KNOW WHAT SPICY FOOD DOES TO HIM?!

FWROOOOM!!

WELL...

THE GOOD NEWS IS WE KNOW WHERE HE IS!

CED-MORIN

THE MONSTERS THROUGHOUT THE LAND CONTINUE TO JOIN STEARAS!

WHAT A PITY HE DIDN'T CHOOSE ME!

WE ARE SO MUCH ALIKE, HE AND I!

LIKE ME, HE WANTS TO CONQUER THE KINGDOM!

LIKE ME, HE IS AN EVIL GENIUS!

LIKE ME, HE IS A POWERFUL SORCERER...

AND I, LIKE HIM, STUDY MAGIC!

HE HAS A CASTLE...

I, TOO, HAVE A CASTLE!

AT LEAST, I LIVE IN ONE...

HE IS SURROUNDED BY FORMIDABLE GUARDS...

AND I...

HE ALSO WEARS A MASK ...

GED-MORIN

OKAY, LET'S GET TO WORK...

LET'S RECAP WHAT I KNOW ABOUT MY ENEMY!

STEARAS HAS SETTLED AT THE TOP OF THE TERRIBLE TOWER!

A STRATEGICALLY STRONG LOCATION!

HERE ARE HIS GUARDS, PROTECTING THE DOOR 24 HOURS A DAY!

HMM... I HAVE TO STUDY THEIR MOVEMENTS...

SAY, YOUR MANSION IS VERY NICE!

THANK YOU! IT JUST SO HAPPENS I'M GIVING A RECEPTION TONIGHT. YOU SHOULD COME!

OH NO, I WOULDN'T DARE! I HAVE NOTHING TO WEAR!

JUST COME AS YOU ARE— YOU ARE PERFECT! OR, I CAN BUY YOU A DRESS!

OH, NO, I COULDN'T ACCEPT!

COME, COME, LET ME TAKE YOU TO THE BALL AND...

...

I WON'T SAY ANYTHING TO THE OTHERS IF YOU LET ME PLAY WITH YOU!

GRAB A UNICORN!

CED-MORIN

SCRATCH
SCRATCH

SAY, SLURP... YOU WOULDN'T HAVE HELPED YOURSELF TO THE REFRIGERATOR LAST NIGHT, WOULD YOU?

HO... HOW DID YOU KNOW?

CED-MORIN

WITH STEARAS IN FULL RECRUITMENT FOR HIS EVIL ARMY, THE STREETS OF THE CITY HAVE BECOME FULL OF BAD PEOPLE!

THERE ARE VAMPIRES, ORCS, AND TROLLS EVERYWHERE...AREN'T YOU AFRAID HE'LL BEAT US?

BAH...

DON'T FORGET THAT WE HAVE A DRAGON! AND GONZAG IS A GOBLIN. A GOBLIN!

THERE IS NO CRUELER CREATURE! GONZAG COULD BEAT ANY TROLL WHO DARES CONFRONT HIM!!

AND THEN, YOU, YOU ARE...

UH...WHAT EXACTLY ARE YOU?

I DON'T KNOW, MASTER!

HUH?

I AM THE ONLY ONE OF MY KIND. I WAS FOUND AS A BABY IN A BASKET...

I WAS CALLED "SLURP" BECAUSE THAT'S THE NOISE I MADE WHEN I WAS TAKEN FROM THE BLANKET THAT I WAS WRAPPED IN!

OH, I'M SORRY... I DIDN'T KNOW!

IT'S OKAY, I GOT USED TO IT!

...

MANY TIMES I TELL MYSELF THAT I SHOULD TRY TO GET TO KNOW YOU BETTER, BOTH OF YOU! AND BE KINDER TO YOU!

DON'T WORRY ABOUT US, BOSS. YOU'RE VERY GOOD AS IT IS!

BONK

OH, LOOK WHO WE RAN INTO! ONE OF THOSE ROTTEN TROLLS THAT GONZAG COULD DEFEAT IN ONE FELL SWOOP!

I'LL TELL YOU WHAT YOU ARE, SLURP...

YOU'RE A FOOL!

CED-MORIN

58

WHAT ARE YOU DOING, MASTER?

I'M PRACTICING MY MAGIC!

ON HUBERT?

YES, I AM TRYING TO CAST A KIND OF MONSTER SPELL ON HIM! I WANT HIM TO BE BIG AND TERRIFYING!

BUT AS USUAL WITH THIS SPELLBOOK, IT DOESN'T WORK!

OR MAYBE... IT'S ME! I'M NOT CUT OUT FOR SORCERY...

NOW, NOW, DON'T SAY THAT!

YOU'LL TRY AGAIN LATER!

AND WHO KNOWS, MAYBE ONE DAY YOU WILL CAST A SPELL THAT WILL WORK!

SIRE, SIRE! THE CITY IS BEING ATTACKED!!

IS IT STEARAS?!

UH, NO...

IT'S A SIDE TABLE!

CED-MORIN

59

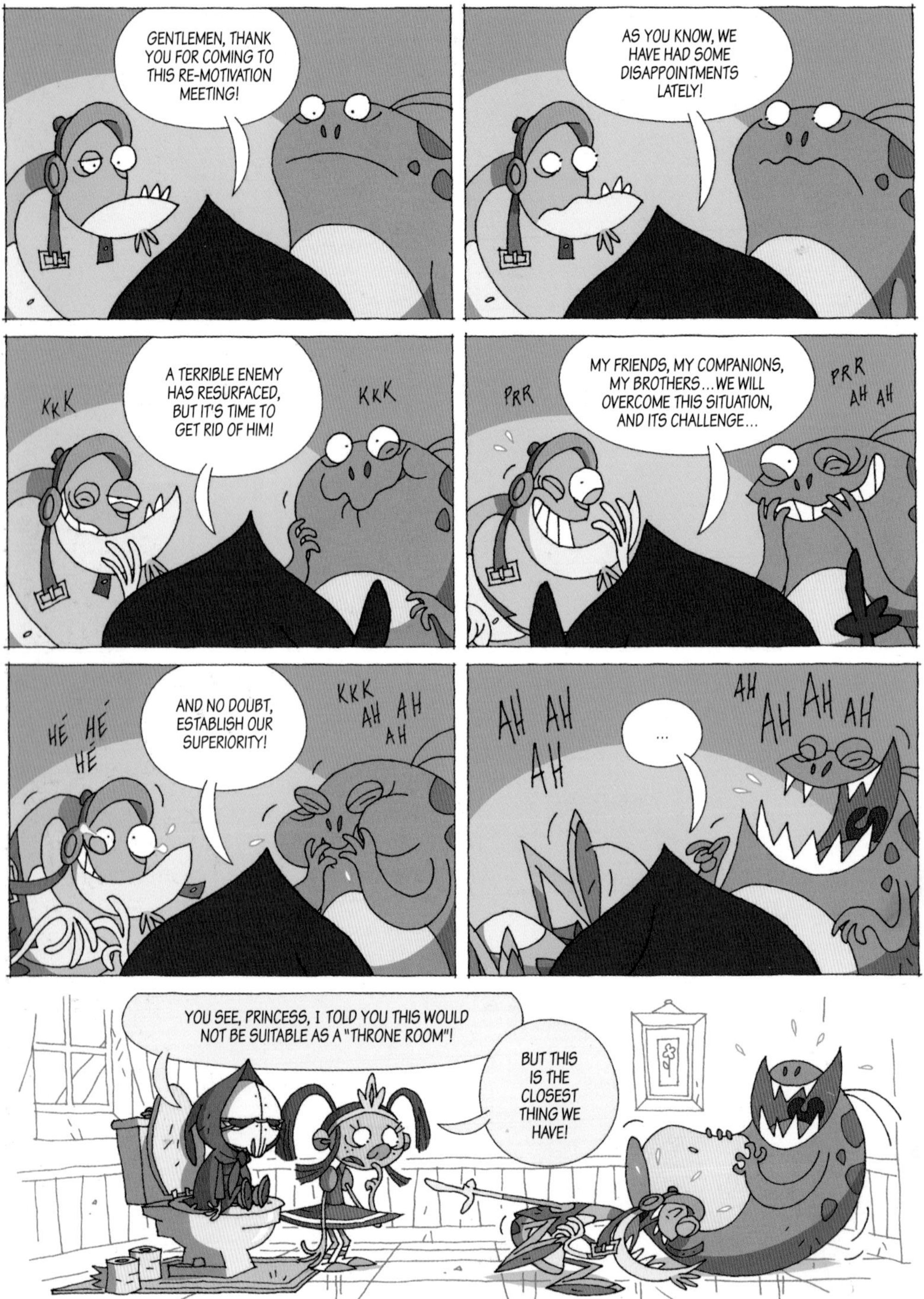
GENTLEMEN, THANK YOU FOR COMING TO THIS RE-MOTIVATION MEETING!
AS YOU KNOW, WE HAVE HAD SOME DISAPPOINTMENTS LATELY!
KKK
A TERRIBLE ENEMY HAS RESURFACED, BUT IT'S TIME TO GET RID OF HIM!
KKK
PRR
MY FRIENDS, MY COMPANIONS, MY BROTHERS...WE WILL OVERCOME THIS SITUATION, AND ITS CHALLENGE...
PRR AH AH
HÉ HÉ HÉ
AND NO DOUBT, ESTABLISH OUR SUPERIORITY!
KKK AH AH AH
AH AH AH
...
AH AH AH AH AH
YOU SEE, PRINCESS, I TOLD YOU THIS WOULD NOT BE SUITABLE AS A "THRONE ROOM"!
BUT THIS IS THE CLOSEST THING WE HAVE!
CED-MORIN

IT'S BEEN AWHILE SINCE STEARAS HAS SAID ANYTHING! HE'S PREPARING SOMETHING...

SO WE WILL GO TO STEARAS'S TERRIBLE TOWER TO SPY ON HIM AND FIGURE IT OUT...

?

GONZAG, WHAT IS THIS?

THAT'S MY DAUGHTER, PERNILLA! AT SCHOOL, THEY HAVE "TAKE YOUR CHILD TO WORK" DAY! SHE HAS TO SPEND THE DAY AT WORK WITH ME!

DOES IT BOTHER YOU?

I GUESS I HAVE NO CHOICE...IN SHORT, WE WILL SET UP BY NIGHT AND THEN...

YOU MEAN "BY DAY"!

EXCUSE ME?

MOST OF STEARAS'S GUARDS ARE VAMPIRES! IT'S BETTER TO START IN THE MORNING...

MAY I?

BY CHOOSING TO ACT AT DAWN, WE WILL HAVE ADVANTAGES OVER STEARAS'S DEFENSES: IT WILL BE THE TIME WHEN THE CREATURES OF THE NIGHT, VAMPIRES AND OTHER ZOMBIES, WILL GO TO BED, EVEN THOUGH THE NEXT GUARDS WILL NOT BE UP YET! WE SHOULD ARRIVE UNDER COVER BY WAY OF THE WOODS, FROM THE NORTH! ALTHOUGH THE WALLS WILL CERTAINLY BE HARDER TO CLIMB, SLURP'S STICKY PROPERTIES WILL COMPENSATE FOR THIS INCONVENIENCE! WE WILL LEAVE BY THE SAME PATH! EASY AS PIE!

...

ARE YOU SURE SHE'S YOUR DAUGHTER?

WHY DOES EVERYONE ALWAYS ASK ME THAT?!!

CED-MORIN

61

HERE WE ARE! THERE'S THE CASTLE!

MORE PRECISELY, IT'S A TOWER!

SHE IS RIGHT. BE PRECISE, SLURP!

SLURP, STICK TO THE WALL AND PULL US UP!

GONZAG, YOU STAND GUARD!

IF YOU SEE SOMETHING STRANGE, WHISTLE!

HOW'S IT GOING, SLURP? WE'RE NOT TOO HEAVY?

A PIECE OF CAKE, BOSS! THERE ARE SOME THINGS YOU DON'T LEARN FROM BOOKS, HUH?!

WAIT, SLURP! YOU JUST PASSED A BIG BEAM!

BUT IT'S TOO BIG FOR US TO CLIMB! WE WILL HAVE TO JUMP AT THE SAME TIME!

AND ONE, TWO...

SLURP, I DIDN'T MEAN YOU!!

YOU DIDN'T WHISTLE, PAPA?

NO, EVERYTHING SEEMED NORMAL HERE!

JUST THE USUAL...

CED-MORIN

62

GO FASTER! WHAT ARE THEY DOING?!

AH, THEY ARE FINALLY AT THE WINDOW OF THE THRONE ROOM!

THEY'RE COMING DOWN!

RUN!!!

SO WHAT DID YOU LEARN?

WE SAW STEARAS!

AND I HAVE INFO JUST FOR YOU, MASTER! JUST WAIT...

...THE HORNS OF HIS HELMET LOOK JUST LIKE CROISSANTS!

THERE YOU GO.

IN PARTICULAR WE SAW THAT HIS CLOSEST GUARDS ARE VAMPIRES! THERE WERE ALSO PLANS ON A BOARD. IT CONCERNED A SWORD!

I JOTTED IT ALL DOWN IN DETAIL!

HMM... NO DOUBT THE MAGIC SWORD OF THE PROPHECY...

YOU SEE SLURP, PERNILLA'S REPORT IS MUCH MORE COMPLETE THAN YOURS! AND SHE HAS NOT FORGOTTEN ANYTHING!

?

HMM...

CED·MORIN

I AM VERY HAPPY THAT PERNILLA IS LEAVING TODAY! SHE GETS ON MY NERVES!

IT'S PROBABLY BECAUSE SHE POINTS OUT HOW INCAPABLE YOU ARE, RIGHT?

HEY, WHAT ARE YOU DOING?!!

READING YOUR MAGIC SPELL BOOK! IT LOOKS PRETTY EASY...

YOU THINK SO? I NEVER MANAGED TO CAST A SPELL WITH THIS THING!

REALLY? THE INSTRUCTIONS ARE RATHER CLEAR!

IT'S SIMPLE. WE MUST MENTION THE OBJECT TARGETED IN THE SPELL: "AKTA CHAIR"!

CAN'T YOU READ, OR WHAT?

YES, YES, WELL...

SLURP IS RIGHT, YOU CAN BE ANNOYING SOMETIMES...

YOUR SPELL DIDN'T WORK ANY BETTER THAN MINE!

DID YOU SEE, SIRE?

SIGH...

IT WOULD SEEM THAT THE TABLE HAS FOUND A PARTNER!

AH, LOVE...

CED-MORIN

64

ARE YOU GRUMBLING BECAUSE THE PRINCESS ASKED US TO DO HOUSEWORK, MASTER?

I'M GRUMBLING BECAUSE SLURP IS NOT HERE TODAY. WE COULD HAVE GIVEN ALL THE WORK TO HIM, AND WHAT'S MORE, THAT FOOL WOULD HAVE DONE IT AS A FAVOR!

UH...SORRY, BOSS, I WON'T BE ABLE TO DO THE WINDOWS...

SO WHAT'S YOUR EXCUSE? THERE'S A BEE? YOUR ARM HURTS? YOU'RE ALLERGIC TO THE CLEANING FLUID?...

NO, THERE IS A WEIRDO AT THE WINDOW!

WHAT DID YOU SAY?

LOOK!

HMM...IT'S ONE OF STEARAS'S VAMPIRES! HE SENT IT TO INTIMIDATE US!

WHY IS HE NOT DOING ANYTHING? WHY DOESN'T HE COME IN?

VAMPIRES CAN'T ENTER A ROOM IF THEY'RE NOT INVITED! DO NOT SAY ANYTHING AND HE WILL LEAVE WHEN THE SUN RISES!

THE FUNNY THING IS THAT ONCE ASKED, THEY ARE FORCED TO COMPLY!

HMM...

I INVITE YOU TO...

GONZAG, NOOOO!!

...CLEAN THE WINDOWS OF THE CASTLE!

YOU KNOW, GONZAG, SOMETIMES YOU SURPRISE ME...

THEN, I INVITE YOU TO CLEAN THE ROOF! THEN I INVITE YOU TO...

CED-MORIN

COME AND SEE, SLURP! THE PROPHECY SPEAKS OF A HERO WIELDING A SWORD WHO WILL DRIVE OUT STEARAS!

BUT WE CAN'T SEE WHO'S HOLDING IT!

LOOK, HE'S PUSHING HIM TOWARD THIS OPENING, WHICH MUST BE THE DOOR OF THE VORTEX LOCATED IN THE TERRIBLE TOWER!

WE MUST FIND THIS SWORD... BUT IT'S BEEN 200 YEARS—IT COULD BE ANYWHERE!!?

WHAT DO I HEAR ?!!

YOU WENT TO SPY ON STEARAS WITHOUT ME?!

THAT WAS NOT OUR AGREEMENT!

I MUST BE PART OF THE TEAM!

BUT, PRINCESS... WE DIDN'T WANT TO PUT YOU IN DANGER...

IN DANGER ?! I AM JUST AS CAPABLE AS ANYONE ELSE!

SO WHAT IS THE REST OF THE PLAN? WHAT IS THE NEXT MISSION ?

UH... FIND THE MAGIC SWORD, I GUESS...

STAY RIGHT THERE!

HERE IS YOUR SWORD!!

TAHAC!

...

BUT...HOW CAN WE BE SURE THIS IS THE RIGHT ONE?

Well, are you just going to leave me stuck here forever?

IT'S GOOD, NEVER MIND!

CED-MORIN

THE MAGIC SWORD?! BUT WHERE DID YOU FIND IT?

BAH, MY FATHER KEPT IT IN THE CELLAR, WITH OTHER ANTIQUES…

I was forged by the wizard Kinion for a single objective to vanquish Stearas, the master of evil!

I'm remembering correctly, right? It has been 200 years after all…

BUT HOW DOES IT WORK?

It's enough for me to touch Stearas!

He will then be swallowed up and imprisoned in the sword, by me of course!

HMM…

AND WHAT OTHER POWERS DO YOU HAVE?

Uhh….Well, that's it!

Ah, yes, I can warn of the dangers that have just occurred!

PREDICT SOMETHING AFTER IT HAPPENED? THAT IS USELESS!

WHAT'S IT MADE OF?

WAIT, WAIT…

YOU ARE MY DAUGHTER'S KIDNAPPERS! GUARDS! GRAB THEM!

See, there, for example:

"Be careful! The king is about to enter and catch you"!

67

CED-MORIN

I'M SORRY! ARE YOU ALL OKAY?

OH YES, YUM-*CRUNCH*...WE ARE... *CRUNCH*...SU-PER WELL TREATED!

APART FROM SLURP, WHO LOVES THE FOOD SERVED IN PRISON, WE CANNOT SAY THAT THE SITUATION IS IDEAL, NO!

I ASKED MY FATHER FOR AN AUDIENCE SO THAT YOU COULD EXPLAIN YOURSELF. I HOPE HE WILL ACCEPT!

PRINCESS, CAN I ASK YOU A FAVOR?

OF COURSE...

I WOULD LIKE YOUR FATHER TO TAKE ME A LITTLE MORE SERIOUSLY, BUT MY ROBE IS ALL DIRTY AND I'M AFRAID THAT...

OH, IS JAIL DIRTY?

NO, IT'S JUST THAT WHEN SLURP EATS, HE SPITS EVERYWHERE!

NICE, WE HAVE SAUSAGES TODAY!

NO PROBLEM. GIVE IT TO ME, I'LL CLEAN IT UP!

AH! AND WHILE I'M AT IT, I'LL MAKE YOU ANOTHER SPARE ROBE!

A LITTLE LATER...... ...

GOOD NEWS: THE AUDIENCE HAS BEEN GRANTED! BAD NEWS: YOUR ROBE IS NOT READY...

BUT PRINCESS...

NO PLAYING AROUND. COME ON, HURRY! HE'S COMING!

YOU HAVE FIVE MINUTES TO EXPLAIN YOURSELF!

YOU HAVE KIDNAPPED MY DAUGHTER. I AM NOT HERE FOR FUN...

?!!!

IF YOU WANTED TO BE TAKEN SERIOUSLY...

...YOU SHOULDN'T HAVE WORN PAJAMAS.

CED-MORIN

68

AND THERE, PERFECT!

HEE, HEE, HEE!

TAP! TAP! TAP!

?

MEANWHILE, IN THE DUNGEON...

YOU MUST KNOW WE ARE FRIENDS OF THE PRINCESS!

AND ABOVE ALL, YOU KNOW HOW TO BEAT STEARAS!

SORRY, SIRE, BUT IT SEEMS YOU DIDN'T UNDERSTAND ME?

PFFFT!!! EX... EXCUSE ME! AHAHAHA! I ... BUT... WITH YOUR OUTFIT I CAN'T CONCENTRATE!

WELL, GONZAG, SLURP, GO EXPLAIN IT TO HIM! HE WILL NOT LISTEN TO ME!

I SEE...

ACTUALLY, THESE PAJAMAS ARE SURPRISINGLY COMFORTABLE!

BUT I DO WONDER WHAT THE PRINCESS IS DOING...

CED-MORIN

SIRE! SIRE! IT'S THE PRINCESS!!!

?

SHE WAS KIDNAPPED AGAIN!

HOW!? BUT WHO DARES!?

THE GUARDS SAW A VAMPIRE FLY AWAY WITH THE PRINCESS THROWN OVER HIS SHOULDER!

SHE WAS WEARING A CAPE WITH A HOOD!

LIKE HIM, THE...UH...

WELL, LIKE HE WAS BEFORE!

IT'S STEARAS!

OH NO, HE THOUGHT SHE WAS ME!

SIRE, I WILL SURRENDER! HE WILL FREE HER!

...GUARD, OPEN!

RIGHT AWAY, SIRE! DRAT, I CAN'T FIND THE KEYS!

HURRY UP AND FIND THEM!!!

DO YOU NEED HELP?

SPLOOP

LET'S SEE THERE!

CAN YOU LOOK IN MY BACK POCKET?

BUT???...

BUT SLURP, YOU COULD'VE ESCAPED AT ANYTIME?!!

NAH, NOT JUST ANYTIME, BOSS!!

NOT BEFORE I ATE MY CUPCAKE FOR DESSERT!

CED-MORIN

70

YOU ARE COMPLETELY INCAPABLE!

I TOLD YOU TO BRING BACK THE PIPSQUEAK! CAN'T YOU SEE THIS IS NOT HIM!

SORRY, MASTER! BUT... TO ME, ALL MORTALS LOOK ALIKE, YOU KNOW!

IF YOU WEREN'T WEARING YOUR HELMET WITH HORNS IN THE SHAPE OF CROISSANTS, WELL...

THEY ARE NOT CR...

FINE, FINE, LET'S JUST KEEP CALM!

WE HAVE THE PRINCESS, AFTER ALL!

LET'S THINK HOW TO TAKE ADVANTAGE OF THIS SITUATION!

THEY'RE GOING TO COME AND SAVE ME, YOU KNOW.

NOT YOUR FATHER! HIS ROYAL GUARD IS WORTHLESS! THERE HAS BEEN NO ARMY IN THE KINGDOM OF ALKYLL FOR 200 YEARS!

YOUR BAND OF FOOLS, ON THE OTHER HAND... THEY HAVE ALREADY COME HERE ONCE AND THEY CAN DO IT AGAIN!

YOU! POST TROLLS ALL AROUND THE CASTLE AND MAKE SURE THAT NO ONE CLIMBS THE WALLS!

YES, O GREAT STEARAS!

AND YOU, PUT MORE GUARDS AT THE FOOT OF THE TOWER! AND DO A HEAD COUNT! MAYBE THEY WILL DISGUISE THEMSELVES AS SOLDIERS TO INFILTRATE US! THAT'S A CLASSIC MOVE!

VERY GOOD, O STEARAS!

CHECK EVERYTHING! ASK EVERYONE! NOTHING SHOULD BE LEFT TO CHANCE! THEY WILL DEFINITELY USE CUNNING TO INFILTRATE US...

UH, MASTER...

WE FOUND THEM!! THEY WERE WALKING ALONG THE CORRIDOR AGAINST THE WALL. THEY SAID IT WAS "MORE DISCREET"...

YEAH... I'M NOT SURE WHAT I WAS HOPING FOR!

CED-MORIN

71

IT'S ONLY YOU? WHERE IS YOUR MASTER? WHAT RIDICULOUS SCHEME IS HE PLANNING?

WE AREN'T SAYING ANYTHING!

ESPECIALLY SINCE WE DIDN'T REALLY UNDERSTAND HIS PLAN ...

STEARAS...HE'S HEADING STRAIGHT FOR US!

HOW? RIDING A GIANT EAGLE? A VULTURE?

UH, NO...

ON ACCENT FURNITURE!

SO THAT'S YOUR STRATEGY, PIPSQUEAK? ATTACK ME WITH A CHEAP COFFEE TABLE?

ABSOLUTELY NOT, IT'S AN AUTHENTIC ALKYLLIAN SIDE TABLE!

AND YOU KNOW WHAT "LITTLE FEATURE" MAKES IT DIFFERENT FROM COMMON TABLES?

FWOOP!

THE DRAWER!

CED-MORIN

ARE YOU OKAY, PRINCESS?

I BROUGHT YOUR PRETTY DRESS BACK!

OH, UH... SUPER.

SO, STEARAS, MASTER OF EVIL! DO YOU RECOGNIZE THIS?

YOU MAY HAVE THE MAGIC SWORD, BUT I...

SNAP!

I HAVE A VAMPIRE ARMY!

HAHA! DO YOU HAVE ANYTHING TO SAY TO THAT?

WELL, ACTUALLY...

YES!

SIRE, I DON'T KNOW IF THEY WILL SUCCEED IN BEATING STEARAS...

BUT IN ANY CASE, THE WINDOWS OF THE PALACE HAVE NEVER BEEN SO CLEAN!

CED-MORIN

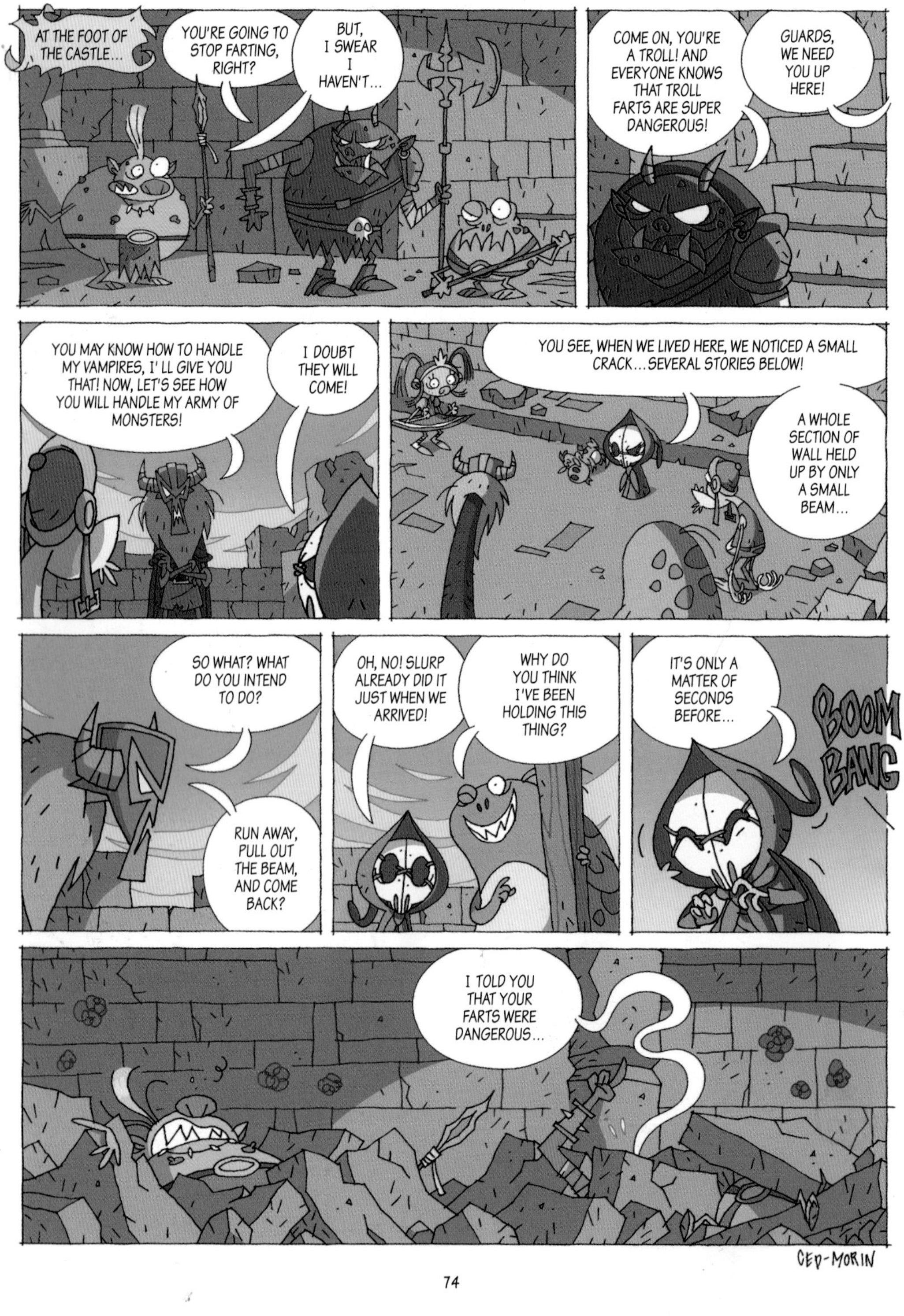
AT THE FOOT OF THE CASTLE...
YOU'RE GOING TO STOP FARTING, RIGHT?
BUT, I SWEAR I HAVEN'T...
COME ON, YOU'RE A TROLL! AND EVERYONE KNOWS THAT TROLL FARTS ARE SUPER DANGEROUS!
GUARDS, WE NEED YOU UP HERE!
YOU MAY KNOW HOW TO HANDLE MY VAMPIRES, I' LL GIVE YOU THAT! NOW, LET'S SEE HOW YOU WILL HANDLE MY ARMY OF MONSTERS!
I DOUBT THEY WILL COME!
YOU SEE, WHEN WE LIVED HERE, WE NOTICED A SMALL CRACK... SEVERAL STORIES BELOW!
A WHOLE SECTION OF WALL HELD UP BY ONLY A SMALL BEAM...
SO WHAT? WHAT DO YOU INTEND TO DO?
RUN AWAY, PULL OUT THE BEAM, AND COME BACK?
OH, NO! SLURP ALREADY DID IT JUST WHEN WE ARRIVED!
WHY DO YOU THINK I'VE BEEN HOLDING THIS THING?
IT'S ONLY A MATTER OF SECONDS BEFORE...
BOOM
BANG
I TOLD YOU THAT YOUR FARTS WERE DANGEROUS...
CED-MORIN

OKAY! NOW, YOU REALLY ARE GETTING ON MY NERVES!

YOU WILL BE DEFENSELESS AGAINST MY FIREBALLS!

GONZAG! A CHILI PEPPER!

THERE WE GO, EAT THAT, MY LITTLE HUBERT!

YOU KNOW, SIRE, I KNOW THAT THE FATE OF YOUR DAUGHTER DEPENDS ON THIS BATTLE...

AND ALSO THE FATE OF THE WORLD!

BUT I CAN'T STOP MYSELF FROM FINDING SOMETHING BEAUTIFUL ABOUT THIS EPIC CONFLICT!

HERE NOW, DON'T SAY SUCH SILLY THINGS!

FIZZ BOOM

OOOOOOOOOOOOOH!

CED-MORIN

I... I HAVE NO MORE ENERGY!

BUT I STILL HAVE... UH...

YOUR PRECIOUS PRINCESS!

HELP!

ARE YOU SO SURE ABOUT THAT?

BECAUSE I HAVE THE IMPRESSION THAT SHE IS DOING RATHER WELL!

?!

DON'T HURT ME!

HAVE YOU DISGUISED ONE OF YOUR ...ER

IT WON'T STOP ME FROM STRANGLING IT!

HERE WE ARE!

FINE, THIS IS GETTING RIDICULOUS, SO LET'S END IT!

WHO IS HIDING UNDER THIS SUIT?!

Surprise!

OH, NO!

POOF!

CLINK CLINK

CED-MORIN

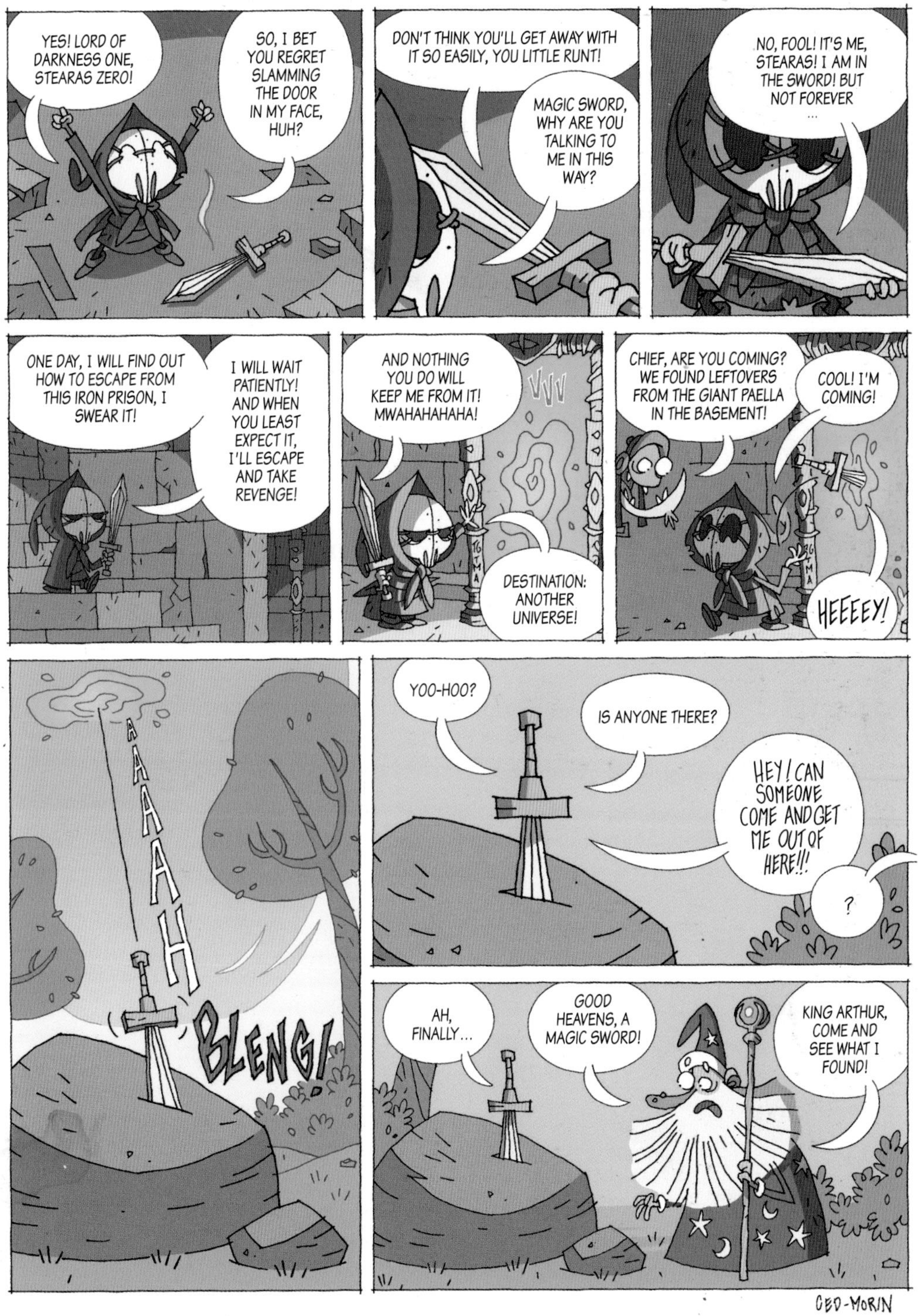
YES! LORD OF DARKNESS ONE, STEARAS ZERO!
SO, I BET YOU REGRET SLAMMING THE DOOR IN MY FACE, HUH?
DON'T THINK YOU'LL GET AWAY WITH IT SO EASILY, YOU LITTLE RUNT!
MAGIC SWORD, WHY ARE YOU TALKING TO ME IN THIS WAY?
NO, FOOL! IT'S ME, STEARAS! I AM IN THE SWORD! BUT NOT FOREVER …
ONE DAY, I WILL FIND OUT HOW TO ESCAPE FROM THIS IRON PRISON, I SWEAR IT!
I WILL WAIT PATIENTLY! AND WHEN YOU LEAST EXPECT IT, I'LL ESCAPE AND TAKE REVENGE!
AND NOTHING YOU DO WILL KEEP ME FROM IT! MWAHAHAHAHA!
DESTINATION: ANOTHER UNIVERSE!
CHIEF, ARE YOU COMING? WE FOUND LEFTOVERS FROM THE GIANT PAELLA IN THE BASEMENT!
COOL! I'M COMING!
HEEEEY!
AAAAAH
BLENG!
YOO-HOO?
IS ANYONE THERE?
HEY! CAN SOMEONE COME AND GET ME OUT OF HERE!!!
?
AH, FINALLY…
GOOD HEAVENS, A MAGIC SWORD!
KING ARTHUR, COME AND SEE WHAT I FOUND!
CED-MORIN

LOOK, EVERYBODY!

STEARAS'S TROOPS ARE RUNNING AWAY!

COME ON!

WE'RE GOING HOME!

HEY, I JUST THOUGHT OF SOMETHING!

IN THE END, THANKS TO THE MAGIC SWORD, YOU DEFEATED STEARAS!

SO, THE HERO OF THE PROPHECY IS YOU!

YOU, A HERO! CAN YOU IMAGINE?

PRINCESS, IF YOU REPEAT THAT TO ANYONE...

I WILL BE FORCED TO KIDNAP YOU AGAIN!

CED-MORIN

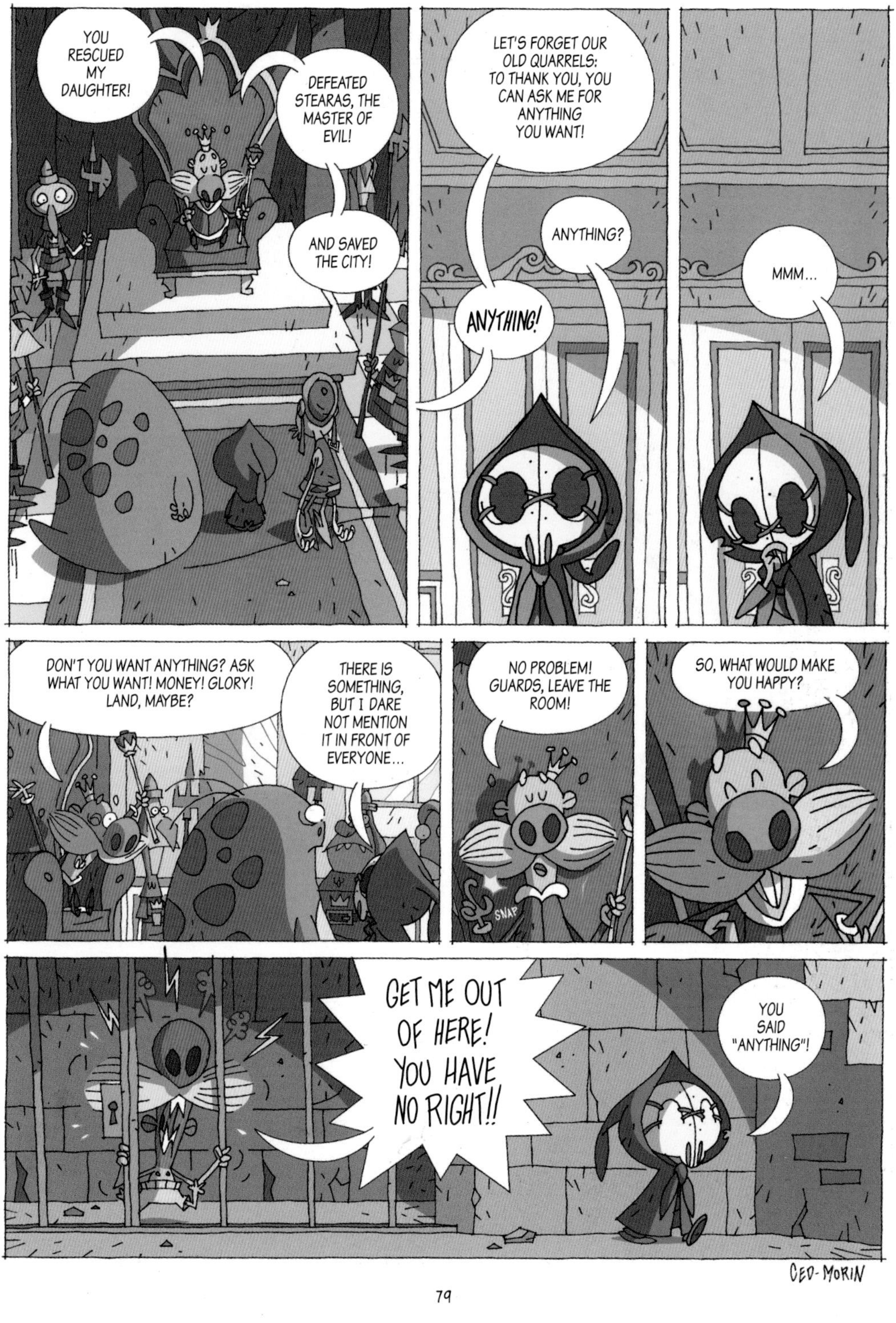
YOU RESCUED MY DAUGHTER!
DEFEATED STEARAS, THE MASTER OF EVIL!
AND SAVED THE CITY!
LET'S FORGET OUR OLD QUARRELS: TO THANK YOU, YOU CAN ASK ME FOR ANYTHING YOU WANT!
ANYTHING?
ANYTHING!
MMM...
DON'T YOU WANT ANYTHING? ASK WHAT YOU WANT! MONEY! GLORY! LAND, MAYBE?
THERE IS SOMETHING, BUT I DARE NOT MENTION IT IN FRONT OF EVERYONE...
NO PROBLEM! GUARDS, LEAVE THE ROOM!
SNAP
SO, WHAT WOULD MAKE YOU HAPPY?
GET ME OUT OF HERE! YOU HAVE NO RIGHT!!
YOU SAID "ANYTHING"!
CED-MORIN

WHAT DO WE DO NOW, BOSS?

WE START BY REVIEWING OUR TITLES!

DON'T YOU SEE THAT WE SUCCEEDED? FORGET APPRENTICE...

FROM NOW ON, I AM THE ONE AND ONLY...

...LORD OF DARKNESS!!

CED-MORIN

80

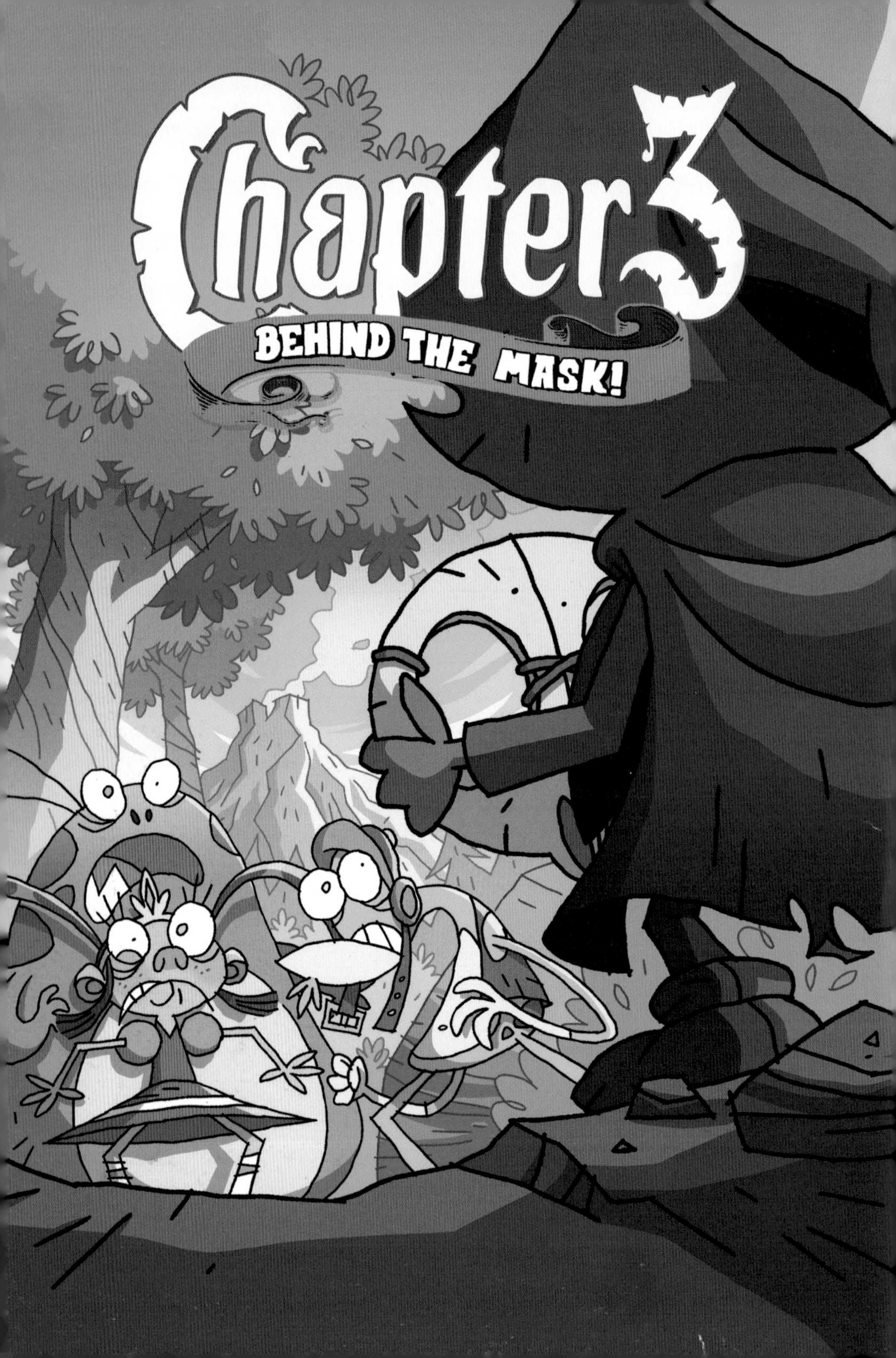
Chapter 3
BEHIND THE MASK!

WELCOME, DEAR READER, TO THE LAND OF ALKYLL, AND ITS CAPITAL, BOURGVILLE: A PROSPEROUS CITY, WHERE PROUDLY STANDS THE ROYAL PALACE, AN ELEGANT MONUMENT WITHOUT EQUAL.

THE STAFF AT THE CASTLE ARE REPUTED TO BE THE BEST. WHO HASN'T HEARD OF THE PRESTIGIOUS SWORDS FORGED BY THE KING'S ARMORY? OR OF THE COOK AND HIS FAMOUS WARM POTATO SALAD?

THE ONLY THING MISSING IS ENTERTAINMENT.

PLUNK PLUNK PLUNK

And a good day to you, guard. I am Gontran, the smiling bard!

OH, THERE YOU ARE. WE'VE BEEN WAITING FOR YOU!

YOU SPEAK A LITTLE STRANGE, NO?

In my work, all the time, I must constantly rhyme!

HERE WE ARE.

Thank you, my friend, you were nice to the end!

KNOCK KNOCK

YES?

OH, IT'S YOU, THE NEW BARD?

I made this trip to entertain your lordship!

You are wearing such strange attire!

Was your jester's hood selected by his sire?

KNOW THIS, DEAR DING-A-LING, FOR I AM THE KING!

FOR WHOEVER TREATS ME IN SUCH A WAY, WILL BECOME THE NEXT MEAL FOR MY DRAGON TODAY!

CED-MORIN

For my first song, I'll sing about flowers as i go along...

WHAT? STOP!

HERE I WILL TELL YOU WHAT TO SAY!

HERE, THESE ARE THE WORDS.

Oh, a sad twist, to limit such an artist.

Very well. After your line, I demand to say mine!

YOU DEMAND?

HAHA...GO AHEAD. YOU WILL UNDERSTAND.

HMM... HMM...

"Gents, ladies, and young lords, if you can, listen to the story of this dreary man."

"Called the Apprentice Lord of Darkness,

"He wants to be the master of evil, and bring the world into chaotic upheaval."

"He hired two big lugs, Gonzag the goblin and Slurp the slug.

"Together with them he took the throne and holds the king iron clad,

"Aided by the princess, who betrayed her dad.

"Now a tyrant he has become.

"He throws people into the dungeon.

"And if with this act you don't agree,

"Into prison you'll come to be!"

Hey, but...

Wait...

"One thing is sure about this sire,

if I said he's nice, I'd be a liar."

CED-MORIN

84

HMPH...

IS THERE SOMETHING WRONG?

IN FACT, PRINCESS, EVERYTHING IS GREAT!

EVER SINCE I TOOK THE CROWN, EVERYTHING HAS BEEN GREAT!

I'VE DONE EVERYTHING I CAN! I HAVE IMPOSED TAXES AND RAISED THEM EVERY DAY...

I REQUIRE THE PEOPLE TO WORK FOR ME!

AND WHAT DO I SEE? NEVER HAS THE COUNTRY BEEN SO PROSPEROUS AND THE PEOPLE SO HAPPY!

NOTHING HAS CHANGED, AND THAT MAKES ME ANGRY!

MY ONLY CONSOLATION IS THAT I GET TO THROW PEOPLE IN PRISON!

OH, SPEAKING OF THAT, WE HAVE A PROBLEM WITH THE PRISON CELL.

WHAT? THERE'S NOT A SINGLE PROBLEM!

YOU'VE THROWN EVERYONE IN PRISON. YESTERDAY YOU IMPRISONED AN ENTIRE CIRCUS ACT BECAUSE YOU DIDN'T LIKE THE NUMBER OF SEALS THEY USED.

AND SO WHAT? I AM THE KING. I DO WHAT I WANT.

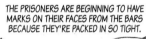

THE PRISONERS ARE BEGINNING TO HAVE MARKS ON THEIR FACES FROM THE BARS BECAUSE THEY'RE PACKED IN SO TIGHT.

SO WHAT? THROW THEM INTO THE PIT!

THAT'S IMPOSSIBLE! SLURP AND GONZAG TOLD ME THEY ARE USING IT FOR THEMSELVES.

WHAT? WHAT HAVE THESE TWO SIMPLETONS DONE WITH THE HOLE IN THE FLOOR?

ARE YOU SURE THEY WON'T DISCOVER US?

OF COURSE NOT! KEEP GOING— THIS IS REALLY GREAT!

CED-MORIN

YOUR HIGHNESS, HERE ARE TODAY'S POLLS!

FINALLY!

HERE ARE THE RESULTS...PEOPLE FIND YOU FAIR, GOOD, AND QUITE CUTE!

WHAT?!

BUT...HOW CAN THESE FOOLS FIND ME FAIR? ME, A TYRANT!!

AND...CUTE, REALLY?

THE ONLY PLACE THEY SEE YOU IS ON THE FRONT OF THE COINS.

SHOW ME THAT!

IS THIS... A JOKE?

BUT I'M SMILING ON THE FRONT!

IT'S BECAUSE OF THIS SMALL LINE OF TEXT HERE!

WHO ENGRAVED THIS ON THE ROYAL COINS?

WELL, I WANTED TO DO IT, BUT YOU PREFERRED TO ASK SLURP AND GON...

SLURP! GONZAG!

YES, BOSS!

ONCE AGAIN, YOU ARE PATHETIC!

YOU'RE GOING TO CORRECT THE DESIGN OF THESE COINS AT THE SILVERSMITH'S, PRONTO! I WANT TO APPEAR HORRRRIBLE!

AND WHILE YOU'RE AT IT, TELL MY MINISTERS TO DOUBLE FEES!

AND...AND TO TRIPLE TAXES!

AFTER THIS, WE'LL SEE IF THEY STILL FIND ME CUTE!

OH, GEE, I HATE IT WHEN HE SENDS US ON A MISSION! I NEVER REMEMBER WHAT TO DO!

OH, BUT NOOO, THIS ONE IS EASY! FIRST, WE JUST HAVE TO RAISE FEES ON THE MINISTERS!

TWO, GET IN A TAXI! ...

THREE, FIX THESE COINS!

I'M TORN BETWEEN RAISING HIS EYEBROWS OR GIVING HIM LARGER EYES! MMMM, NOT BAD!

THERE WE GO. TO THE SILVERSMITH! HE'S LUCKY TO HAVE US!

CED-MORIN

I ANNOUNCE THE OPENING OF GRAND COUNSEL OF THE MINISTERS.

PRINCESS, WHY DOES THE NEW KING NEVER COME TO THE MEETING OF THE MINISTERS?

HE SAYS IF HE SEES YOUR FACES HE'LL BE TOO TEMPTED TO THROW YOU IN THE DUNGEON.

BUT DON'T WORRY, THERE'S NOT ENOUGH ROOM...

DOES HE KEEP INCREASING OUR FEES BECAUSE HE DOESN'T LIKE US?

THAT'S ENOUGH! HE WANTS A PRECISE REPORT. HOW IS THE COUNTRY DOING?

EVERYTHING IS GOING GREAT!

LET'S START WITH THE UNEMPLOYMENT NUMBERS.

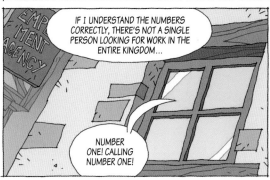

IF I UNDERSTAND THE NUMBERS CORRECTLY, THERE'S NOT A SINGLE PERSON LOOKING FOR WORK IN THE ENTIRE KINGDOM...

NUMBER ONE! CALLING NUMBER ONE!

UH, WIZARD KINION...

I BELIEVE IT'S YOUR TURN!

ARE YOU SURE?

SO... I READ IN YOUR FILE THAT YOU'VE BEEN OUT OF WORK FOR 200 YEARS.

YOU DIDN'T USE MY SERVICES IT SEEMS, MMM?

IT'S JUST THAT I AM A TRAINER OF HEROES, AND SINCE NO ONE NEEDS THAT ANYMORE...

BINGO! I HAVE THE PERFECT CANDIDATE FOR YOU! HIS NAME IS KROKK.

IT WILL BE UP TO YOU TO TRAIN HIM.

YOU WILL BE HIS GUIDE, HIS COUNSELOR, HIS GURU...

YOU MUST BEGIN BY HELPING HIM CONTROL HIS ANGER...

THIS PLANT LOOKED AT ME THE WRONG WAY!

SO I SMASHED IT!!!

...

WHEN DO I GET VACATION?

CED-MORIN

YOU SUMMONED US, MASTER?

YES, YES, HE SUMMONED US-US-MA-MASTER!

WHAT'S WITH THE BABY TALK, SLURP?

YOU ASKED ME TO RAISE OUR BABY DRAGON, SO I'M TAKING A NEW APPROACH.

I ASKED YOU TO TEACH HIM HOW TO STEAL AND BREATHE FIRE, NOT TO STUTTER.

I MUST FACE THE FACTS... I REPLACED THE KING AND IT'S BEEN A FAILURE.

SEE, HUBERT, A FAIL-URE!

FOR REASONS I CAN'T EXPLAIN, ALL MY DECISIONS, AS DIABOLICAL AS THEY'VE BEEN, ARE ACCEPTED AS GOOD BY THE PEOPLE!

AM I WEAKENING? TURNING SOFT?

AWWWW! BUT WHO IS TURNING TOO SOFT?

MY DECISION IS MADE!

I'M RETURNING THE CROWN IMMEDIATELY AND LEAVING. BUUUUT I WILL BE BACK... TO CONQUER!

I WILL BE STRONGER!

MORE RUTHLESS!

RIGHT, HUBERT, MORE RUTH-LESS!

FACING NEW CHALLENGES WILL TOUGHEN ME!

AS A RESULT... I'LL BE EVEN MORE POWERFUL!

THIS IS WHAT I MUST DO... IT'S A QUEST!

IF YOU SAY ONE WORD I'LL STRANGLE YOU!

ZzZZ

HERE WE ARE!

WHAT IS THIS PLACE?

REALLY, SLURP? YOU'VE NEVER BEEN IN A LIBRARY?

THE LIBRARY OF THE PALACE IS THE MOST FAMOUS IN THE KINGDOM.

IT CONTAINS WITHIN IT ALL THE BOOKS OF THE ENTIRE WORLD!

BLOM

UH, WHAT'S WRONG WITH HIM? IS HE HAVING AN ATTACK?

THIS JUST HAPPENED ALL OF A SUDDEN. IT'S TOO MUCH FOR HIM.

GGG...

LET'S GET TO WORK!

ARE YOU OKAY?

YES, YES.

FIND ME A QUEST! AND I DON'T WANT A WORTHLESS PROPHECY QUEST, OKAY?

A GOOD OLD MAGIC OBJECT TO SEARCH FOR WILL BE PERFECT.

YOU'RE DOING THINGS WITHOUT ME?!

WHAT? NO, NO, NOT AT ALL, WE...

I HAVE WHAT IT TAKES!

STOP LEAVING ME OUT OF THE GROUP!

BUT PRINCESS, WE WEREN'T... WE WERE LOOKING FOR...

WONDERFUL.

The Big Book of Quests.
More than 1,000 alphabetized quests.
The most popular quests.

CED-MORIN

89

THIS ONE IS PERFECT!

WE'RE GOING TO SEARCH FOR THIS RELIC!

The Big Book of Quests

More than 1,0 alphabetize quests.

The mos popular qu

"An excellent quest!"

"Perfect from beginning to end"

THE DEMON'S HAND IS A POWERFUL ARTIFACT FOUND ON DEVIL'S MOUNTAIN.

OH, SURE... THAT SOUNDS LIKE FUN.

IT GETS EVEN BETTER! "WHOEVER POSSESSES THIS DEMON'S HAND WILL HOLD COLOSSAL POWERS OF DESTRUCTION!"

THIS SURPASSES ALL MY EXPECTATIONS. I WON'T JUST BE THE MASTER OF THE KINGDOM...

BUT MASTER OF THE WORLD!

GREAT! I'LL PACK SOME LUNCHES!

I'LL GET SOME HATS!

WE'RE GOING ON A HIKING TRIP!

MY PROBLEM IS THAT IN MY HEAD I'M TERRIFYING, BUT ALL OF YOU ALWAYS MANAGE TO RUIN IT!

CED-MORIN

YOU MUST LEARN TO CONCENTRATE, HUH, CROC, THAT'S IT?

KROKK! BUT YOU CAN CALL ME THE A.B.H.,

FOR APPRENTICE BARBARIAN HERO.

THERE'S ONE!!

SPLASH SPLASH SPLASH

DRAT! MISSED IT!

PATIENCE IS KEY!

WATCH, KROC, SEE HOW THE BEAR FISHES.

HE CAN STAY LIKE THAT FOR HOURS.

AND ONLY AT THE RIGHT MOMENT ...

HE MAKES HIS MOVE!

SPLISH

TELL ME KHROK, WHAT IS YOUR MISSION RIGHT NOW?

I WANT TO GET RID OF THE NEW KING. HE'S "EVIL."

AND ME, I FIGHT THOSE WHO ARE "EVIL."

SPLASH

THAT'S ENOUGH! I'LL SHOW YOU HOW I FISH!

RAAAAH!

BONK

YOU CAUGHT... THE BEAR?

YEAH.

I DON'T LIKE FISH.

CED-MORIN

91

LET'S GO, OUTSIDE, ALL OF YOU.

I'M SETTING YOU FREE.

BUT, YOU'RE NOT LEAVING?

WHY WOULD I LEAVE?

IT'S GREAT HERE.

EVEN IF IT DOES SMELL LIKE A PIGSTY.

IT'S FINISHED, SIRE, I'M SETTING YOU FREE. I'M LEAVING THE KINGDOM.

TAKE BACK YOUR CROWN.

CERTAINLY NOT!

I EAT WELL, I SLEEP WELL, I SEE MY DAUGHTER EVERY DAY!

I HAVE EVERY ADVANTAGE AND NO INCONVENIENCES!

AND "ZERO" RESPONSIBILITIES...

BESIDES, I'VE JUST HEARD THE RUMOR...

THAT YOU ARE A BETTER KING THAN I EVER WAS!

I KNOW, I'M A COMPLETE DISGRACE TO MY PROFESSION.

GIVE ME JUST ONE REASON WHY I SHOULD ACCEPT!

I'LL PUT THE BARD IN THE CELL WITH YOU.

Once again, time with the king I get to spend?

SIGH.

GED-MORIN

ENOUGH TRAINING! I'M GOING TO SLAY THE TYRANT!

BUT... WHY? HE'S SO GOOD WITH THE PEOPLE!

WHERE IS THE KING?!!

CALM DOWN! HERE I AM!

BUT YOU'RE BACK?

IF YOU'RE LOOKING FOR THE GUY WHO REPLACED ME, HE JUST LEFT WITH HIS FRIENDS.

AND THEY TOOK MY DAUGHTER.

I KNEW IT!

THESE DOUBLE-CROSSERS KIDNAPPED HER? TIED HER UP?

WITH HER KNAPSACK. DOES THAT COUNT?

HMM.

BUT WHERE DID THEY GO?

ONE THING IS CERTAIN...

WHATEVER THEIR DIABOLICAL PLAN IS, THESE ARE FORMIDABLE ADVERSARIES!

SLURP, GONZAG ...

STOP THROWING THAT FOX DUNG!

CED-MORIN

SLURP, SEEING THAT YOUR "METHOD" DIDN'T WORK WITH HUBERT, I WOULD LIKE TO TRY ANOTHER WAY.

AH?

I READ THAT MOTHER DRAGONS TOSS THEIR BABIES INTO THE AIR TO TEACH THEM HOW TO FLY.

WE'RE GOING TO TRY THAT.

I DON'T THINK THIS IS A GOOD IDEA.

IT WON'T HURT HIM. HIS SKIN IS INDESTRUCTIBLE.

AND THIS IS A SMALL CLIFF.

YES, BUT ANYTHING WILL STILL DROP FAST TO THE BOTTOM!

HERE WE GO!

BU...WHAT? HE DIDN'T FLY...

OUCH!!

MGGNNN...

YOU NEVER SHOULD INTERRUPT MY SNACK!

ARE YOU THE ONE WHO THREW THIS AT ME WHILE I WAS HAVING MY SNACK?

I'M...SORRY, SIR. IT WAS AN ACCIDENT!

NO! I ASSURE YOU, IT WON'T HAPPEN AGAIN!

IT'S OKAY THIS TIME.

CRUNCH

PHEW!

YOU MIGHT LISTEN TO ME FROM TIME TO TIME.

ONE DAY, YOU'LL BE IN A REAL JAM.

OED-MORIN

YOUR PACKED LUNCH IS DELICIOUS, SLURP!

BUT THIS ISN'T OVER. LET'S LOOK AT THE PLAN!

WE HAVE TO GO THROUGH THE FORBIDDEN FOREST.

WHOA, WHOA, WHOA!

WHAT?

LIKE...WE CAN'T PASS THROUGH THERE IF IT'S FORBIDDEN, RIGHT?

I MEAN, WON'T WE HAVE TO PAY A FINE?

OH, NO! MOST OF THESE NAMES ARE PHONY! IT'S JUST TO SCARE AWAY TRAVELERS.

SO WE CAN GO THROUGH THE MINES OF DESPAIR, THEN...

OH, NO! CAN WE GO AROUND THAT?

THERE'S NOT A "FESTIVE WELCOMING TUNNEL"?

RELAX! IT'S NOT REAL.

BUT BEFORE ALL THAT, WE HAVE TO CROSS THE PLAINS OF NEVER-ENDING STORMS.

UMM...

FOR THE LAST TIME, PRINCESS, IT'S JUST A NAME!

JUST A NAME, HUH?

THAT'S WHAT I SAID. IT'S NOT A PLAIN...

...IT'S A PLATEAU!

GED-MORIN

IT'S SO PRETTY HERE!

LET'S BE CAREFUL!

WE DON'T KNOW WHO, OR WHAT, LIVES HERE.

LOOK, HUMANS!

AH, YES, YOU'RE RIGHT.

?

WHY? ONLY HUMANS KNOW HOW TO MAKE A SNOWMAN?

I KNOW HOW, TOO!

USUALLY PEOPLE BUILD A SNOWMAN TO LOOK LIKE THEM, RIGHT?

YOU WOULD HAVE BUILT A SNOWSLUG, FOR EXAMPLE.

IT HAS A HEAD, A NOSE, TWO ARMS, IT'S TALL.

EVERYTHING INDICATES IT WAS BUILT BY A HUMAN.

IT'S SIMPLE DEDUCTION, YOU SEE, SLURP? NOTHING AGAINST YOU...

HEY!

THAT'S MY HUSBAND YOU'RE MESSING WITH?!!!

?

CED-MORIN

HA HA HA HA HA!

YOU HAVE A VERY NICE COMMUNITY HERE!

PLEASE KNOW WE APPRECIATE YOUR HOSPITALITY...

IT'S SO NICE FOR YOU TO PUT US UP FOR THE NIGHT!

BUT IT'S TIME FOR US TO GO TO BED!

WE HAVE TO GET UP EARLY TOMORROW!

SO...WHERE ARE YOU GOING EXACTLY?

TO LOOK FOR A RELIC TO DESTROY THE WORL—

HA HA!

WE'RE... SEARCHING FOR UNICORNS!

GOOD NIGHT, THEN!

SEE YOU TOMORROW! AND THANKS AGAIN!

IT'S IMPOSSIBLE TO SPEND THE NIGHT HERE. I'M LITERALLY FREEZING!

I AGREE. EVEN THEIR BLANKETS ARE MADE OF ICE!

LOOK, MY BEAUTIFUL SLIME IS FORMING ICICLES ON MY ARM!

ME, I LIKE IT!

THEY LEFT US SOME SNOW TO SNACK ON. IT'S LIKE EATING ICE CREAM!

SLURP

WHERE DID YOU FIND THAT?

IN A TRAY OVER THERE.

I'M TAKING OUR LITTER BOX.

I FORGOT AND LEFT IT IN YOUR ROOM.

CED-MORIN

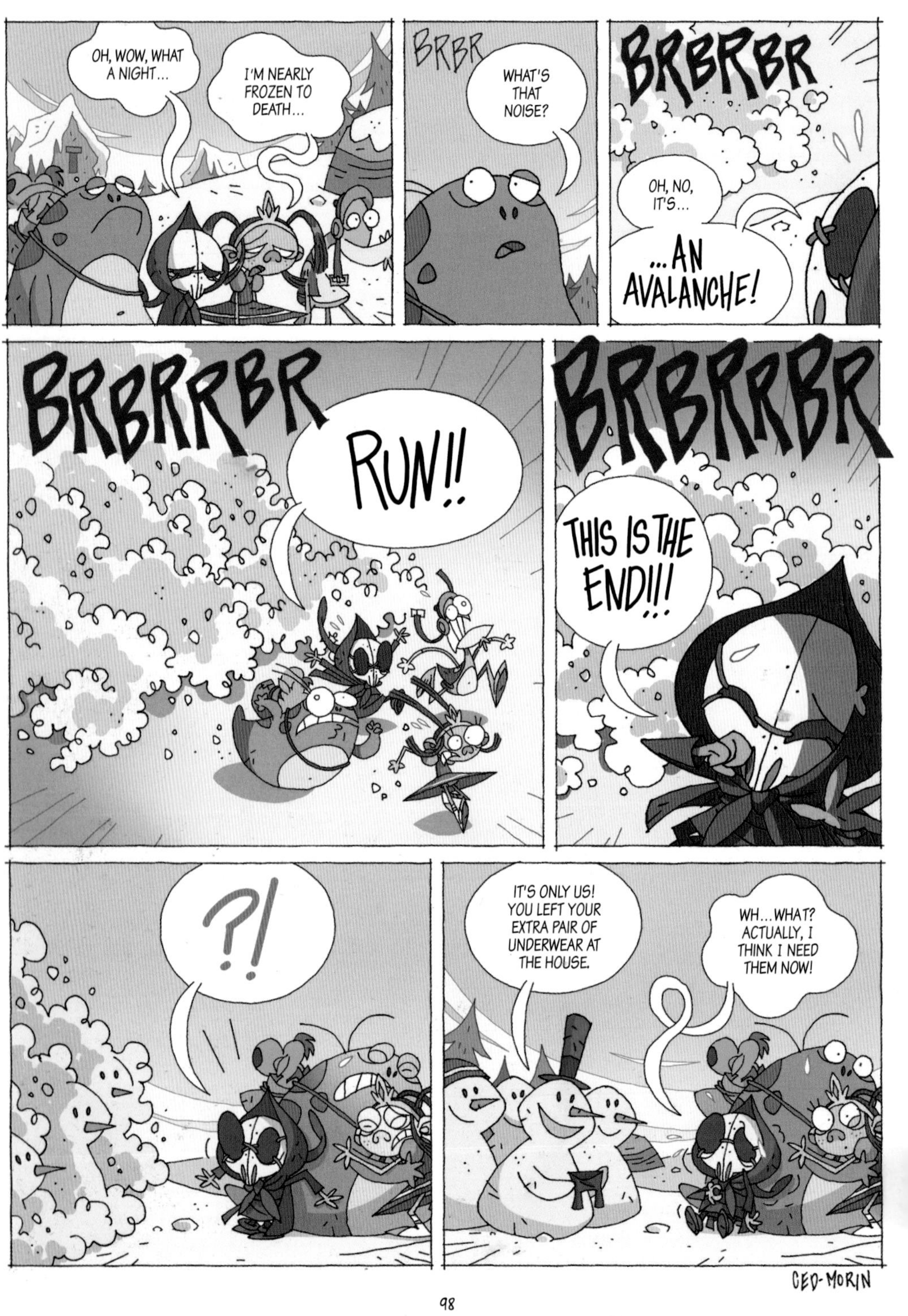
OH, WOW, WHAT A NIGHT...
I'M NEARLY FROZEN TO DEATH...
BRBR
WHAT'S THAT NOISE?
BRBRBR
OH, NO, IT'S...
...AN AVALANCHE!
BRBRRBR
RUN!!
BRBRRRBR
THIS IS THE END!!!
?!
IT'S ONLY US! YOU LEFT YOUR EXTRA PAIR OF UNDERWEAR AT THE HOUSE.
WH...WHAT? ACTUALLY, I THINK I NEED THEM NOW!
CED-MORIN

I WON'T BE UNHAPPY TO LEAVE THAT ICY PLACE!

FINALLY, WE'VE REACHED THE FORBIDDEN FOREST!

WE SHOULD TURN AROUND, DON'T YOU THINK?

BUT WHY?! DEVIL'S MOUNTAIN IS JUST ON THE OTHER SIDE!

BECAUSE THESE WOODS ARE THOUGHT TO BE VERY DANGEROUS!

WHOEVER DARES ENTER THEM WON'T COME OUT!

AND LEGEND SAYS THERE ARE FEROCIOUS WEREWOLVES!

THAT'S SILLY. THOSE ARE JUST MYTHS!

ARGH, THAT DOES IT! YOU NEVER LISTEN TO ME!!!

YOU CAN DO WHAT YOU LIKE!!

?

YOU CONSTANTLY CRITICIZE SLURP AND GONZAG, BUT YOU'RE JUST AS FOOLISH AS THEY ARE!

HEY!

WELL NOW!

GOING THROUGH THERE MAKES NO SENSE! BUT NONE OF YOUR IDEAS MAKE ANY SENSE!

PROVE TO ME THAT I'M WRONG!

JUST **FOR ONCE**, MAKE ONE GROWN-UP DECISION!

SHOULD WE DO "ROCK, PAPER, SCISSORS"?

OED-MORIN

ARE YOU SURE YOU DON'T WANT TO COVER YOURSELF UP SOME?

I DON'T NEED IT!

I BATTLE THE COLD!

HERE, COLD, TAKE THAT!

BECAUSE IF YOU FEEL LIKE TURNING AROUND SOON AND GOING BACK TO A WARMER PLACE, I'LL UNDERSTAND.

JUST SAY THE WORD.

I'M LISTENING ...

ONE LOOK WILL SUFFICE!

OR ONE THOUGHT!

OKAY, IF YOU DON'T SAY ANYTHING WITHIN THE NEXT SECOND, THAT WILL MEAN YOU WANT TO TURN BACK.

SHHH!

THERE! THEY ARE DOWN THE HILL AT THE EDGE OF THE FOREST.

BUT FROM HERE, I CAN'T REALLY SEE WHAT THEY'RE DOING. IT LOOKS LIKE SOME SORT OF DANCE?

SCISSORS! SCISSORS!

I WON-HA!!

CED-MORIN

100

WE'RE IN FRONT OF THE TREE FORTRESS OF THE SYLVAIN ELVES!

WE SHOULD RING THE BELL...

DON'T TOUCH THAT, IT'S BAD LUCK!

IT'S A TRAP!

THE BOOKS SAYS YOU'LL FIND AN EXCLUSIVE COMMUNITY OF WOMEN IN THIS PLACE.

THEIR LAIR WILL HAVE A DEFENSE SYSTEM AGAINST ALL MEN.

IF A GUY TOUCHES THE BELL A THORNY VINE WILL SUDDENLY APPEAR AND CHOKE HIM...

EEEK!

THEN, THE BRANCHES WILL WRAP AROUND HIM!

AND THEN THE HUGE ROOTS WILL FINISH HIM BY CRUSHING HIM!

OH, WOW...

AND ONLY THEN WILL THE TREE FINALLY RELEASE HIM.

G.

UNLESS SOMEONE YELLS "OPEN ME!"

AND IN THIS CASE, IT WILL START OVER.

CED-MORIN

HEY, YOU THERE!

ARE YOU DONE PLAYING WITH THAT BELL?

WE LOVE AND RESPECT THIS FOREST.

TO HONOR IT, WE LIVE IN THE TREETOPS AND ARE CALLED "SYLVAIN."

YOU MADE A MISTAKE COMING TO OUR SANCTUARY...

PLEASE LET US GO! THEY AREN'T BAD, JUST FOOLISH!

NONSENSE! I **AM** EVIL!

YOU DON'T CONCERN US, MY SISTER. YOU ARE FREE TO GO.

OH, REALLY?

AS FOR THE REST OF YOU, YOU'RE OUR PRISONERS!

HEY! SYLVAIN!

YES?

THAT HAPPENS EVERY TIME...

CED-MORIN

102

THIS IS GOOD! I THINK WE LOST THEM!

OOF! WE ARE OUT OF DANGER!

LET'S CONTINUE OUR QUEST!

YOU GO ON.

I'M GOING BACK.

PRINCESS?!

MAEVA! YOU DON'T EVEN KNOW MY NAME. IT'S MAEVA!

JUST BECAUSE I'M THE PRINCESS, YOU THINK NONE OF MY IDEAS COUNT. NONE OF MY SUGGESTIONS ARE ACCEPTED. I'VE HAD ENOUGH. I'M JUST AS GOOD AS YOU!

ONE DAY, YOU WILL KICK YOURSELF, MISTER APPRENTICE LORD OF DARKNESS.

I'M LEAVING TO GO LIVE WITH THE SYLVAIN ELVES, AND DON'T COME FIND ME UNTIL YOU'VE CHANGED.

...

VERY WELL, GO AHEAD! ANYWAY, YOU'RE JUST SLOWING US DOWN.

BUT, MASTER...

YOU CAN'T...

LET HER GO.

GOOD RIDDANCE.

CED-MORIN

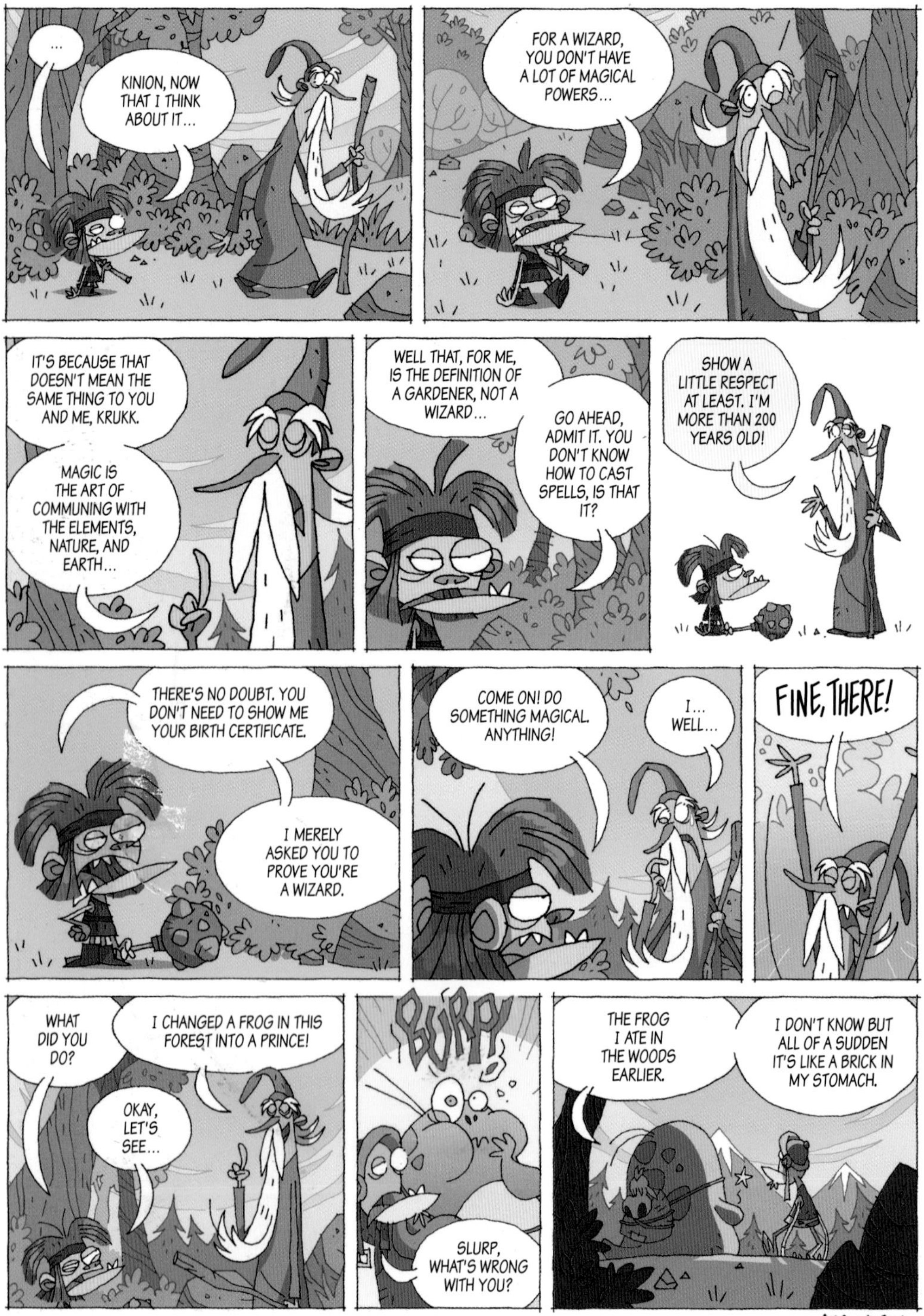
...
KINION, NOW THAT I THINK ABOUT IT...
FOR A WIZARD, YOU DON'T HAVE A LOT OF MAGICAL POWERS...
IT'S BECAUSE THAT DOESN'T MEAN THE SAME THING TO YOU AND ME, KRUKK.
MAGIC IS THE ART OF COMMUNING WITH THE ELEMENTS, NATURE, AND EARTH...
WELL THAT, FOR ME, IS THE DEFINITION OF A GARDENER, NOT A WIZARD...
GO AHEAD, ADMIT IT. YOU DON'T KNOW HOW TO CAST SPELLS, IS THAT IT?
SHOW A LITTLE RESPECT AT LEAST. I'M MORE THAN 200 YEARS OLD!
THERE'S NO DOUBT. YOU DON'T NEED TO SHOW ME YOUR BIRTH CERTIFICATE.
I MERELY ASKED YOU TO PROVE YOU'RE A WIZARD.
COME ON! DO SOMETHING MAGICAL. ANYTHING!
I... WELL...
FINE, THERE!
WHAT DID YOU DO?
I CHANGED A FROG IN THIS FOREST INTO A PRINCE!
OKAY, LET'S SEE...
BURP
SLURP, WHAT'S WRONG WITH YOU?
THE FROG I ATE IN THE WOODS EARLIER.
I DON'T KNOW BUT ALL OF A SUDDEN IT'S LIKE A BRICK IN MY STOMACH.
CED- MORIN

WE'RE APPROACHING THE MINES OF DESPAIR!

THE... THE MINES... AS IN "UNDERGROUND?"

IT SOUNDS LIKE A BUNCH OF BLOODTHIRSTY OGRES GROWLING!

IT'S A GOOD THING THAT OGRES ARE NO LONGER OUR ENEMIES.

LET'S GO THIS WAY. IT'S A GOOD SHORTCUT.

I... I DON'T KNOW, MASTER...

DO WE HAVE TO?

YOU NEED A LITTLE COURAGE!

LOOK, IT SEEMS SOMEONE HAS BEEN WATCHING US.

HELLO.

AAAAHH!!

HAHA! CALM DOWN, BOYS, OGRES HAVE CHANGED!

TODAY, WE PRESENT TO YOU A TOUR OF OUR MINES WHERE YOU CAN OBSERVE UNIQUE LIMESTONE FORMATIONS AND SURPRISING HISTORIC PLACES.

WHEN THE TOUR IS OVER, DON'T FORGET TO TIP YOUR GUIDE.

YOU SEE, THERE IS NOTHING TO FEAR.

IT'S WORSE. IT'S...IT'S...

EDUCATIONAL!!!

CED-MORIN

ARE WE STILL ON THE RIGHT PATH?

YES, THERE ARE THE REMAINS OF THEIR DISGUSTING SACK LUNCHES!

WHERE DOES YOUR OBSESSION WITH STOPPING THIS TYRANT COME FROM, KROLL?

BAH, I WANT TO BE A HERO.

AND HEROES WANT TO STOP LORDS OF EVIL.

YES, OF COURSE...

BUT IN YOUR CASE, IT SEEMS PERSONAL.

DID SOMEONE ELSE "EVIL" HURT YOU A LONG TIME AGO?

YOU HAVE SEEN THROUGH ME. YOU ARE TALENTED, MASTER KINION.

IT STARTED WHEN I WAS A KID.

MY PARENTS CAME TO PICK ME UP AT BARBARIAN SCHOOL AND...

OH MY GOODNESS! AN EVILDOER KILLED YOUR PARENTS!!!

HUH? OH, NO! THEY'RE FINE. THEY ARE IN A RETIREMENT HOME FOR BARBARIANS.

LONG STORY SHORT, THEY CAME WITH MY YOUNGER SISTER, AND...

WHAT?!! THIS MONSTER TOOK YOUR SISTER AND DEVOURED HER!!

THAT'S AWFUL!

WHAT? NOT AT ALL...SHE'S ON A SCHOOL TRIP TO LEARN HOW TO CAPTURE MAMMOTHS!

SO...MY SISTER HAD A CAT, AND...

THIS TERRIBLE ONE...SKINNED THE CAT?

NO...HE SCARED HER AND IT MADE THE CAT ATTACK THE HAMSTER.

SO YOU'RE SAYING WE'RE HERE BECAUSE A TERRIBLE PERSON SCARED A CAT THAT ATE YOUR HAMSTER?

I WILL AVENGE YOU, MISTER WHISKERS!

CED-MORIN

AND?

I STILL CAN'T FIND ANYTHING!

WITH ALL DUE RESPECT...

IT WOULD BE A GOOD IDEA TO HURRY!

YES, BUT I'M DOING WHAT I CAN!

NOTHING HERE...

I CAN'T HOLD ON TOO MUCH LONGER!

DRAT. SOMEWHERE IT MUST TALK ABOUT IT!

THIS IS BECOMING URGENT!

GNN!

HOLD ON JUST A LITTLE LONGER.

THIS OLD SPELL BOOK IS LOUSY...

BOSS, DO SOME- THING!

I TOLD YOU, I'VE LOOKED EVERYWHERE ...

THERE IS NOTHING IN HERE ABOUT SLEEPWALKING DRAGONS!

FLAP FLAP

ZZZ

CED-MORIN

I KNOW WHERE THEY ARE GOING!

?

THEY ARE ON *THEIR* WAY TO DEVIL'S MOUNTAIN, CROCC!

AAAAGGH! YOU'RE HURTING ME!

ON TOP OF DEVIL'S MOUNTAIN IS THE SACRED DEMON'S HAND!

AN ANCIENT RELIC THAT GIVES ANYONE WHO POSSESSES IT THE POWER TO DESTROY EVERYTHING!

BY THE GODS, THEN WE HAVE TO HURRY!

YES, BUT BEFORE WE DO, YOU MUST KNOW ONE THING ABOUT THIS EVIL OBJECT!

THIS ONE BASIC THING THAT CAN MAKE ALL THE DIFFERENCE!

LISTEN CAREFULLY, IT'S...

DING!

AH?! OKAY, WELL, THIS IS THE END OF THE LESSON. WE'VE REACHED THE TIME LIMIT FOR TODAY!

IT WAS A PLEASURE GETTING TO WORK WITH YOU, KROLL! GOOD LUCK WITH SAVING THE WORLD AND ALL THAT!

?!

...

KINION?

CED- MORIN

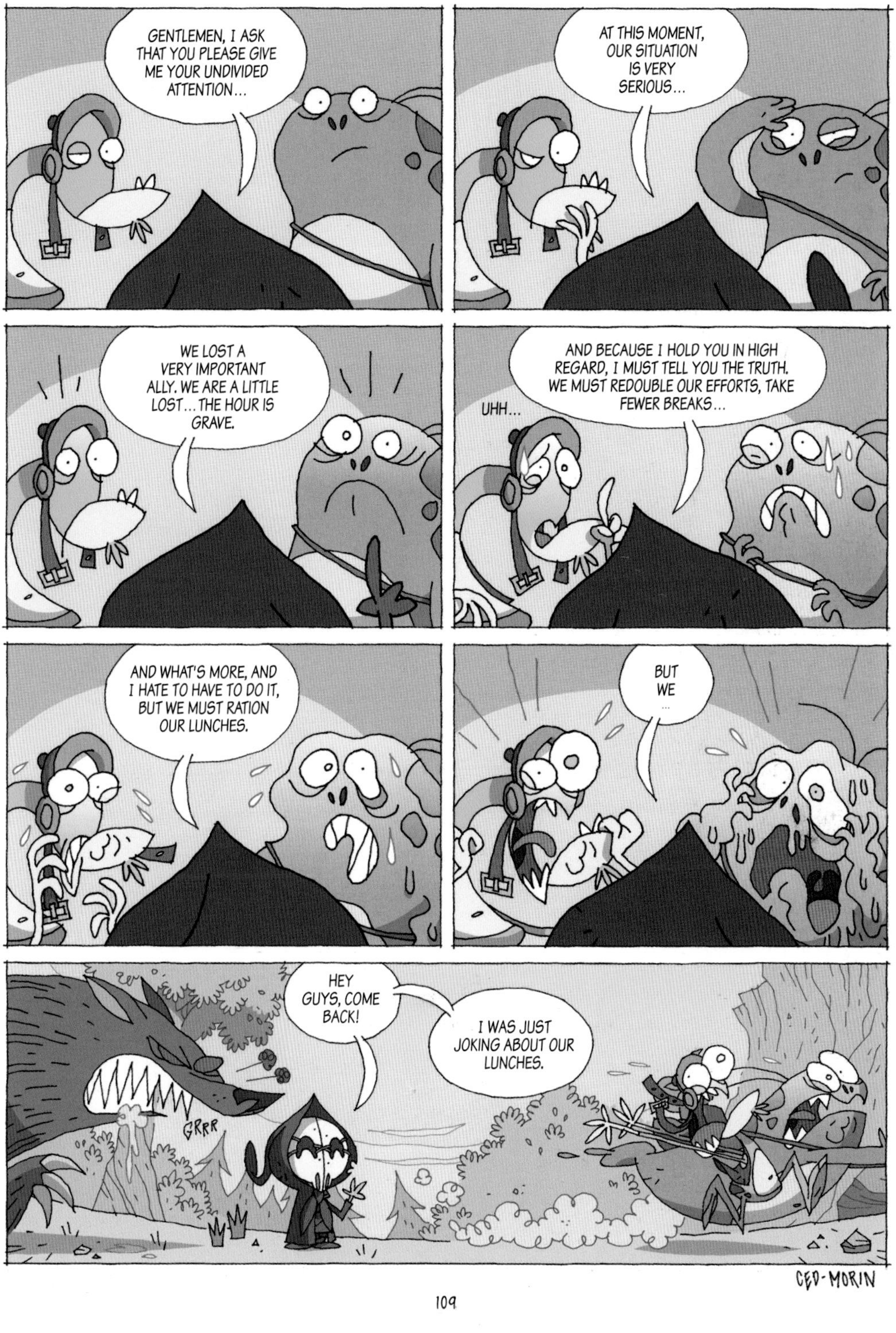
GENTLEMEN, I ASK THAT YOU PLEASE GIVE ME YOUR UNDIVIDED ATTENTION...
AT THIS MOMENT, OUR SITUATION IS VERY SERIOUS...
WE LOST A VERY IMPORTANT ALLY. WE ARE A LITTLE LOST... THE HOUR IS GRAVE.
UHH...
AND BECAUSE I HOLD YOU IN HIGH REGARD, I MUST TELL YOU THE TRUTH. WE MUST REDOUBLE OUR EFFORTS, TAKE FEWER BREAKS...
AND WHAT'S MORE, AND I HATE TO HAVE TO DO IT, BUT WE MUST RATION OUR LUNCHES.
BUT WE ...
GRRR
HEY GUYS, COME BACK!
I WAS JUST JOKING ABOUT OUR LUNCHES.
CED-MORIN

AAAH!!

IT'S A WEREWOLF!!!

SLURP, WHAT'S HAPPENING TO YOU?

WHEN I'M VERY SCARED, I LIQUEFY!

HE'S GETTING CLOSER!

ZIP

?

ZIP ZIP ZIP ZIP ZIP

UN...UNBELIEVABLE. HE SLID ON YOU, SLURP, LIKE A SKATING RINK...

WHAT DID HE FALL ON?

WHAT IS THIS HOUND WHO FELL ON ME AND DISTURBED ME DURING MY SNACK TIME?

IS THERE A GIANT THAT LIVES AT THE BOTTOM OF EVERY CLIFF HERE OR WHAT?

DADDY'S GOING TO BRUSH YOU AND MAKE YOUR HAIR INTO PRETTY CURLS, MY LITTLE DOGGY!

YIP YIPPP

CED-MORIN

FINALLY, WE MADE IT.

DEVIL'S MOUNTAIN...

MMM...IT LOOKS LIKE THERE IS SOMEONE AT THE TOP.

YOU CAN BE SO SUSPICIOUS!

YOU ALWAYS OVERDRAMATIZE EVERYTHING! LET'S FOLLOW THE INSTRUCTIONS IN THE SPELL BOOK: "THE PATH IS LONG AND FILLED WITH DEATH TRAPS."

"BEWARE OF THE STAIRS. THE STONES ARE LOOSE."

CRRR

"...AND YOU COULD BE CRUSHED AT ANY MOMENT."

"YOU WILL NOTICE, AT THE ENTRANCE OF THE CAVE, A FEROCIOUS BAT THAT GUARDS IT."

"IF YOU MANAGE TO GET PAST THE ENTRANCE, BEWARE OF THE BOTTOMLESS CANYON!"

"ONE TIP: HOLD THE GUARDRAIL AND NEVER MOVE MORE THAN THREE STEPS TO THE RIGHT."

AND THERE WE GO, WE'RE HERE!

YOU SEE, THAT WASN'T SO HARD!

OH, DARN!

I HAVE A ROCK IN MY SHOE.

AND OF COURSE, THERE'S NO ONE TO HELP ME!

CED-MORIN

"WHOEVER TAKES POSSESSION OF THE DEMON'S HAND WILL REALIZE ALL HIS WISHES, BOTH GOOD AND TERRIBLE."

SLURP, GONZAG, I HAVE IT!!

FINALLY, I HAVE IT!!

MY POWER KNOWS NO LIMIT!!

CRAAACK

BLOOP

WHOEVER CROSSES MY PATH WILL BE CRUSHED!

HEY!

EXCUSE ME?

WHO IS THIS PEASANT?

MISTER WHISKERS, I SHALL FINALLY AVENGE YOU.

CED-MORIN

LET THAT GO!

SLUUURP!

POF

TAKE CARE OF HIM, GONZAG!

PAF

I'M GOING TO LET GO, MASTER!

HANG ON TO THE EDGE, SLURP!

I CAN'T! I'M TOO SCARED. I'M GOING TO LIQUEFY!

HERE, GIVE ME YOUR HAND!

THERE, I HAVE IT...

HERE...

OH NO, SLURP...

THIS ISN'T THE HAND I MEANT...

CED-MORIN

GET BACK, YOU LOUSE!

HEY!

YOU'LL NEVER GET AWAY WITH THAT HAND!

IF YOU LIKE IT SO MUCH, TAKE IT!

YOU'RE WITH ME, GONZAG!

WHERE ARE WE GOING, BOSS?

TO SAVE SLURP, OF COURSE!

WHAT? TO THE BOTTOM OF THE BOTTOMLESS CANYON? BUT THAT'S IMPOSSIBLE!!

I'M NOT EXACTLY THE SMARTEST, BUT EVEN I KNOW THAT...

NO! I REFUSE TO ABANDON EITHER ONE OF YOU!!!

WE MUST FIND A WAY TO SAVE HIM. DO YOU HEAR ME!?

HEY, GUYS!

FLAP

FLAP

DID I MISS SOMETHING?

114

CED-MORIN

SLURP!!!

FLAP FLAP FLAP

ARE YOU OKAY?

JUST GREAT, BOSS! AND EVEN MORE, IT WAS GREAT AT THE BOTTOM. THERE WAS PLENTY OF LIGHT!!

YOU ARE THE BEST, HUBERT!

HEY, THERE'S LIGHT? AT THE BOTTOM? BUT THAT MEANS THAT...

IT'S A VOLCANO...

ABOUT TO ERUPT!

WE MUST GET OUT OF HERE!

AND FAST!!

BUT MASTER...

WHAT ABOUT THE HAND?

THAT'S THE LEAST OF MY WORRIES! IT'S UP TO KROKK TO DEAL WITH IT!

CED-MORIN

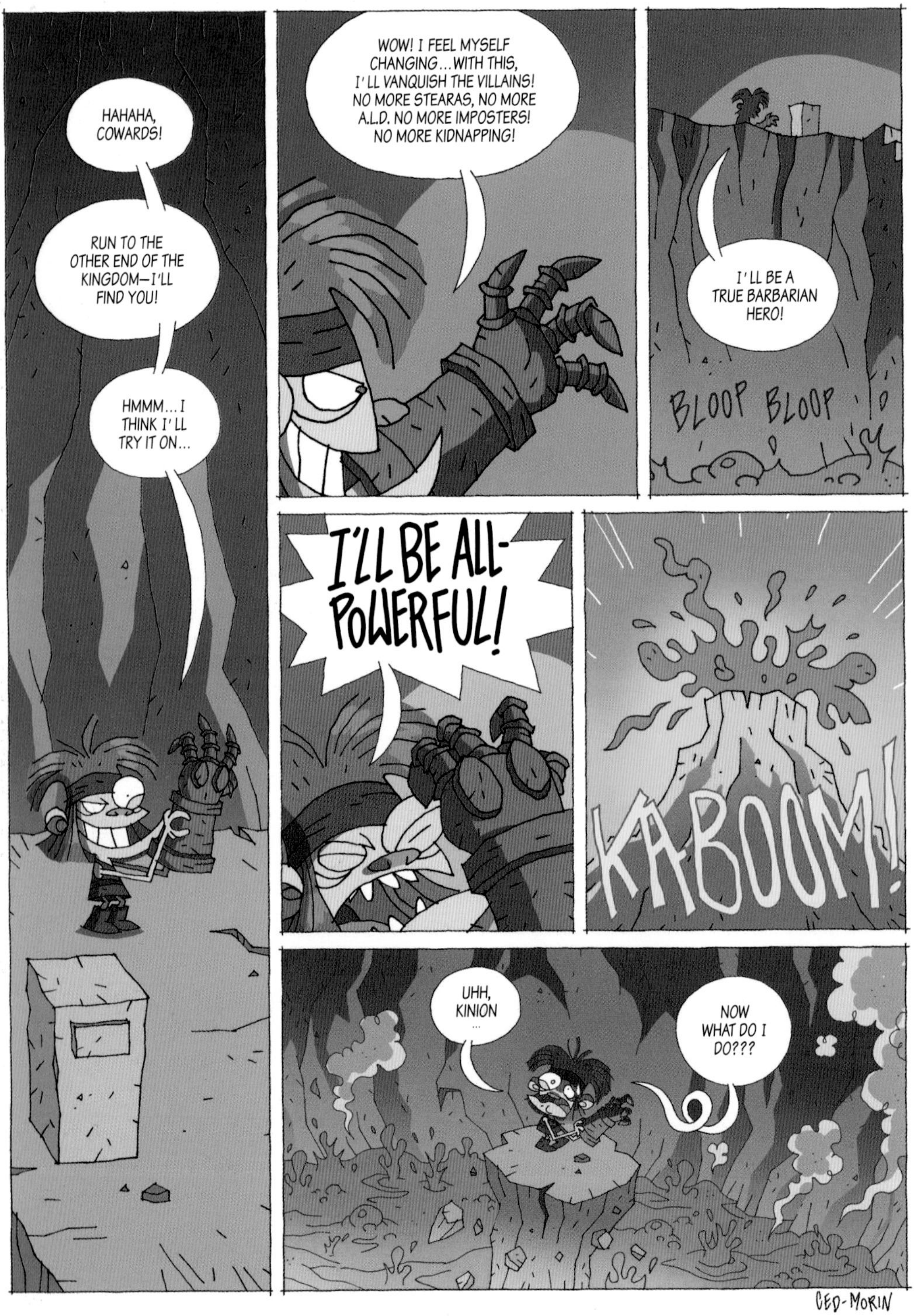
HAHAHA, COWARDS!
RUN TO THE OTHER END OF THE KINGDOM—I'LL FIND YOU!
HMMM… I THINK I'LL TRY IT ON…
WOW! I FEEL MYSELF CHANGING… WITH THIS, I'LL VANQUISH THE VILLAINS! NO MORE STEARAS, NO MORE A.L.D. NO MORE IMPOSTERS! NO MORE KIDNAPPING!
I'LL BE A TRUE BARBARIAN HERO!
BLOOP BLOOP
I'LL BE ALL-POWERFUL!
KABOOM!
UHH, KINION …
NOW WHAT DO I DO???
CED-MORIN

RUN!!

LET'S TAKE SHELTER IN THE FOREST!

THE TREES ARE ON FIRE!!

THIS ISN'T THE RIGHT TIME TO LIQUEFY, SLURP! FOCUS!

I'M TRYING!

AAAH! WE'RE TRAPPED!

THIS WAY! I HAVE AN IDEA!

WE'LL ASK THE SYLVAIN ELVES TO TAKE US IN.

WHAT?!

I THINK I PREFER THE FIIIRRRRE!!

CED-MORIN

117

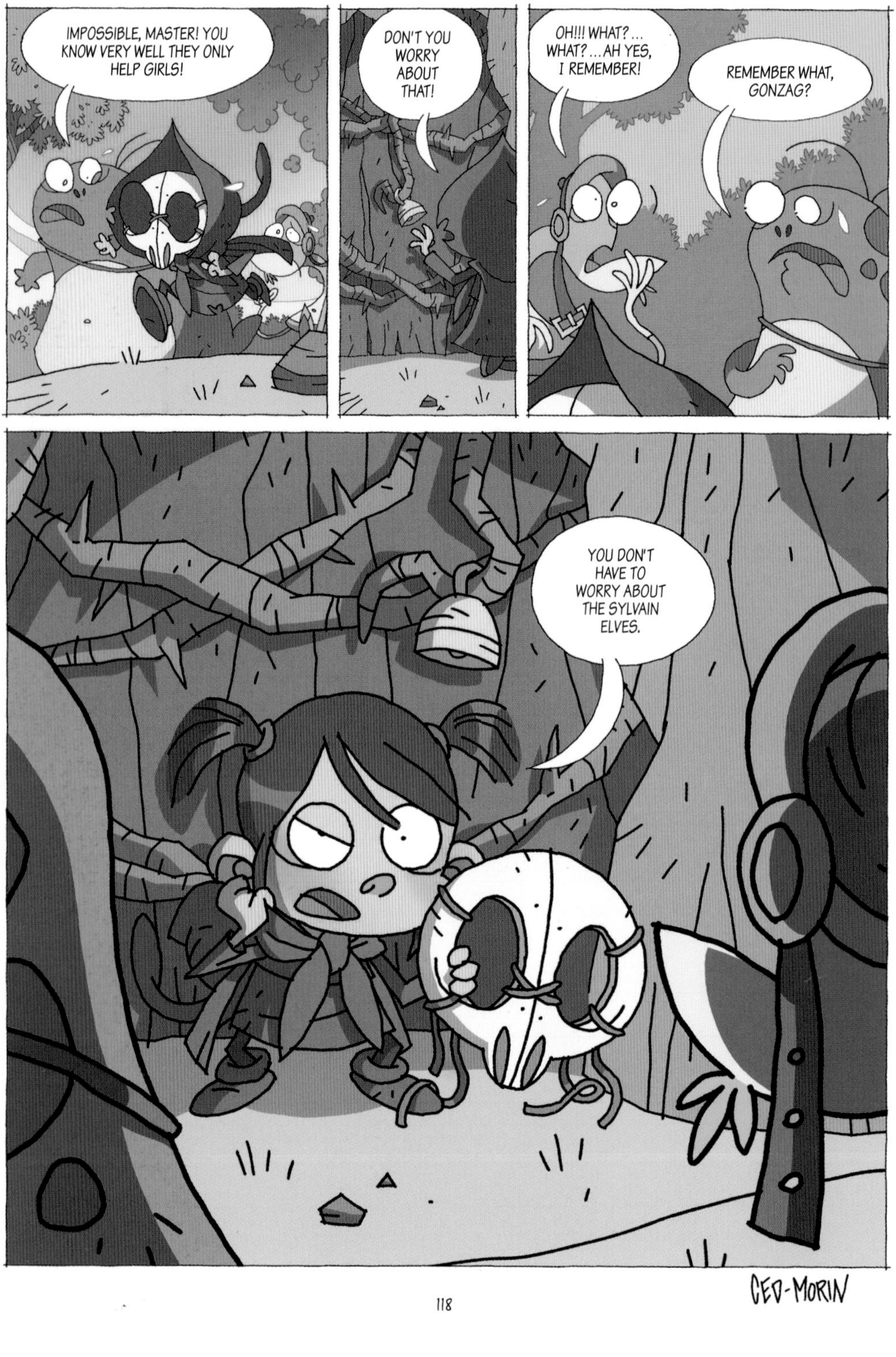
IMPOSSIBLE, MASTER! YOU KNOW VERY WELL THEY ONLY HELP GIRLS!
DON'T YOU WORRY ABOUT THAT!
OH!!! WHAT? ... WHAT? ... AH YES, I REMEMBER!
REMEMBER WHAT, GONZAG?
YOU DON'T HAVE TO WORRY ABOUT THE SYLVAIN ELVES.
CED-MORIN

Chapter 4

HOT ON THEIR HEELS!

DEAR READER, BEFORE WE DIVE INTO THE HEART OF THIS STORY, LET'S GO BACK IN TIME, LONG BEFORE THE BEGINNING OF THIS WACKY ADVENTURE ...

IT WILL BE PERFECT!

HELLO! ARE YOU THERE?

YOO-HOO!

OH! IS SOMEONE THERE?

OH, IT'S YOU AGAIN. WHAT DO YOU WANT?

ARE YOU COMING OUT TO PLAY WITH ME?

I'VE ALREADY TOLD YOU. I HAVE BETTER THINGS TO DO!

BUT...

THERE IS NO BUT! NO. I SAID NO!

YOU NEVER WANT TO! IT'S NOT FAIR!!!

LIFE IS NOT FAIR! NOW GO HOME!

I'M NOT USED TO BEING TOLD NO!

WELL, GET USED TO IT ...

...PRINCESS.

CED-MORIN

121

TODAY.

KABOOM!

RUN!!

THE TREES ARE ON FIRE!!

AAAH! WE'RE TRAPPED!

THIS WAY, I HAVE AN IDEA!

WE'LL ASK THE SYLVAIN ELVES FOR HELP!

IMPOSSIBLE, MASTER! YOU KNOW VERY WELL THEY ONLY HELP GIRLS!

DON'T WORRY ABOUT THAT!

I'VE GOT IT COVERED.

WHAAATT?!

YOU HAVE PIGTAILS?

CED-MORIN

122

YOU AREN'T VERY OBSERVANT, SLURP.

WAIT, YOU KNEW THE MASTER HAD HAIR?

ARE YOU DONE?

WE'RE IN THE MIDDLE OF A FOREST FIRE!

NOW FOLLOW ME!

AND KEEP MY IDENTITY SECRET!

HALT THERE!

HOW DID YOU GET IN?

ONLY WOMEN CAN OPEN THE DOOR!

WELL, ACTUALLY...

I CAST A SPELL ON YOUR DOOR!

SO IT WAS YOU WHO AWAKENED DEVIL'S MOUNTAIN?

NO! THERE WAS A BARBARIAN! HE STOLE A MAGICAL RELIC—THAT'S WHAT CAUSED THE ERUPTION!

AND THE FIRE IN THE WOODS?

SAME THING! IT'S THAT GUY! NOT US! I PROMISE!

SO WHO LEFT THE DOOR OPEN AND LET IN THE FLAMES?

OKAY, THAT WAS US.

CED-MORIN

FIRE!

SYLVAIN SISTERS! HURRY! I NEED HELP HERE!

COME ON, LET'S GO!

WHERE ARE WE GOING, BOSS?

TO FIND THE PRINCESS AND LEAVE!

BY THE WAY, NOW THAT WE'VE SEEN YOUR FACE, WHAT SHOULD WE CALL YOU?

UGH!

EVERYTHING IS EXACTLY THE SAME! I REMAIN LORD OF DARKNESS AND YOU, MY LACKEYS! WE WON'T SAY ANYTHING TO THE PRINCESS!

WHY? SHE'LL BE MAD IF SHE'S LEFT OUT.

I KNOW THAT, THANK YOU! BUT THE FACE BEHIND THIS MASK...

...IS WANTED.

PINK HERTON
Private Detective

KNOCK KNOCK

YES?

AH, IT'S YOU! COME IN!

IT ALWAYS SURPRISES ME THAT YOU ARE A GHOST!

IT'S VERY PRACTICAL IN THIS BUSINESS! I CAN MAKE MYSELF INVISIBLE, WALK THROUGH WALLS...

YESTERDAY, YOU CAME TO ME WITH THIS POSTER AND SAID, "FIND THEM."

AND I DID!

ALREADY? I'M IMPRESSED! WHERE?

I FOUND THIS ONE GLUED TO A POLE ACROSS THE STREET.

IT'S THE PERSON THAT YOU NEED TO FIND, NOT THE POSTER...

CED-MORIN

THE TREE FORTRESS IS SURROUNDED BY FLAMES!

COME ON, SISTERS, LET'S PUSH BACK THIS FIRE!

FASTER!

?

ARE YOU FIGHTING THE FIRE WITH ARROWS?

OH... YES, UH... IT'S A HABIT...

WHAT SHOULD WE DO, THEN?

YOU DON'T KNOW HOW TO EXTINGUISH A FIRE?!!

WHERE ARE YOUR WATER RESERVES?

WE DON'T HAVE ANY! WHEN WE WANT WATER, WE WAIT FOR IT TO RAIN. WHEN WE'RE HUNGRY, WE PICK FRUIT. WE TRUST MOTHER NATURE!

AND WHEN EVERYTHING'S ON FIRE, WHAT DOES MOTHER NATURE DO?

SHE COULD... UH... MAKE A RIVER FLOOD?

AAAAH! THIS PLACE IS THE WORST!

PRINCESS!

OH, IT'S YOU!

PRINCESS, I APOLOGIZE... IT IS MY FAULT IF THE TREE FORTRESS IS DESTROYED...

I'M SO HAPPY TO SEE YOU!!

125

CED-MORIN

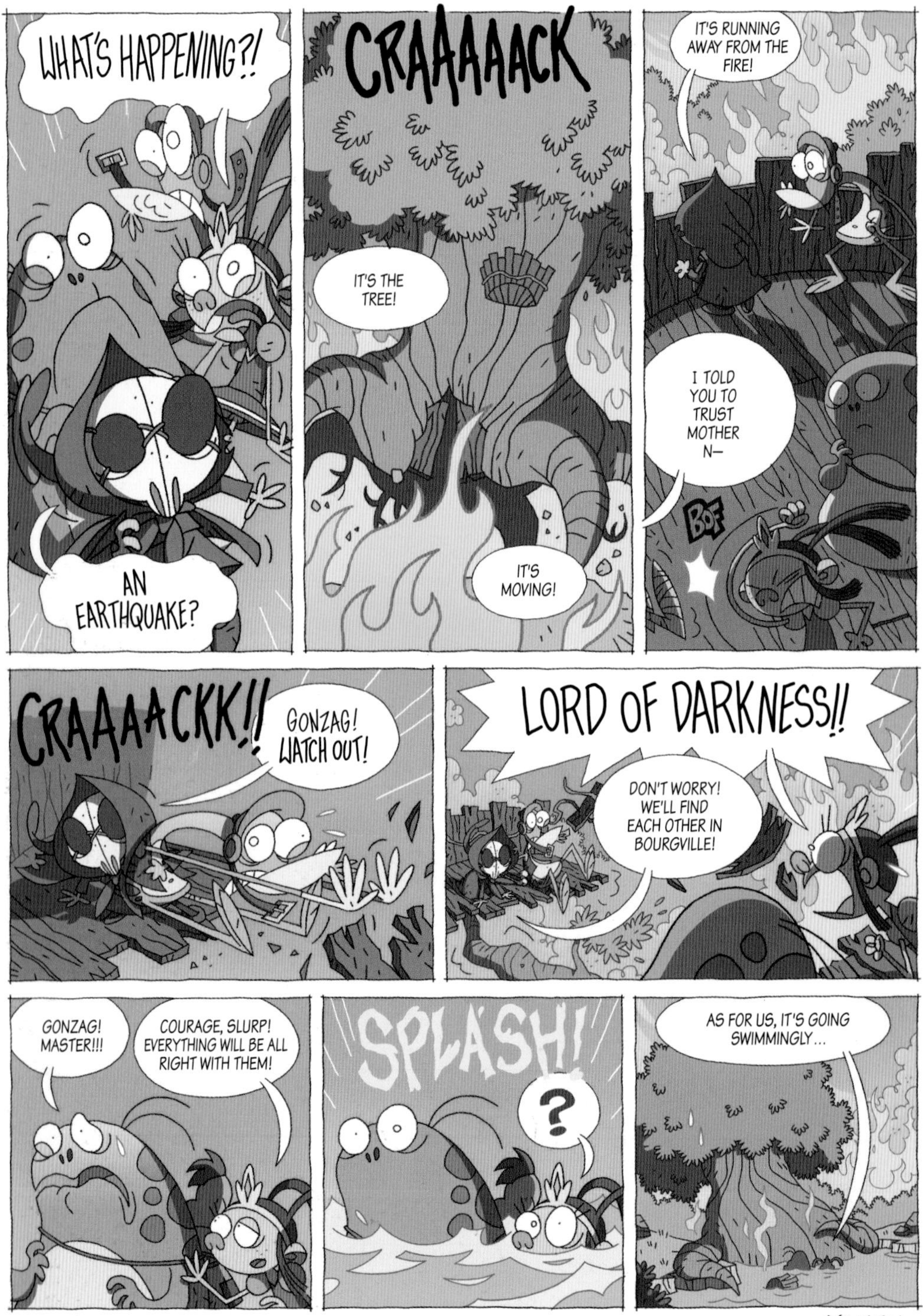
WHAT'S HAPPENING?!
AN EARTHQUAKE?
CRAAAAACK
IT'S THE TREE!
IT'S MOVING!
IT'S RUNNING AWAY FROM THE FIRE!
I TOLD YOU TO TRUST MOTHER N—
BOF
CRAAAACKK!!
GONZAG! WATCH OUT!
LORD OF DARKNESS!!
DON'T WORRY! WE'LL FIND EACH OTHER IN BOURGVILLE!
GONZAG! MASTER!!!
COURAGE, SLURP! EVERYTHING WILL BE ALL RIGHT WITH THEM!
SPLASH!
?
AS FOR US, IT'S GOING SWIMMINGLY...

CED-MORIN

AAAAH!

IT'S OKAY, GONZAG. YOU CAN STOP SCREAMING.

OH, YES. SORRY.

UM, MY MISTAKE, YOU CAN CONTINUE.

CED-MORIN

127

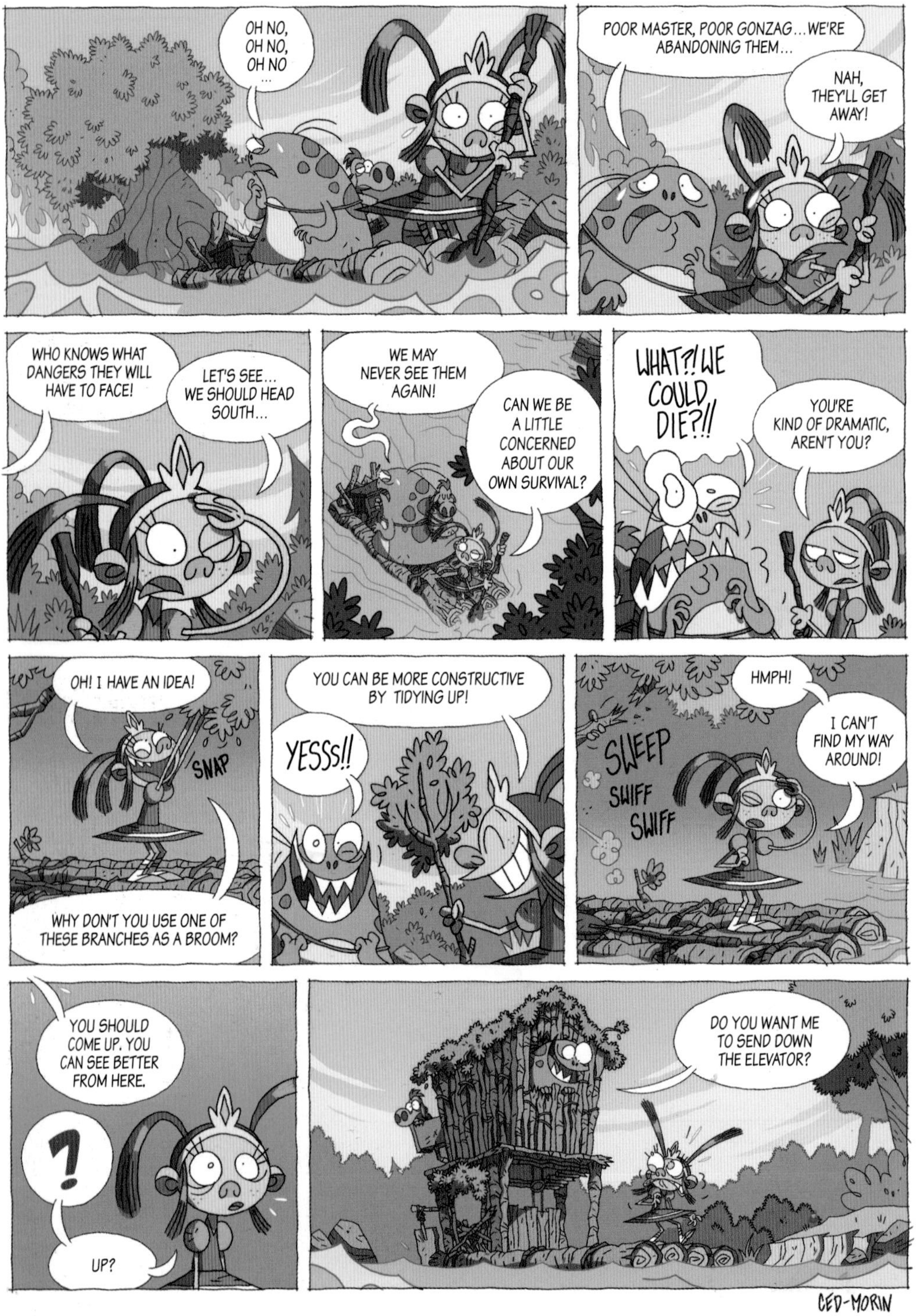
OH NO, OH NO, OH NO …
POOR MASTER, POOR GONZAG…WE'RE ABANDONING THEM…
NAH, THEY'LL GET AWAY!
WHO KNOWS WHAT DANGERS THEY WILL HAVE TO FACE!
LET'S SEE… WE SHOULD HEAD SOUTH…
WE MAY NEVER SEE THEM AGAIN!
CAN WE BE A LITTLE CONCERNED ABOUT OUR OWN SURVIVAL?
WHAT?! WE COULD DIE?!!
YOU'RE KIND OF DRAMATIC, AREN'T YOU?
OH! I HAVE AN IDEA!
SNAP
WHY DON'T YOU USE ONE OF THESE BRANCHES AS A BROOM?
YOU CAN BE MORE CONSTRUCTIVE BY TIDYING UP!
YESSS!!
HMPH!
SWEEP
SWIFF
SWIFF
I CAN'T FIND MY WAY AROUND!
YOU SHOULD COME UP. YOU CAN SEE BETTER FROM HERE.
?
UP?
DO YOU WANT ME TO SEND DOWN THE ELEVATOR?

CED-MORIN

WHEN YOU DON'T KNOW WHERE TO START YOUR INVESTIGATION...

THERE IS ONLY ONE SOLUTION: THE STREET.

HEY! YOU!

?

HAVE YOU SEEN THIS GIRL?

HMM...

I WOULD LOVE TO HELP YOU, BUT I'M LOOKING FOR MY DOG...

I'LL GIVE YOU A HAND, IF YOU DO THE SAME FOR ME!

OKAY! I'LL KEEP A LOOK OUT!

I'M LOOKING FOR THIS GIRL. AND THIS DOG, TOO.

AND SOMEONE STOLE MY COLLECTION OF ANIMAL HATS...

I'M LOOKING...

PLEASE HELP ME FIND MY PARAKEETS!

I...

MY BABYSITTER QUIT. I HAVE TO FIND ANOTHER ONE!

SO, HOW'S THE SEARCH GOING?

AS YOU CAN SEE, IT'S MOVING FORWARD!

CED-MORIN

AAAAH!!

I KNEW I WOULD END UP LIKE THIS! DEVOURED BY HIM!

DO YOU KNOW EACH OTHER?

ALL THE GOBLINS FEAR HIM! MOMS SCARE THEIR CHILDREN BY SAYING THAT IF THEY ARE NOT GOOD, THE "BIG PURPLE HAMSTER" WILL GET THEM!

AND THEY TAKE THIS SERIOUSLY?

HE'S THE ENEMY OF MY PEOPLE! OUR ANCESTORS EVEN BUILT TRAPS AGAINST HIM IN THESE TUNNELS!

TO ELIMINATE HIM?

OH NO, HE'S WAY TOO STRONG! JUST TO DISTRACT HIM!

AND WHAT DO THESE TRAPS LOOK LIKE?

WELL, ACTUALLY...

I THINK WE'RE IN ONE!

CED-MORIN

SLURP, DO YOU THINK THIS RAFT WILL HOLD?

IN WHAT WAY?

I DON'T KNOW... OVER A WATERFALL, FOR EXAMPLE?

WHY DO YOU ASK THAT?

SPLASH

AMAZING! IT IS STILL INTACT!

BUT WILL IT BE AFTER A STORM?

KRAAKOOM

A LITTLE WET BUT STILL STANDING!

WOW! YOU SHOULD BE AN ENGINEER!

AA AAA AAA

BOOM

APPARENTLY NOTHING CAN WITHSTAND A DRAGON WITH A COLD...

WE ALL HAVE AT LEAST ONE WEAKNESS...

131

CED-MORIN

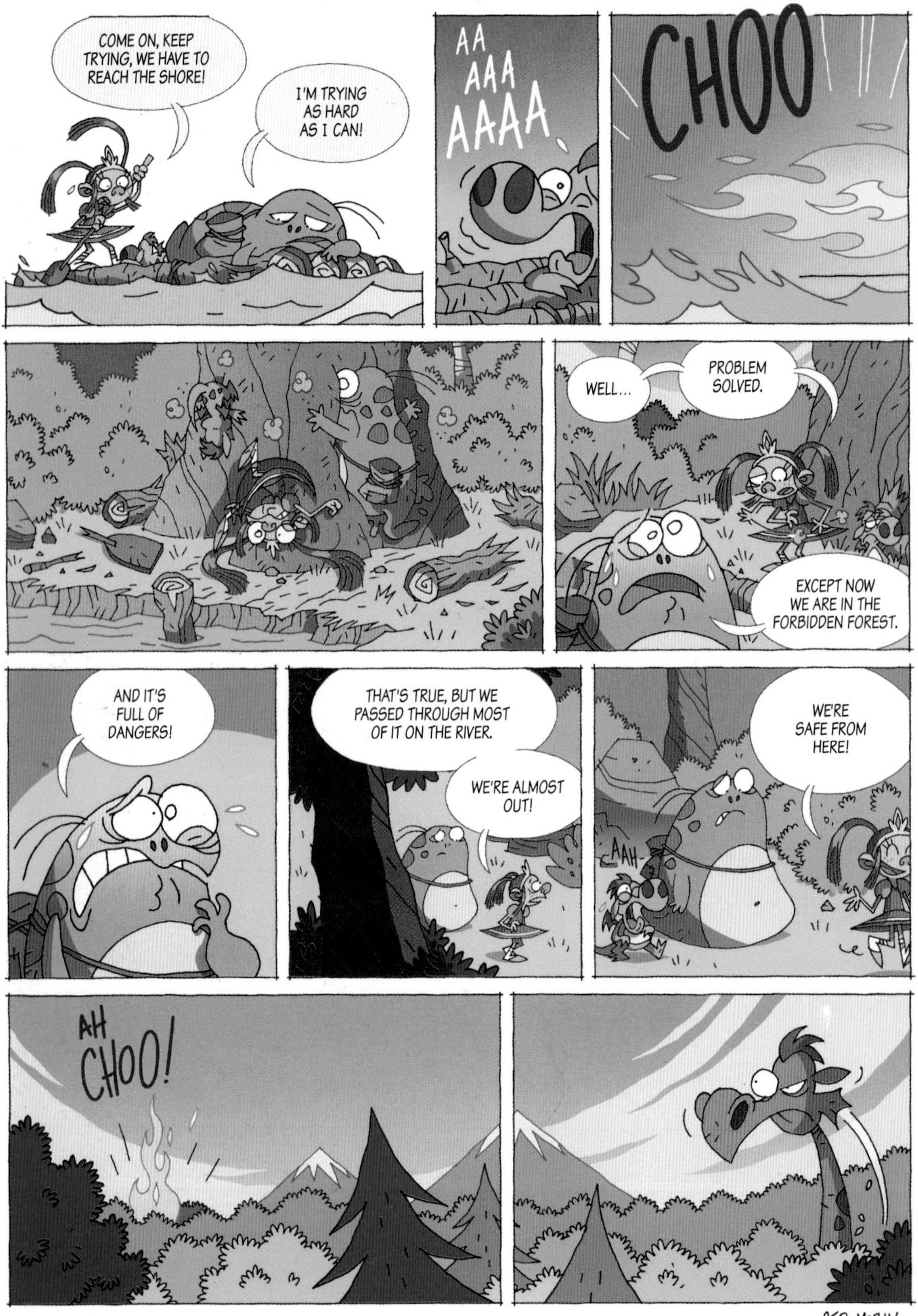
COME ON, KEEP TRYING, WE HAVE TO REACH THE SHORE!
I'M TRYING AS HARD AS I CAN!
AA AAA AAAA
CHOO
WELL...
PROBLEM SOLVED.
EXCEPT NOW WE ARE IN THE FORBIDDEN FOREST.
AND IT'S FULL OF DANGERS!
THAT'S TRUE, BUT WE PASSED THROUGH MOST OF IT ON THE RIVER.
WE'RE ALMOST OUT!
WE'RE SAFE FROM HERE!
AAH-
AH CHOO!
CED-MORIN

ARE YOU SURE WE'RE GOING IN THE RIGHT DIRECTION?

TRUST ME!

SUCH A NICE, SUNNY DAY...

...EXCEPT FOR THAT BIG CLOUD...

THAT'S NOT A CLOUD. IT'S A...

DRAGON!

FLAP FLAP FLAP FLAP

FLAP FLAP FLAP

AAAH

THAT WAY!

SHHH, I THINK WE LOST HIM!

NOTHING ON THE RIGHT.

NOTHING ON THE LEFT.

NEXT TIME, WE'LL HAVE TO REMEMBER TO LOOK UP WHEN SEARCHING FOR A DRAGON...

FLAP

FLAP

DON'T WORRY ...

THERE WON'T BE A NEXT TIME.

CED-MORIN

WE ARE NO LONGER BEING FOLLOWED!

FOR NOW! BUT THE JAWS OF TERROR IS STILL ON THE PROWL...

THIS CRITTER COULD BE USEFUL TO ME, IF I CAPTURED IT...

NO ONE CAN TAME HIM! BRRRR...

WE ARE VERY CLOSE TO YOUR PEOPLE. LOOK!

GOBLIN KINGDOM 3 MILES

GREAT!

MY WIFE AND CHILDREN ARE THERE RIGHT NOW, IN OUR VACATION STALAGMITE!

PERFECT! WE CAN REST HERE A LITTLE...

I NEED QUIET TO THINK ABOUT NEW EVIL PLANS.

AND TO ENJOY YOUR FAMILY'S DELICIOUS BEET COOKIES!

GOBLIN KINGDOM 6 MILES

?

SIX MILES! BUT BACK THERE IT SAID THREE!

OH, YES!

GOBLIN KINGDOM 6 MILES

IT'S A GOBLIN TRICK TO CONFUSE OUR ENEMIES.

OUR SIGNS MAKE NO SENSE AT ALL!

7M   9M

3M

CLEVER.

BUT HOW DO YOU FIND YOUR WAY?

IT'S EASY WHEN YOU KNOW THE TRICK!

YOU HAVE TO FOLLOW THOSE, YOU SEE!

NOT THE WAY TO THE GOBLIN KINGDOM 2 MILES

WE PROMISE THE GOBLIN KINGDOM IS NOT THIS WAY!

I SEE THAT YOUR PEOPLE ARE JUST AS SMART AS YOU ARE...

ARE YOU KIDDING? I'M CONSIDERED A GENIUS AMONG THEM.

CED-MORIN

WE'RE ALMOST THERE.

GOBLIN KINGDOM NOT THIS WAY NOT AT ALL!

SO I SEE.

OH!

SKELETON SOLDIERS!

HEY! YOU!

LET'S RUN!

YOU DIDN'T TELL ME WE MIGHT MEET THEM HERE!

THAT'S NEW!

?

SO, WHAT DO THEY DO?

MMM...

YOU'RE BACK! WE'RE GOING TO ROAST YOU!

GO AHEAD. COME ON!

UH...

NO. YOU APPROACH.

I BET YOU CAN'T TAKE ONE STEP.

OH, YEAH?

THERE...ATTACK GUYS...

CLACK CLACK CLACK

LET'S GO, GONZAG. LET'S LEAVE THESE WRETCHES.

YOU TRIPPED US WITH A WIRE OR SOMETHING...

YOU'RE LUCKY THE GROUND ISN'T SLOPING OR WE'D BE ROLLING AFTER YOU!

HEY, COME BACK HERE!

CED-MORIN

135

HERE WE ARE!

BEFORE WE ENTER, I NEED TO WARN YOU...

?

THE OTHER GOBLINS HAVE A FUNNY REACTION WHEN THEY SEE ME.

HOW'S THAT? THEY MAKE FUN OF YOU?

BECAUSE THAT WOULD BE UNDERSTANDABLE.

NO, NO.

HOW DO THEY REACT?

IT'S THE HERO!

THE HERO!

THE HERO

THE HERO

THE HERO

THE HERO

AND HIS FRIEND

I DID NOT EXPECT THAT...

CED-MORIN

I ENDED UP FINDING SOMEONE WHO KNEW THE GIRL...

BUT NOT EVERYTHING WENT AS PLANNED...

FIND THE DETECTIVE AND SURROUND HIM!

!!

OH NO, HERE THEY COME!

BOSS!!! HE'S IN THE ALLEY!

CATCH HIM!

THERE HE IS!

THERE ARE TOO MANY OF THEM!

I CAN'T ESCAPE...

TAG, YOU'RE IT!

TAP

YEEAAHH!!

ONE LAST TIME, BUT AFTER YOU ANSWER MY QUESTIONS, OK?

CED-MORIN

OH NO, OH NO, OH NO!

WE'RE GOING TO BE EATEN!

WOULD YOU STOP WHINING?

I CAN'T THINK!

WELL, OBVIOUSLY WE'RE TOO HIGH UP.

WE CAN'T JUMP FROM HERE...

SO OUR CHOICES ARE BEING EATEN OR JUMPING INTO NOTHIING?

OH NO ...

THE DRAGON. HE'S BACK.

FLAP

FLAP

BWAAAA

NO! GET AWAY! LEAVE US ALONE!

WAAAa

FLAP

FLAP

AAAAAH!

BWAAAaa

FLAP

FLAP

?

SLURP, EVERYTHING IS FINE. HE JUST BROUGHT US FOOD.

I KNOOOOW! I SAAAAWWW!

THEN WHY ARE YOU CRYING?

BECAUSE HE ONLY BROUGHT VEGEETABLLESS!

CED-MORIN

138

HE'S GONE AGAIN. WHAT'S THIS DRAGON UP TO?

HE WANTS TO FATTEN US UP!

CROUNCH

WITH CABBAGES AND PUMPKINS?

IT LOOKS MORE LIKE HE WANTS TO KEEP US HEALTHY!

I THINK I'VE SEEN HIM SOMEWHERE BEFORE, ACTUALLY...

FLAP

FLAP

WHERE'S HE GETTING ALL THIS FOOD?

MEANWHILE...

THANK YOU FOR COMING SO FAST, OFFICER...?

OFFICER BERRY, DEPARTMENT OF UNEXPLAINED VEGETABLE DISAPPEARANCE!

YA SEE, I WAS GARDENING THERE, LIKE THIS!

THEN I TURNED AROUND AND ALL OF A SUDDEN! POOF! HALF OF MY PLANTS HAD DISAPPEARED!

YOU CALLED THE RIGHT PERSON! THIS FITS PERFECTLY WITHIN MY JURISDICTION.

BAM

WHOOSH

THERE! DID YOU SEE?! WHAT ARE YOU GOING TO DO?!!

MMM.

NOTHING.

WHAT DO YOU MEAN "NOTHING"?!

YOU HAVE TO CONTACT THE DEPARTMENT OF THEFT BY GIANT REPTILES.

NOW, HERE'S YOUR FINE FOR FILING A FALSE CLAIM.

CED-MORIN

YES, YES, THANK YOU FOR THE WELCOME! HEE!

WHAT WAS THAT ALL ABOUT?

THE HERO THE HERO

THE HERO

THEY BELIEVE THAT MY FATHER WILL SAVE OUR PEOPLE FROM AN UKNOWN THREAT SOMETIME IN THE FUTURE.

PERNILLA!

FATHER.

PRISCILLA, MY DARLING!

CHTON! GOL! BRINGO!

MY BOYS!

IS IT TRUE WHAT THEY SAY ABOUT YOU?

OH NO, AN ELDER MADE THAT PREDICTION WHEN I WAS BORN.

WE MOVED TO THE CITY SO WE WOULDN'T HAVE TO HEAR ABOUT IT ANYMORE!

HOWEVER, WE DO NEED A HERO AT THE MOMENT...

HOW'S THAT?

RECENTLY, A MYSTERIOUS BEING APPEARED IN THESE CAVES.

THERE WAS A BIG EARTHQUAKE. THE EARTH OPENED UP AND HE APPEARED.

NO ONE KNOWS WHO HE IS...

IF HE'S A SORCERER OR A DEMON...

OR WHY HE IS HERE...

I KNOW YOU'RE THERE...

...APPRENTICE LORD OF DARKNESS!

CED-MORIN

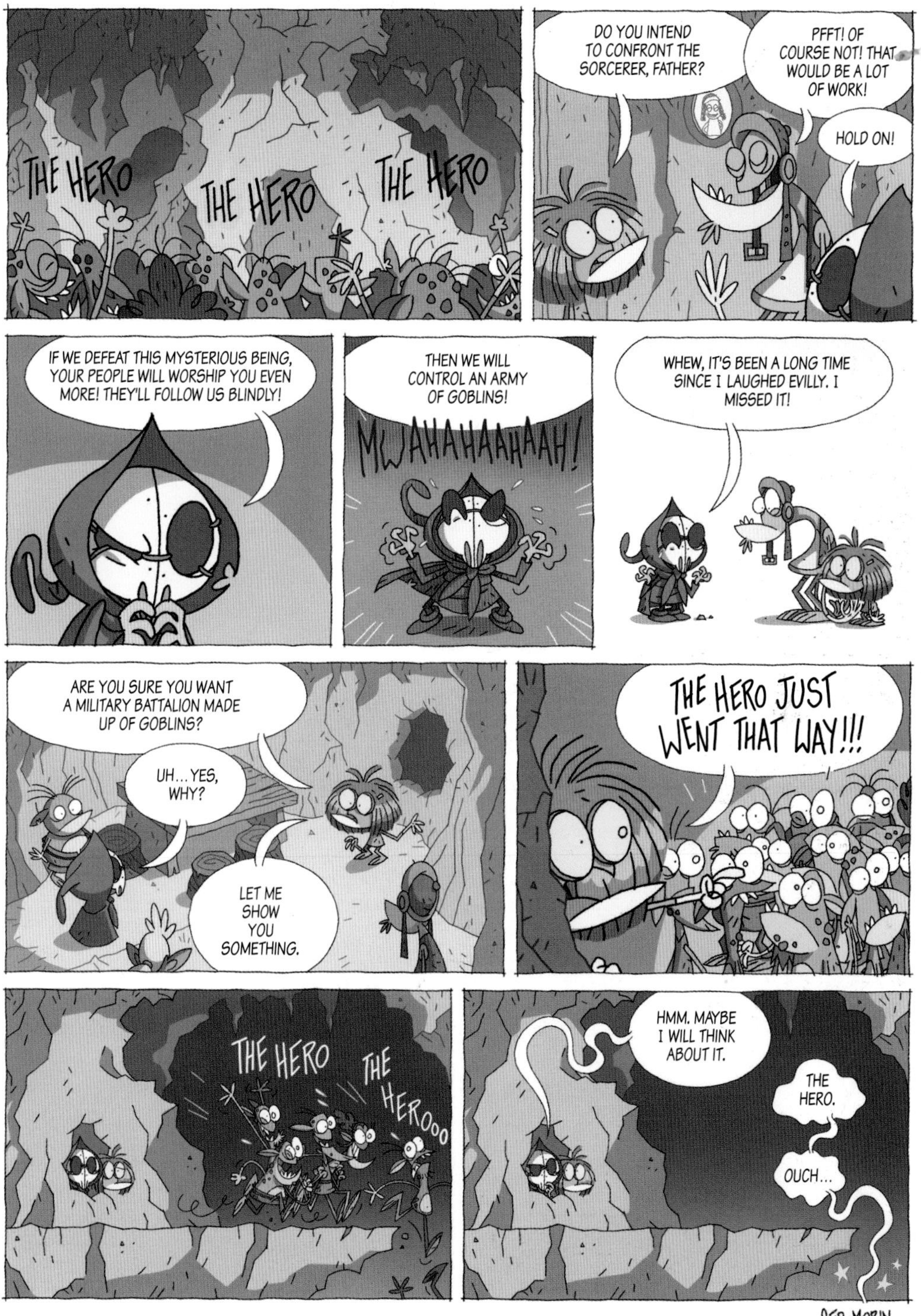
THE HERO
THE HERO
THE HERO
DO YOU INTEND TO CONFRONT THE SORCERER, FATHER?
PFFT! OF COURSE NOT! THAT WOULD BE A LOT OF WORK!
HOLD ON!
IF WE DEFEAT THIS MYSTERIOUS BEING, YOUR PEOPLE WILL WORSHIP YOU EVEN MORE! THEY'LL FOLLOW US BLINDLY!
THEN WE WILL CONTROL AN ARMY OF GOBLINS!
MWAHAHAAHAAH!
WHEW, IT'S BEEN A LONG TIME SINCE I LAUGHED EVILLY. I MISSED IT!
ARE YOU SURE YOU WANT A MILITARY BATTALION MADE UP OF GOBLINS?
UH… YES, WHY?
LET ME SHOW YOU SOMETHING.
THE HERO JUST WENT THAT WAY!!!
THE HERO
THE HEROoo
HMM. MAYBE I WILL THINK ABOUT IT.
THE HERO.
OUCH…
CED-MORIN

IT'S DECIDED. LET'S GET RID OF THIS MYSTERIOUS STRANGER!

WELL, OKAY. PFFFT...

WILL YOU TAKE PERNILLA WITH YOU? SHE NEEDS SOME FRESH AIR.

BUT IT'S GOING TO BE SUPER DANGEROUS!

YOU TOOK ME TO FIGHT STEARAS, THE MASTER OF EVIL!

SHE HAS A POINT THERE!

I'LL TAKE YOU TO HIS HIDEOUT.

THE HERO!

ARE YOU SURE YOU CAN WIN?

I BEAT STEARAS! I WILL PARADE AROUND IN MY UNDERWEAR IF I DON'T WIN AGAINST THIS ONE, TOO!

IT'S RIGHT THIS WAY.

THERE YOU ARE ...

FINALLY...

AAH!!

LET'S GET OUT OF HERE!

SO, YOU'RE GIVING UP?

SHOULD I LEND YOU SOME UNDERWEAR?

CED-MORIN

142

WELL, ARE WE GOING TO FIGHT HIM?

GONZAG, DON'T YOU RECOGNIZE HIM?

IT'S THE BARBARIAN WHO SWORE HE'D HAVE MY HIDE! HE STOLE THE DEMON'S HAND THAT GIVES HIM UNLIMITED POWER!

UH...

REMEMBER? IN THE CRATER OF THE VOLCANO!

THAT MAKES SENSE. WE ARE LOCATED GEOGRAPHICALLY UNDER THE VOLCANO.

HE MAY NOT BE THAT STRONG ANYMORE.

MMMM

WAAAAA

ARISE, MY ARMY!

OKAYYY...

I WAS THINKING... IF WE RUN AWAY NOW...

NO ONE WILL SEE...

OR KNOW...

THE HERO THE HERO

143

CED-MORIN

CHOMP CRUNCH SLURP

THAT WAS A CLOSE CALL WITH THE VOLCANO!

IT'S NOT ERUPTING ANYMORE. THAT'S STRANGE.

IT'S AS IF SOMEONE TURNED IT OFF...HEY! ARE YOU LISTENING TO ME OR JUST DROOLING?!

CRUNCH

ACTUALLY, THESE VEGGIES ARE NOT THAT BAD. AH, HERE COMES MORE!

FLAP

FLAP

OH, WAIT!

I'VE GOT IT!

THAT MUST BE HUBERT'S MOM!

SHHH! NOT SO LOUD!

WE STOLE HER EGG A WHILE AGO ...

THAT'S WHY SHE ISN'T HURTING US AND KEEPS BRINGING US FOOD!

SHE THINKS WE'RE HUBERT'S FRIENDS.

SO WE DON'T HAVE ANYTHING TO FEAR AS LONG AS HUBERT IS WITH US!

AH AAH

AHCHOooo

CED-MORIN

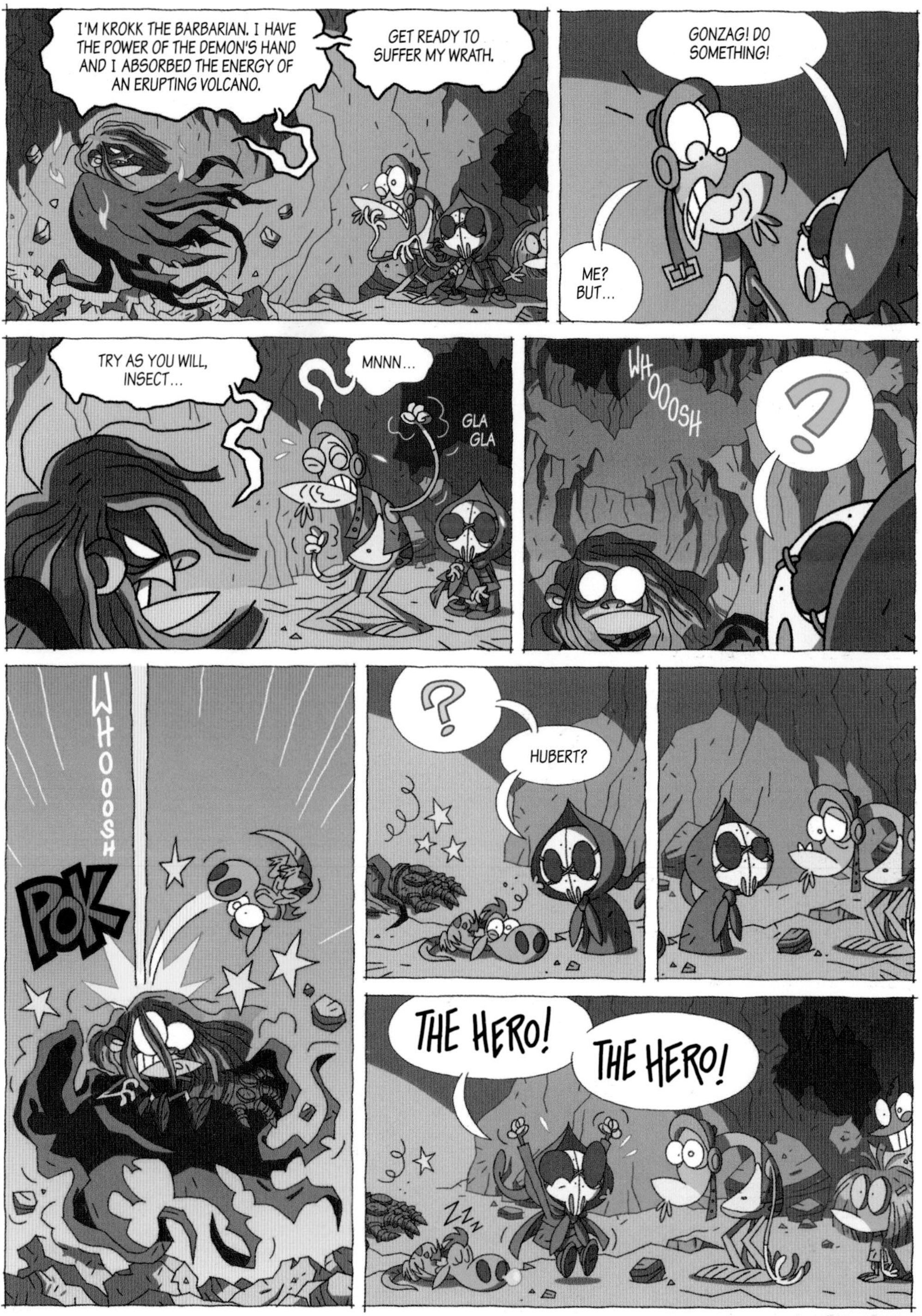
I'M KROKK THE BARBARIAN. I HAVE THE POWER OF THE DEMON'S HAND AND I ABSORBED THE ENERGY OF AN ERUPTING VOLCANO.
GET READY TO SUFFER MY WRATH.
GONZAG! DO SOMETHING!
ME? BUT...
TRY AS YOU WILL, INSECT...
MNNN...
GLA GLA
WHOOOSH
?
WHOOOOSH
POK
?
HUBERT?
THE HERO!
THE HERO!
CED-MORIN

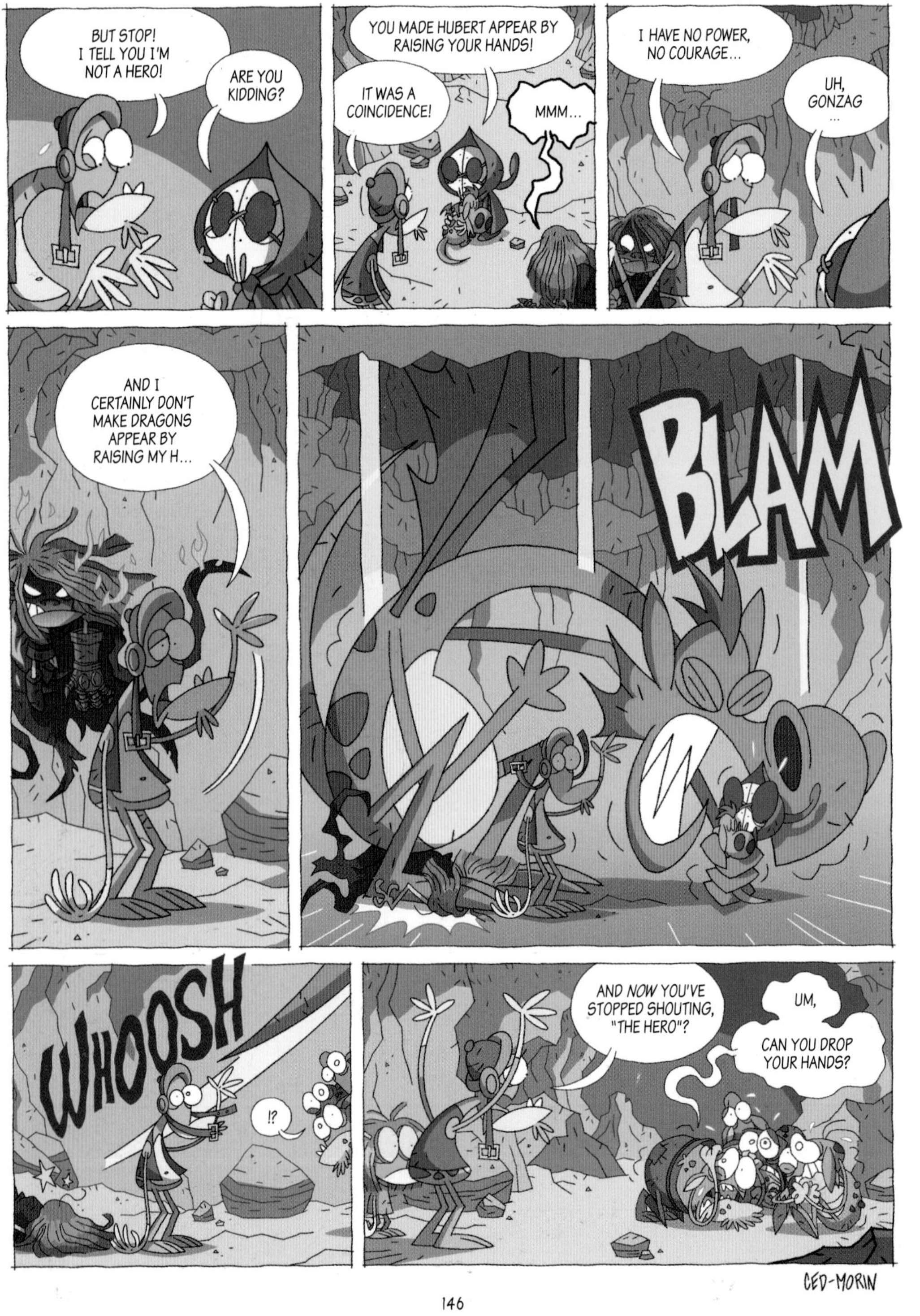
BUT STOP!
I TELL YOU I'M NOT A HERO!
ARE YOU KIDDING?
YOU MADE HUBERT APPEAR BY RAISING YOUR HANDS!
IT WAS A COINCIDENCE!
MMM...
I HAVE NO POWER, NO COURAGE...
UH, GONZAG ...
AND I CERTAINLY DON'T MAKE DRAGONS APPEAR BY RAISING MY H...
BLAM
WHOOSH
!?
AND NOW YOU'VE STOPPED SHOUTING, "THE HERO"?
UM,
CAN YOU DROP YOUR HANDS?
CED-MORIN

FIVE MINUTES EARLIER...

WHAT IS SHE GOING TO DO TO US?

THAT'S IT, I'M LIQUEFYING MYSELF!

OH!

HUBERT FELL INTO THE VOLCANO!

WHOOOSHH

PHEW! SAVED!

FLOP

AAAAH

OH, NO ...

AAAAAH

SO JUST LIKE THAT, YOU'RE TELLING ME A DRAGON DESTROYED YOUR VEGETABLE GARDEN?

YES, HE HAD...

AAAAAAHH

KAFLOOM

LET ME GUESS... I HAVE TO CONTACT THE DEPARTMENT OF DESTRUCTION BY PRINCESS?

HA HA HA

OF COURSE NOT!

THEY'RE ON VACATION THIS WEEK.

CED-MORIN

IT WAS GREAT TO PLAY WITH YOU! FOR A GHOST, YOU'RE PRETTY BAD AT HIDING!

I WASN'T EVEN TRYING! DO YOU HAVE WHAT YOU PROMISED ME?

HERE, THIS NOTEBOOK IS HERS!

"C"? WHAT'S HER NAME?

WE DON'T KNOW REALLY ... SHE WAS WITH US, BUT SHE NEVER SPOKE WITH ANYONE.

THAT'S ALL THERE WAS IN HER LOCKER.

AND IT'S BEEN A WHILE SINCE WE SAW HER!

OKAY, SEE YOU NEXT TIME, POOR SPORT!

DETECTIVE POOR SPORT!

HMM...

MASKS, MASKS, AND MORE MASKS!

FLIP

COSTUMES OF ALL TYPES

HELLO, DID SOMEONE ORDER A MASK LIKE THIS FROM YOU RECENTLY?

WAIT A MINUTE, I'LL CHECK MY RECEIPTS.

YOUR MASKS ARE REALLY TERRIFYING!

THAT'S MY EMPLOYEE...

CAN I HELP YOU?

CED-MORIN

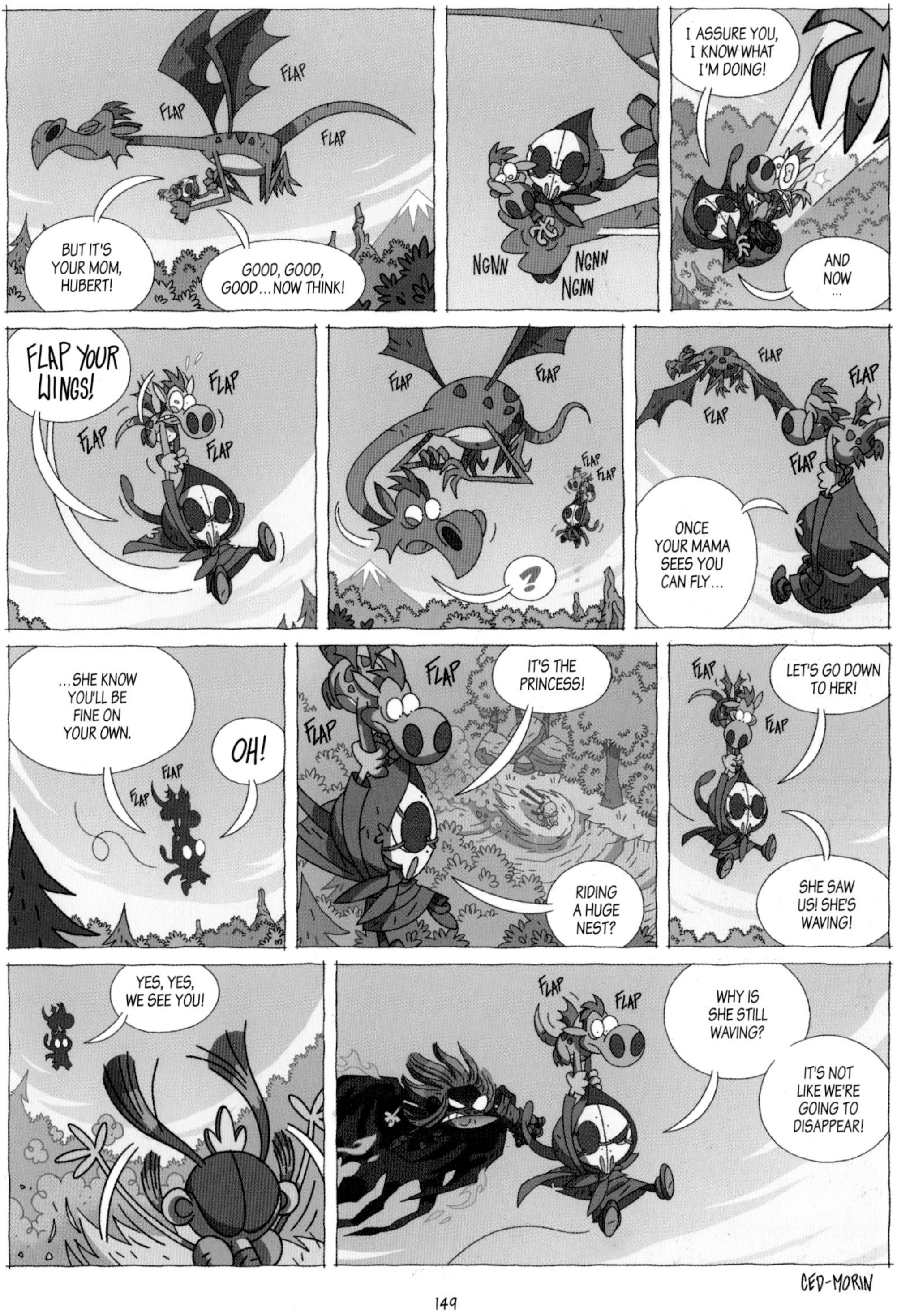
FLAP
FLAP
FLAP
BUT IT'S YOUR MOM, HUBERT!
GOOD, GOOD, GOOD... NOW THINK!
NGNN
NGNN
NGNN
I ASSURE YOU, I KNOW WHAT I'M DOING!
AND NOW ...
FLAP YOUR WINGS!
FLAP
FLAP
FLAP
FLAP
FLAP
FLAP
FLAP
?
FLAP
FLAP
FLAP
FLAP
ONCE YOUR MAMA SEES YOU CAN FLY...
...SHE KNOW YOU'LL BE FINE ON YOUR OWN.
FLAP
FLAP
OH!
FLAP
FLAP
IT'S THE PRINCESS!
RIDING A HUGE NEST?
FLAP
FLAP
LET'S GO DOWN TO HER!
SHE SAW US! SHE'S WAVING!
YES, YES, WE SEE YOU!
FLAP
FLAP
WHY IS SHE STILL WAVING?
IT'S NOT LIKE WE'RE GOING TO DISAPPEAR!
CED-MORIN

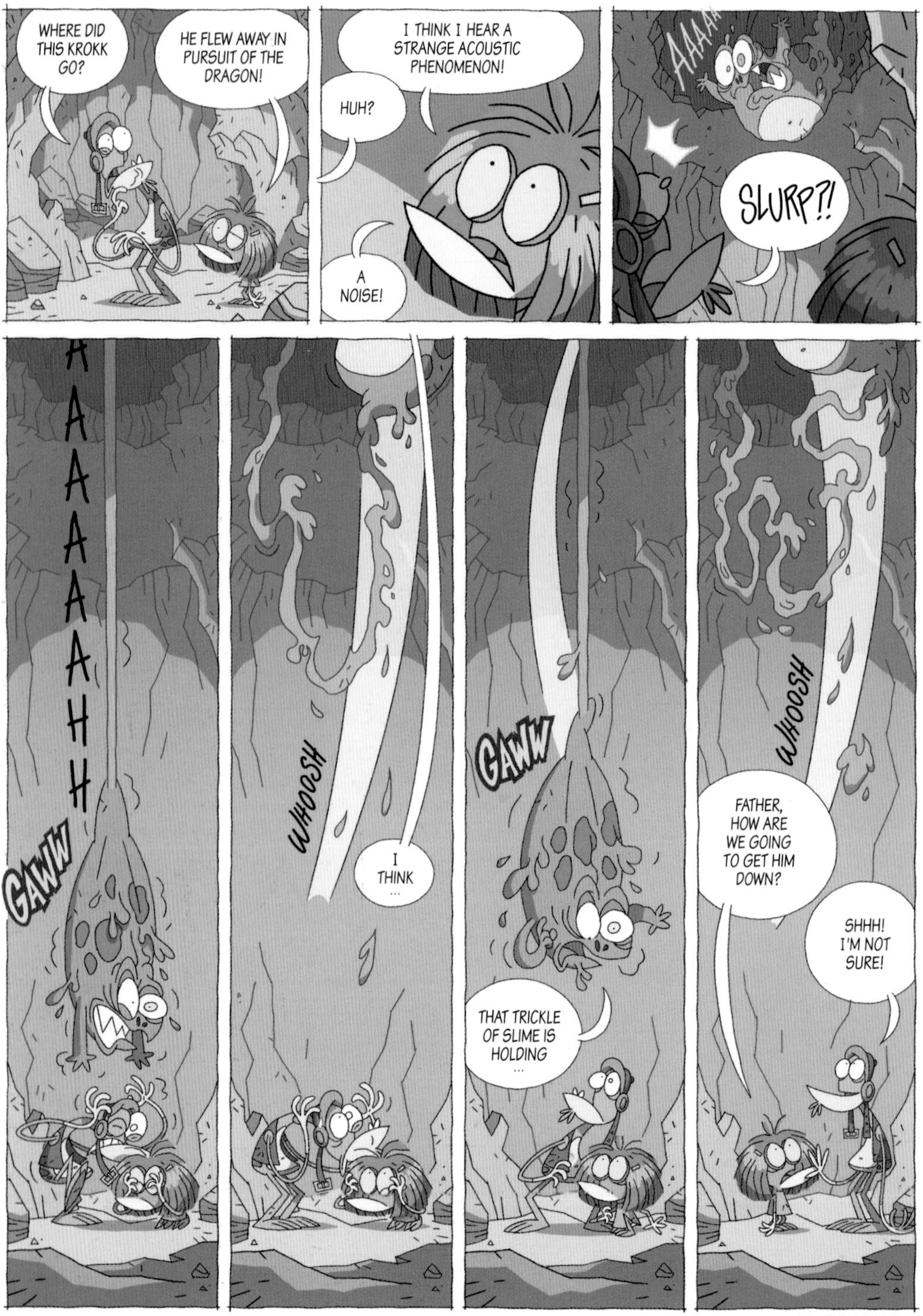
WHERE DID THIS KROKK GO?
HE FLEW AWAY IN PURSUIT OF THE DRAGON!
I THINK I HEAR A STRANGE ACOUSTIC PHENOMENON!
HUH?
A NOISE!
AAAA
SLURP?!
AAAAAAAAH
GAWW
WHOOSH
I THINK ...
GAWW
THAT TRICKLE OF SLIME IS HOLDING ...
WHOOSH
FATHER, HOW ARE WE GOING TO GET HIM DOWN?
SHHH! I'M NOT SURE!
CED-MORIN

MY FRIEND SLURP...

MY DAUGHTER PERNILLA ...

OUR PEOPLE ARE BEING ATTACKED. OUR MASTER IS MISSING...

BUT WE WILL RESIST! I WILL BE THE HERO THAT THIS KINGDOM BELIEVES I AM.

I'LL NEED YOU TO HELP ME THINK THROUGH THIS.

KROKK IS GONE, BUT HIS SOLDIERS ARE STILL AROUND.

HE HAS BROUGHT AN ARMY OF SKELETONS TO LIFE!

BUT WE WON'T GIVE IN!

WE WON'T BE KNOCKED DOWN!

ARE YOU WITH ME?!

YEEESSS!

SIGH.

CED-MORIN

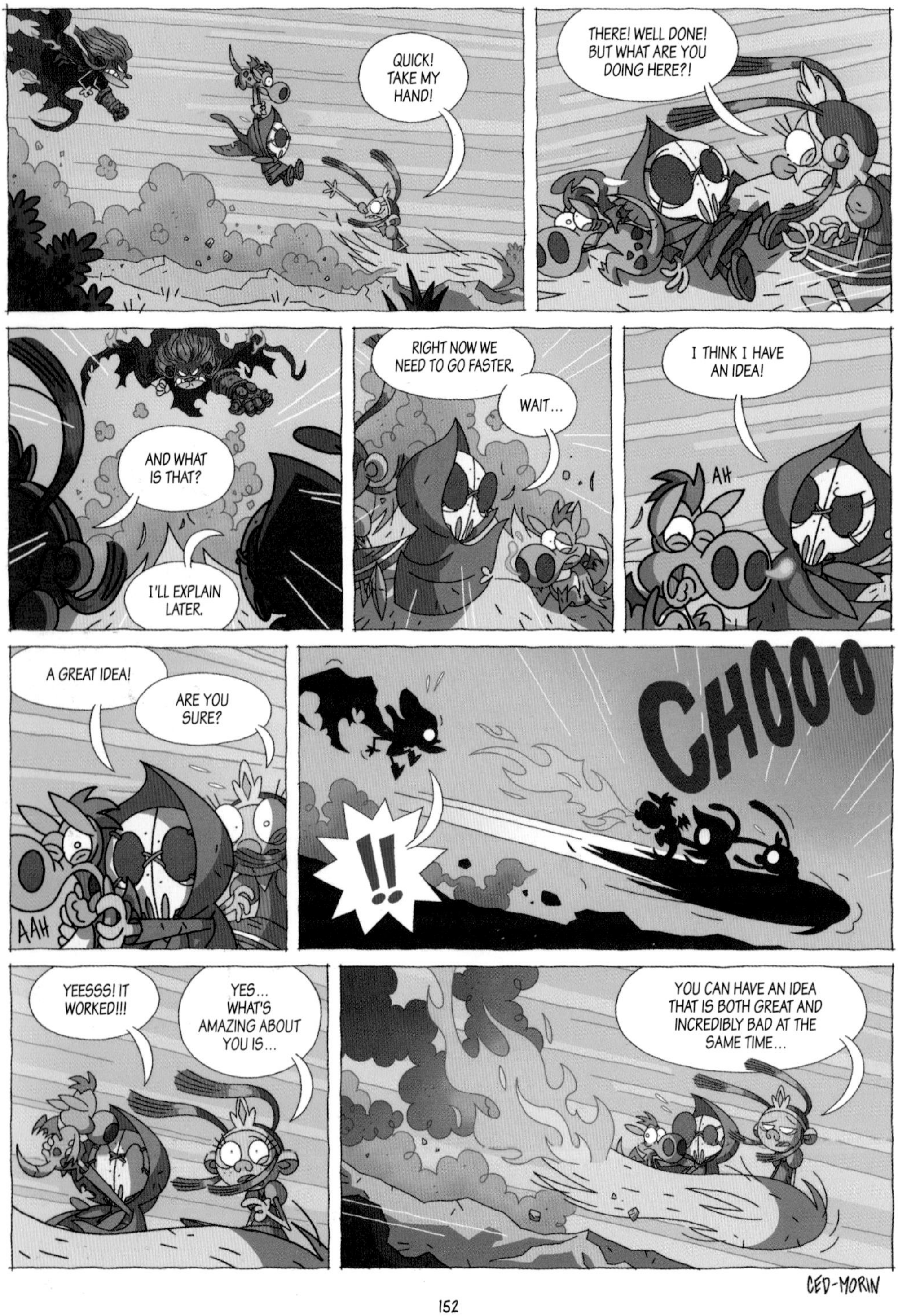
QUICK! TAKE MY HAND!
THERE! WELL DONE! BUT WHAT ARE YOU DOING HERE?!
AND WHAT IS THAT?
I'LL EXPLAIN LATER.
RIGHT NOW WE NEED TO GO FASTER.
WAIT…
I THINK I HAVE AN IDEA!
AH
A GREAT IDEA!
ARE YOU SURE?
AAH
!!
CHOOO
YEESSS! IT WORKED!!!
YES… WHAT'S AMAZING ABOUT YOU IS…
YOU CAN HAVE AN IDEA THAT IS BOTH GREAT AND INCREDIBLY BAD AT THE SAME TIME…
CED-MORIN

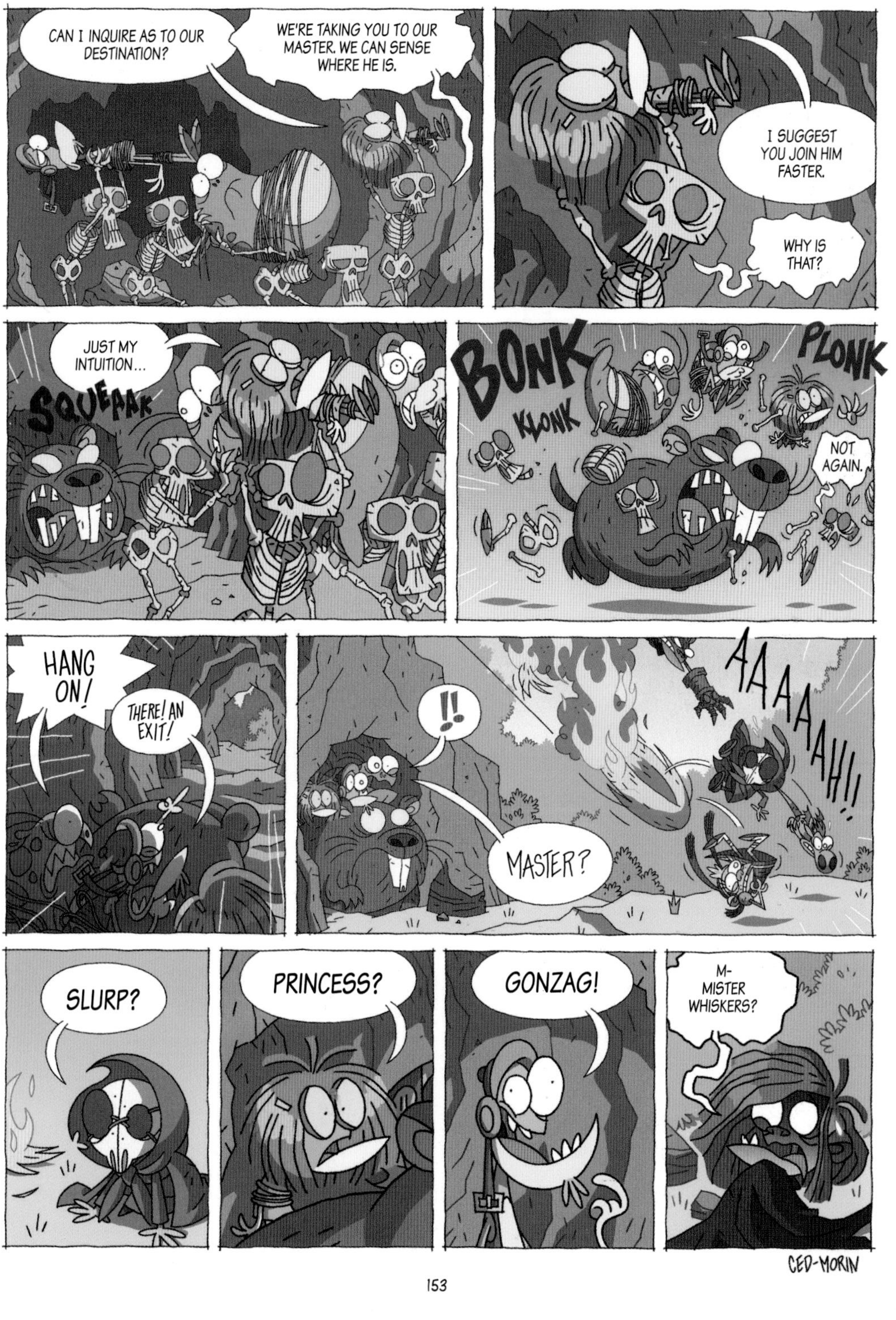
CAN I INQUIRE AS TO OUR DESTINATION?
WE'RE TAKING YOU TO OUR MASTER. WE CAN SENSE WHERE HE IS.
I SUGGEST YOU JOIN HIM FASTER.
WHY IS THAT?
JUST MY INTUITION...
SQUEAAK
BONK
KLONK
PLONK
NOT AGAIN.
HANG ON!
THERE! AN EXIT!
!!
MASTER?
AAAAAAH!!
SLURP?
PRINCESS?
GONZAG!
M-MISTER WHISKERS?
CED-MORIN

MISTER WHISKERS?

WHAT'S HE DOING?

IT LOOKS LIKE KROKK TAKES OUR ANCESTRAL ENEMY FOR A DOMESTIC HAMSTER WHO ONCE BELONGED TO HIM...

BUT THAT'S IMPOSSIBLE.

IT MUST BE 200 YEARS OLD, AND IT WEIGHS THREE TONS. IT CAN'T BE HIS...

HUSH!

WITH THE DEMON'S HAND, HE CAN'T THINK CLEARLY ANYMORE.

SQUEAK

SQUEAK

I HATED THE WORLD AFTER I LOST MISTER WHISKERS.

NOW THAT WE'RE REUNITED, MY FIGHT IS OVER.

WE CAN GO HOME NOW.

BAMF

WELL, ARE THEY GONE, OR...

MMM... SO IT SEEMS.

WHERE IS A DEMON'S HOME?

SQUEEAAK

IT'S STARTING TO GET CROWDED IN HERE.

CELERY ICE CREAM?

CED-MORIN

I WROTE DOWN THE ADDRESS THAT THE CUSTOMER LEFT US WHEN ORDERING HER MASK!

HEH HEH! THANK YOU!

MYSTERY SOLVED!

WOOSH

OH NO ...

IT DOESN'T MATTER. I CAN GO BACK TO THE...

CLOSED
P.S. I DON'T LIKE YOU

FINE...

OH, GEE, I'M GETTING DIZZY

HEY, YOU!!

CRUNCH CRUNCH

WHY DID YOU GIVE ME A PARAKEET?

THE GIRL'S ADDRESS IS INSIDE!

PINK HERTON

CED-MORIN

WE'RE LEAVING FOR BOURGVILLE, MY LITTLE PERNILLA!

SMOOTCH

YOU CAN GO BACK TO THE CAVES ON YOUR OWN. THEY'RE SAFE NOW.

TELL YOUR MOM WE'LL SEE HER AT HOME.

FATHER?

I ADMIT THAT I ALWAYS DOUBTED THAT YOU COULD BE THE HERO OF THE GOBLINS...BUT IN THE END, YOU GOT RID OF THIS DEMON AND THE ENEMY WHO HAS ALWAYS THREATENED US.

I JUST WANTED TO SAY TO YOU...

...THAT I AM VERY PROUD TO BE YOUR DAUGHTER.

ARE YOU OKAY, GONZAG?

YES—SNIFF—I... JUST HAVE A LITTLE DIRT IN MY EYE...

I CAN'T WAIT TO BE IN THE CAPITAL AGAIN!

ME TOO! THIS JOURNEY HAS BEEN TOO LONG!

NO MORE DEMONS, GIANT RODENTS, AND BEING CHASED!

ALL I WANT IS A LITTLE BIT OF...

REST? ...

CHUNK

CHUNK

GUARDS! IT'S THE THIEF WHO STOLE THE KING'S THRONE!!!

I WISH BEING THE LORD OF DARKNESS CAME WITH SOME DAYS OFF.

CHUNK

CED-MORIN

HUFF! HUFF! QUICKLY! THEY'RE COMING!

THERE IS ONLY ONE THING LEFT TO DO!

GO TO THE PALACE AND CONVINCE MY FATHER TO DROP THE CHARGES AGAINST YOU!

I'LL GO AS FAST AS I CAN!

PRINCESS MAEVA, UH ...

I DIDN'T THINK WE WOULD, BUT WE'RE HAVING FUN WITH YOU!

OH, THAT'S NICE! I'M HAVING FUN, TOO!

SEE YOU LATER!

AND US, WHERE ARE WE GOING BOSS... MASTER...UH, RESPONSIBLE AUTHORITY?

HMPH... FOLLOW ME!

I KNOW WHERE TO HIDE!

WE'LL BE SAFE HERE FOR A WHILE!

THANK YOU! I HAVE A TALENT FOR TELLING DISGUSTING STORIES TO ANIMALS!

THAT'S THE FIRST TIME I'VE SEEN SOMEONE MAKE A PARAKEET THROW UP!

CED-MORIN

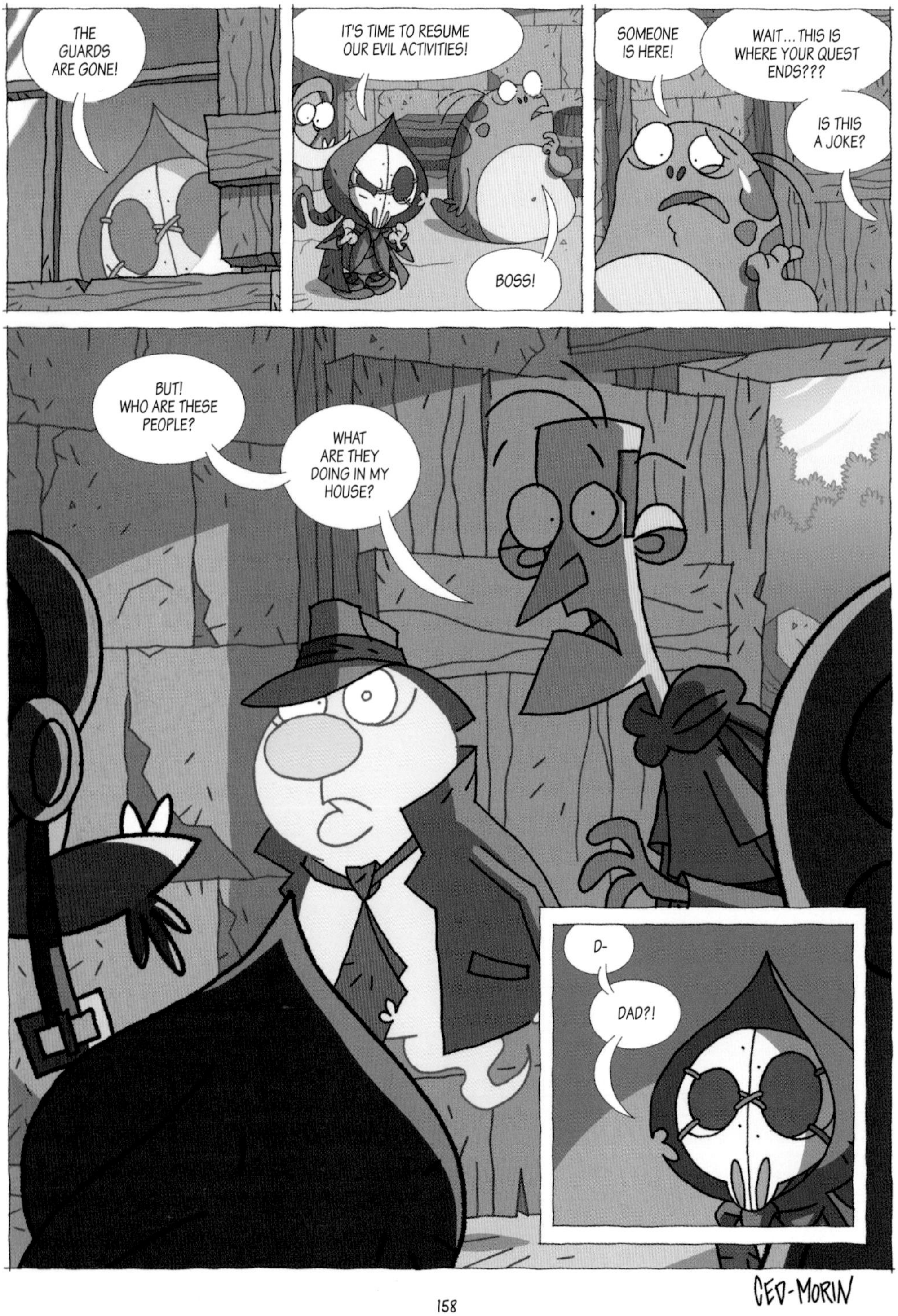
THE GUARDS ARE GONE!
IT'S TIME TO RESUME OUR EVIL ACTIVITIES!
BOSS!
SOMEONE IS HERE!
WAIT... THIS IS WHERE YOUR QUEST ENDS???
IS THIS A JOKE?
BUT! WHO ARE THESE PEOPLE?
WHAT ARE THEY DOING IN MY HOUSE?
D-
DAD?!

CED-MORIN

Chapter 5
SLIMY ADVENTURES

AS YOU RECALL:
200 YEARS AGO, THE LANDS OF ALKYLL WERE PLUNGED INTO FEAR AND DARKNESS.

BOURGVILLE, THE ONCE-SPLENDID CAPITAL, WAS RUINED BY THE CONSTRUCTION OF THE TERRIBLE TOWER.

MWAHAHAHA HAHAHAHA!

STEARAS WAS THE MASTER OF ABSOLUTE EVIL AND CAUSED CHAOS AND DESTRUCTION...

MWAHAHAHA HAHAHA!

MASTER, YOU ARE LAUGHING FOR NO REASON. THAT FRIGHTENS OUR MEN!

UH, NO, NO, WE LIKE IT ...

SO, WHERE IS THE ARMY OF RUTHLESS SOLDIERS THAT I ORDERED FROM YOU, ALCHEMIST?

AH, THAT ARMY, WELL, UH...

I CREATED THE MONSTERS, BUT WE'RE GOING TO HAVE TO WAIT A LITTLE WHILE UNTIL THEY'RE READY...

WAIT?! BUT HOW LONG?

GAGA!

GAGA!

WAAAH!

MAYBE TWENTY... THIRTY YEARS?

CED-MORIN

MASTER, THERE'S SOMETHING ELSE ABOUT YOUR ARMY OF MONSTERS...

WHAT ELSE?!

WELL, I FOLLOWED YOUR INSTRUCTIONS:

THEY WILL BE BLOODTHIRSTY WARRIORS, THEIR FANGS SHARP, THEIR SLOBBER DRIPPING AND CAPABLE OF IMMOBILIZING ENEMIES, THEY CAN STICK TO WALLS...

THEY HAVE NO EMOTIONS...

SO? THEY SOUND PERFECT TO ME!

BUT, ONE OF THEM MAY BE...

...NICE.

NICE?! HOW IS THAT POSSIBLE?

IT'S AN ANOMALY! OR... I MADE A MISTAKE IN THE FORMULA WHEN CREATING IT.

THE SOLUTION IS SIMPLE: SNAP!

SNAP?

YES, OR "CRACK," IF YOU PREFER.

"CRACK." VERY WELL, MASTER.

WELL, ACTUALLY, IT'S NOT CLEAR.

JUST GET RID OF HIM!!!!

CED-MORIN

ARE YOU CERTAIN YOU DON'T WANT TO SEE THEM, YOUR VILENESS?

AN ARMY THAT WON'T BE READY FOR YEARS?

I HAVE BETTER THINGS TO DO, THANK YOU.

GET RID OF HIM AND PLACE THE OTHERS IN HIBERNATION.

LET'S GO. ON WITH IT!

I HAVE TO DEAL WITH THESE RUMORS OF PROPHECIES AND HEROES...

YOU, THERE! COME WITH ME. YOU WILL HELP ME.

WHY ME?!

WHERE ARE WE GOING?

TO THE INCUBATOR TO SEE THE EVIL ARMY.

WHAT? JUST LIKE THAT? WITHOUT WEARING ARMOR?

DON'T WORRY. THEY ARE JUST BABIES. WE WILL IDENTIFY THE GOOD GUY OF THE GROUP, AND WE'LL GET RID OF IT.

GGNNAAAAA ♪♪♪ ARMM GGNNAAARRR

IT'S GOING TO TAKE US HOURS TO FIND HIM!

CED-MORIN

GAGA!

IS THAT UNDERSTOOD? YOU GET RID OF THIS THING!

I CAN'T DECIDE BETWEEN CRUSHING IT, PUSHING IT INTO A VOLCANO, OR HAVING IT DEVOURED BY A VERY, VERY NASTY RACCOON.

IT DOESN'T MATTER.

JUST DON'T GIVE IN TO ITS CUTENESS!

THAT'S A CLASSIC BABY MOVE.

THESE CREATURES ARE DECEITFUL.

JUST LEAVE IT TO ME. KINDNESS IS NOT MY STYLE.

NO, IT DOESN'T AFFECT ME AT ALL.

HERE WE GO. TO THE CRUSHER.

HEY, WELL, IF IT ISN'T BRUX!

BRUX, ARE YOU JOINING US? WE'RE MAKING A GRILLED CHEESE.

OH! WAIT FOR ME. I JUST HAVE TO GO TO...

THERE'S ALMOST NO MORE CHEESE LEFT!

Help yourself!

CED-MORIN

OH, PHILBIN, LOOK! SOMEONE LEFT SOMETHING.

OH NO, NOT AGAIN!

WE'RE NOT GOING TO PICK UP SOMETHING OFF THE STREET!

YOU WERE VERY HAPPY WHEN I FOUND THAT TOASTER.

IT WAS TEEMING WITH RATS! A WHOLE FAMILY OF THEM LIVED IN IT!

YES, BUT IN THE END YOU ENJOYED TOASTED RATS.

THAT'S TRUE. THERE WAS A LITTLE TASTE OF MOLD AND CRISPINESS.

OH, DARLING! IT'S A BABY!

UH...ARE YOU SURE?

WE WANTED TO BE PARENTS!

NOT OF JUST ANYTHING, YOU KNOW!

I ADMIT HE IS CUTE!

AH!

IT'S A LITTLE STICKY...

SLURP

WHAT SHALL WE CALL HIM?

CED-MORIN

SLURP.

SLURP!

?

NOW BACK TO THE PRESENT.

YOU SAT IN THE WRONG PLACE.

THAT'S MY CHAIR!

OH? HOW DO YOU KNOW IT'S YOURS?

...THE FACT THAT I WAS SITTING IN IT.

OH, SORRY BOSS.

I FEEL LIKE A HUMAN HANDKERCHIEF.

SO, LET'S START OUR MEETING.

AFTER ALL OUR RECENT ADVENTURES, IT'S TIME TO REFOCUS.

WE NOW HAVE A NEW HIDEOUT, BUT WE NEED A NEW MISSION.

SUGGESTIONS?

WE COULD HANG A STRING OF LIGHTS!

WE COULD BUILD BIRDHOUSES!

BUILD AN OBSTACLE COURSE!

MAKE SMOOTHIES!

NO...IT HAS TO HAVE SOMETHING TO DO WITH ABSOLUTE EVIL...

REMEMBER WHY I HIRED YOU?

UH...

AH, YES. THIS EXPLAINS A LOT...

CED-MORIN

WELL, IS EVERYBODY HERE?

GONZAG.

HERE.

SLURP.

HERE.

HUBERT.

ZZZZ.

OKAY, SO IF EVERYONE IS HERE, WE'LL GO AHEAD...

WE'RE NOT GOING TO WAIT FOR THE PRINCESS? SHE WON'T BE TOO LATE.

WHAT?! YOU INVITED HER?!

YOU SAID, "EVERYBODY MUST BE THERE!"

BUT THE PRINCESS KNOWS ME! I MEAN, SHE KNOWS THE OTHER "ME" UNDER THE MASK! SHE EVEN KNOWS THAT I LIVED HERE!

A.L.D.? ARE YOU THERE??

ACK!

IT'S HER!

I DON'T REALLY SEE THE PROBLEM. WE KNOW YOUR REAL IDENTITY. WHY NOT HER?

BECAUSE I WAS HORRIBLE TO HER! SHE WILL HATE ME FOREVER!

TOC TOC

I'M COMING, I'M COMING!

PRINCESS... THEY ARE WAITING FOR YOU UP IN THE ATTIC.

YOU'RE HERE?

I'M JUST HOSTING THEM!

THEY'RE WAITING FOR YOU UP THERE!

HMMM...

HUFF! HUFF!

PRINCESS! THERE YOU ARE... HUFF...FINALLY!

WAIT ONE MINUTE. I HAVE SOMETHING TO TELL THE GIRL DOWNSTAIRS!

WAIT! WHAT DID SHE SAY?!

THAT SHE WAS GOING DOWN TO TALK TO YOU, THE OTHER "YOU."

THAT CAN'T BE TRUE!

THAT CAN'T BE TRUE!

HEL-LO! ANYONE HERE?

YES... YES! I'M HERE!

WHAT WERE YOU DOING IN THAT CLOSET?

I WAS LOOKING FOR... SOME... UH...

PICKLED EYE OF NEWT!

YOU SEE! I LOVE IT!

OH, REALLY?

OH, REALLY WHAT?

WHY DON'T YOU EAT IT IF YOU LIKE IT?

I, UH...

SEE, SEE...

SQUISH SQUISH!

MMM...

HMMM... WELL, I'M GOING BACK.

YES, HEEHEE...

HUFF! HUFF!

YUCK!

I'M BACK!

WHAT GOOD NEWS! LET'S GO!

WAIT! IN FACT, I FORGOT TO TALK TO OUR HOSTESS!

AH-AH! I WILL JOIN YOU IN A MINUTE!

ADMIT IT... YOU KNOW THEY'RE THE SAME PERSON, HUH?

YES, BUT I WANT TO SEE HER SUFFER A LITTLE BIT...

CED-MORIN

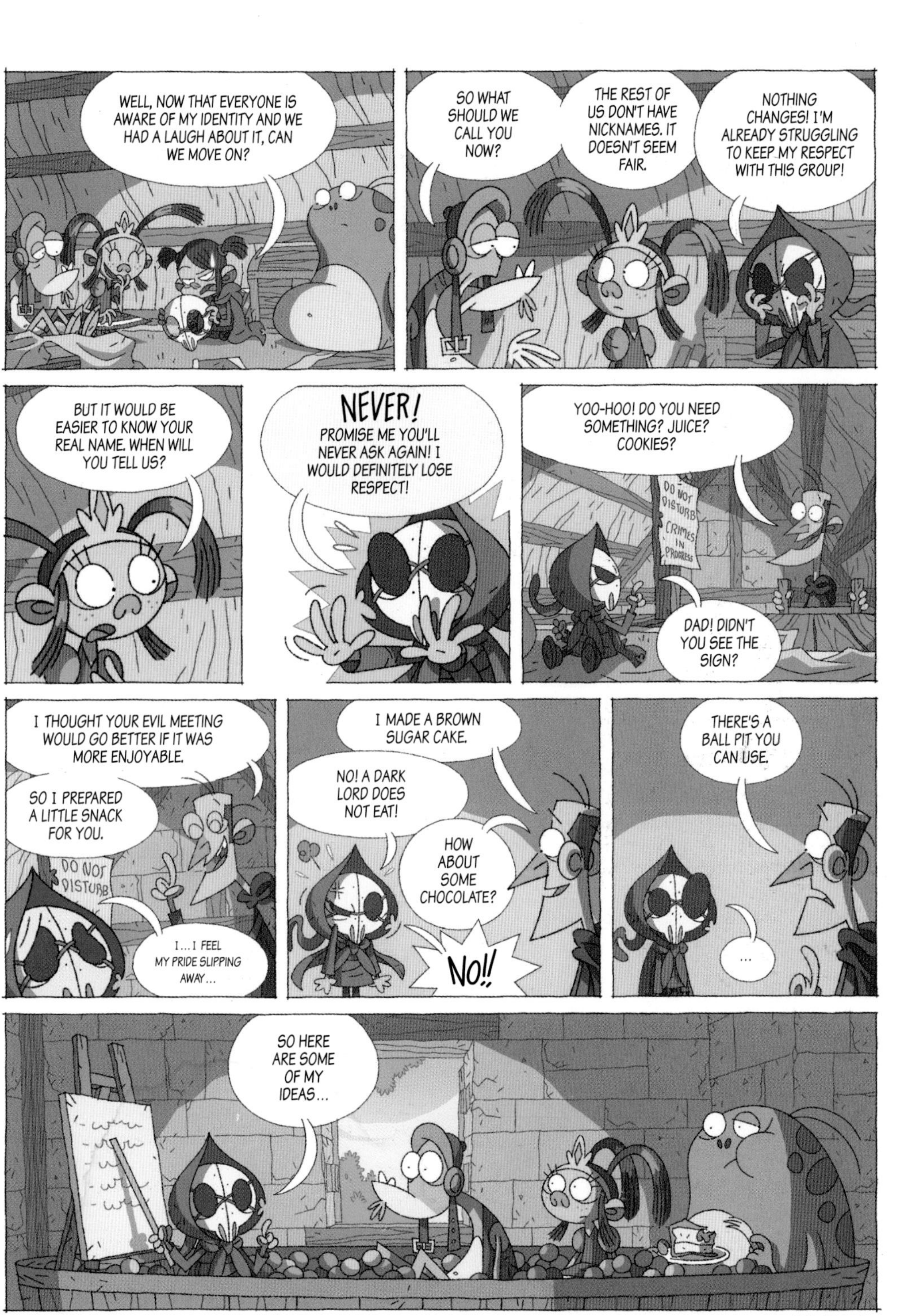

WELL, NOW THAT EVERYONE IS AWARE OF MY IDENTITY AND WE HAD A LAUGH ABOUT IT, CAN WE MOVE ON?
SO WHAT SHOULD WE CALL YOU NOW?
THE REST OF US DON'T HAVE NICKNAMES. IT DOESN'T SEEM FAIR.
NOTHING CHANGES! I'M ALREADY STRUGGLING TO KEEP MY RESPECT WITH THIS GROUP!
BUT IT WOULD BE EASIER TO KNOW YOUR REAL NAME. WHEN WILL YOU TELL US?
NEVER! PROMISE ME YOU'LL NEVER ASK AGAIN! I WOULD DEFINITELY LOSE RESPECT!
YOO-HOO! DO YOU NEED SOMETHING? JUICE? COOKIES?
DO NOT DISTURB
CRIMES IN PROGRESS
DAD! DIDN'T YOU SEE THE SIGN?
I THOUGHT YOUR EVIL MEETING WOULD GO BETTER IF IT WAS MORE ENJOYABLE.
SO I PREPARED A LITTLE SNACK FOR YOU.
DO NOT DISTURB
I... I FEEL MY PRIDE SLIPPING AWAY...
I MADE A BROWN SUGAR CAKE.
NO! A DARK LORD DOES NOT EAT!
HOW ABOUT SOME CHOCOLATE?
NO!!
THERE'S A BALL PIT YOU CAN USE.
...
SO HERE ARE SOME OF MY IDEAS...

CED-MORIN

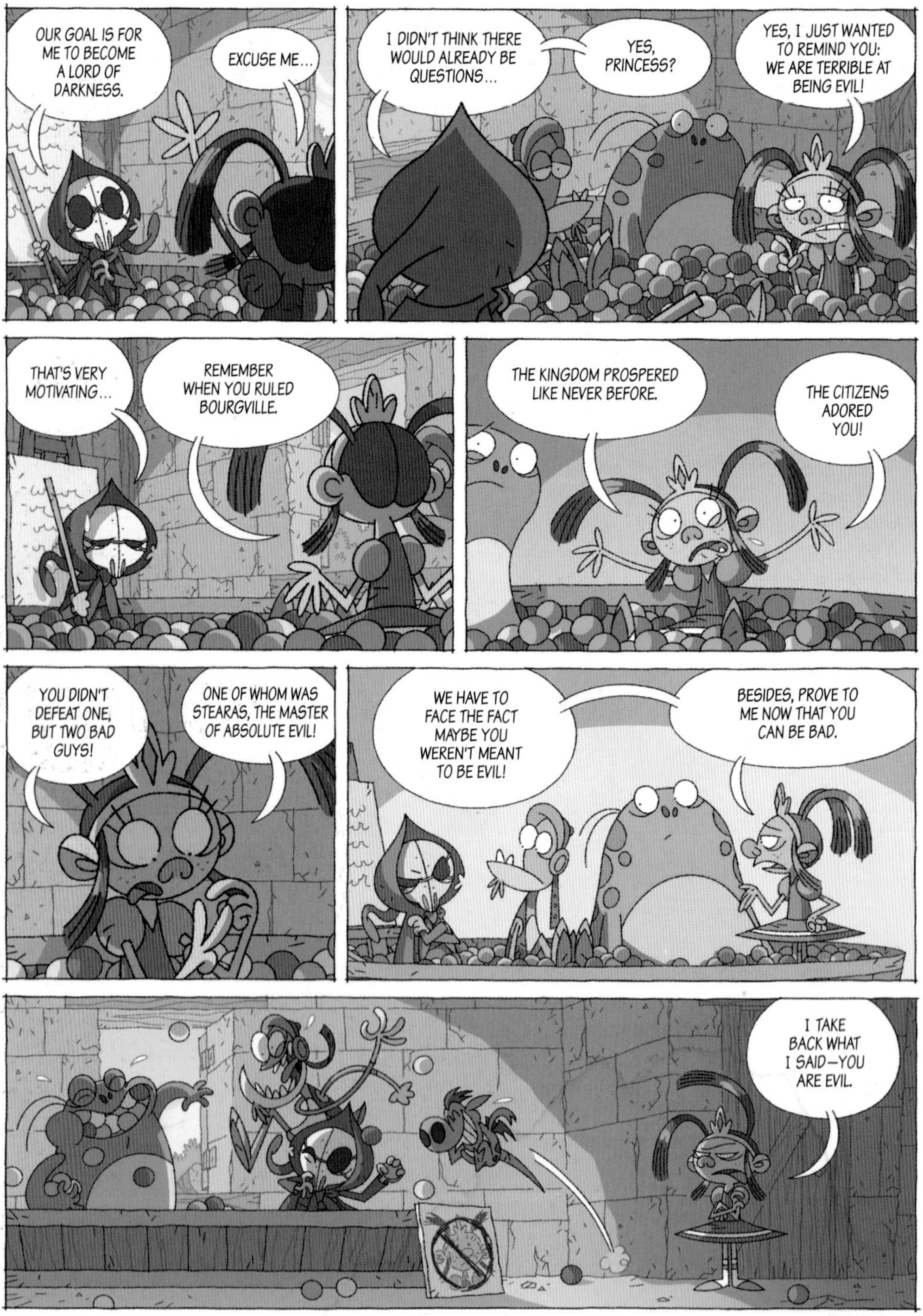
OUR GOAL IS FOR ME TO BECOME A LORD OF DARKNESS.
EXCUSE ME…
I DIDN'T THINK THERE WOULD ALREADY BE QUESTIONS…
YES, PRINCESS?
YES, I JUST WANTED TO REMIND YOU: WE ARE TERRIBLE AT BEING EVIL!
THAT'S VERY MOTIVATING…
REMEMBER WHEN YOU RULED BOURGVILLE.
THE KINGDOM PROSPERED LIKE NEVER BEFORE.
THE CITIZENS ADORED YOU!
YOU DIDN'T DEFEAT ONE, BUT TWO BAD GUYS!
ONE OF WHOM WAS STEARAS, THE MASTER OF ABSOLUTE EVIL!
WE HAVE TO FACE THE FACT MAYBE YOU WEREN'T MEANT TO BE EVIL!
BESIDES, PROVE TO ME NOW THAT YOU CAN BE BAD.
I TAKE BACK WHAT I SAID—YOU ARE EVIL.

CED-MORIN

TO ANSWER YOU SERIOUSLY, PRINCESS...

...THERE'S NOT JUST THIS TINY LITTLE KINGDOM!

THERE ARE OTHER COUNTRIES TO THE NORTH LIKE NAWAK'S GATE, THE KINGDOM OF THE YOUNG KING, AND MIDGARD...

BASICALLY, I WANT TO CONQUER *THE WORLD!*

AND FOR THAT I NEED TO...?

START A ROCK BAND?

START A CLOTHING BRAND?

CREATE TOYS IN YOUR IMAGE?

NO, CREATE AN ARMY!

IT IS CLEAR THAT I'M NOT GOING TO SUCCEED WITH YOU GUYS ALONE.

AND WE NEED MONEY.

UH...DO YOU HAVE ANY?

NOTHING IN MY POCKETS!

YOU DON'T HAVE POCKETS. YOU'RE PULLING ON YOUR SKIN.

THE COFFERS OF THE KINGDOM HAVE BEEN EMPTY SINCE YOUR REIGN.

SO IT'S HOPELESS...

SIGH!

COME ON! I KNOW YOU DON'T GIVE UP SO EASY!

DO YOU THINK BY POUTING AT THE WINDOW YOU'LL FIND THE ANSWER?

MAYBE...

BANK

CED-MORIN

HMMM...

HUM-HMM!

INTERESTING!

...

CAN YOU TELL ME EXACTLY WHAT YOU'RE DOING?

I'M ACTING LIKE YOU. YOU SEEM TO BE THINKING.

SIGH!

HERE'S WHAT I'M THINKING ABOUT.

I'M STUDYING THE NEIGHBORHOOD TO FIND HIDING PLACES IN CASE A QUICK ESCAPE IS NECESSARY.

IF OUR BANK ROBBERY ENDS BADLY.

IF YOU WANT, THERE'S THIS BUILDING. THAT'S WHERE I WAS RAISED.

CLEANERS

PLUM AND PHILBEN

DID YOU GROW UP IN A CLEANING COMPANY?

WHY DOES THAT NOT SURPRISE ME?

THIS PAPER SAYS IT'S BEEN CLOSED FOR MORE THAN 170 YEARS!

SLURP... YOU ARE ALMOST 200 YEARS OLD?

I DON'T LOOK IT, HUH?

BUT I'M STILL AS STRONG AS EVER, LIKE THIS OLD SHACK!

BOOM

CRAAACK

RUMBLE RUMBLE !!

WHAT I DON'T UNDERSTAND...

...IS HOW YOU WERE ABLE TO SURVIVE THIS LONG...

CED-MORIN

HONEY, I WAS TOLD YOU WANT TO ROB THE BANK?

HMMM...

ROB A BANK?

I THINK IT'S GREAT THAT YOU HAVE GOALS!

SMACK!

DAAADD!

IT'S NICE THAT YOUR FATHER SUPPORTS YOU!

YES, THAT'S THE WORD.

HE'S THE NICEST MAN IN THE WORLD! THAT'S WHY I RAN AWAY!

IN FACT, HE ENCOURAGES ME EVEN IN MY EVIL ENDEAVORS!

YOUR FATHER, NICE? ISN'T HE THE KINGDOM EXTERMINATOR?

HE'S THE ONE WHO GOT RID OF RATS AND VERMIN, YES.

HERE'S HOW HE DOES IT:

FIRST OF ALL, HE SETS TRAPS.

AH! THAT'S NOT VERY NICE!

THESE TRAPS ARE SPECIAL! IN EACH ONE THERE IS A SOFA BED, A STACK OF MAGAZINES, AND AN ALL-YOU-CAN-EAT BUFFET.

HE PUTS THE CRITTERS IN A SMALL ROOM TOGETHER.

THERE HE TEACHES THEM MATHEMATICS AND LANGUAGES.

OKAY, READ PAGE TWELVE.

I PREFER TO WORK AS A TEAM.

THEN WHEN THEY GRADUATE, THEY CAN LOOK FOR WORK.

TELL ME YOU'RE JOKING, RIGHT?

KNOCK KNOCK

LORD OF DARKNESS, THERE'S A PACKAGE FOR YOU!

AH, GREAT! I WAS WAITING FOR THIS!

SIGN HERE, PLEASE!

CED-MORIN

IT SHOULD BE THE NEXT STREET ON THE RIGHT.

HMPH, WE ALWAYS HAVE TO DO ALL THE WORK!

WE JUST HAVE TO BUY MASKS!

AND WHY IS THAT? IT'S NOT UH... THE HOLIDAY WHERE WE DRESS UP...

HALLOWEEN!

THE MASTER...SHE SAYS IT'S FOR WHEN WE ROB A BANK.

SO THAT WE ARE NOT RECOGNIZED.

I DON'T SEE WHY I WOULD BE RECOGNIZED. I'VE NEVER SET FOOT IN A BANK!

IT'S WORSE FOR ME.

I DON'T EVEN HAVE A FOOT!

RING RING

AH, HERE IT IS!

HELLO!

WE'VE COME TO BUY MASKS!

ARE YOU SURE YOU NEED THEM?

WHAT STYLE DO YOU WANT?

UH...

AH WELL, WE WEREN'T TOLD THAT...

THEY ARE TAKING A WHILE!

DO YOU STILL THINK IT'S A GOOD IDEA TO SEND THEM ON A MISSION?

ALL I ASKED THEM WAS THAT WE GO IN DISGUISE!

WE'RE BACK!

AND THIS TIME, WE'RE SURE YOU'LL BE PLEASED!

CED-MORIN

174

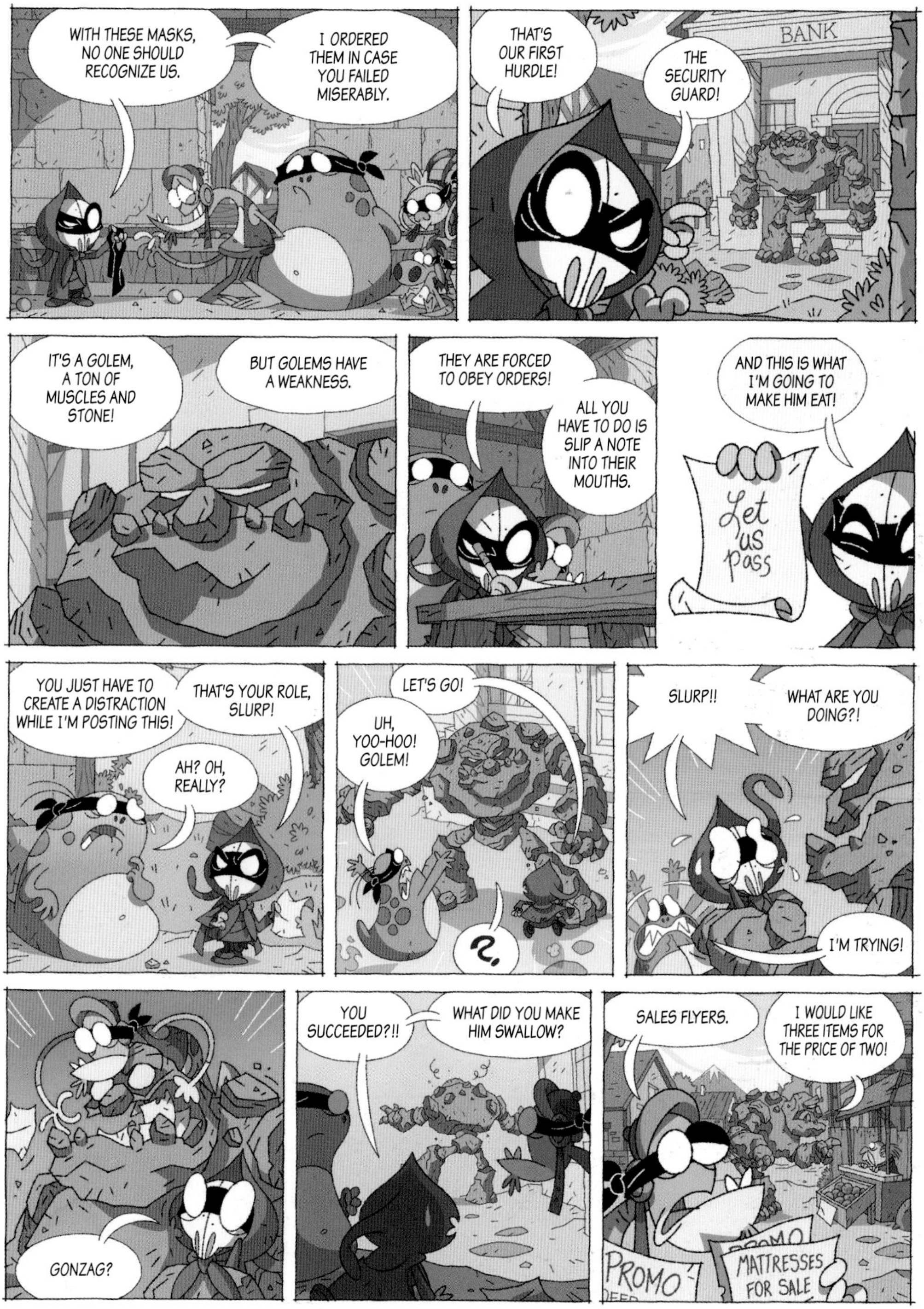
WITH THESE MASKS, NO ONE SHOULD RECOGNIZE US.
I ORDERED THEM IN CASE YOU FAILED MISERABLY.
BANK
THAT'S OUR FIRST HURDLE!
THE SECURITY GUARD!
IT'S A GOLEM, A TON OF MUSCLES AND STONE!
BUT GOLEMS HAVE A WEAKNESS.
THEY ARE FORCED TO OBEY ORDERS!
ALL YOU HAVE TO DO IS SLIP A NOTE INTO THEIR MOUTHS.
AND THIS IS WHAT I'M GOING TO MAKE HIM EAT!
Let us pass
YOU JUST HAVE TO CREATE A DISTRACTION WHILE I'M POSTING THIS!
THAT'S YOUR ROLE, SLURP!
AH? OH, REALLY?
LET'S GO!
UH, YOO-HOO! GOLEM!
?
SLURP!!
WHAT ARE YOU DOING?!
I'M TRYING!
GONZAG?
YOU SUCCEEDED?!!
WHAT DID YOU MAKE HIM SWALLOW?
SALES FLYERS.
I WOULD LIKE THREE ITEMS FOR THE PRICE OF TWO!
PROMO
PROMO
MATTRESSES FOR SALE
CED-MORIN

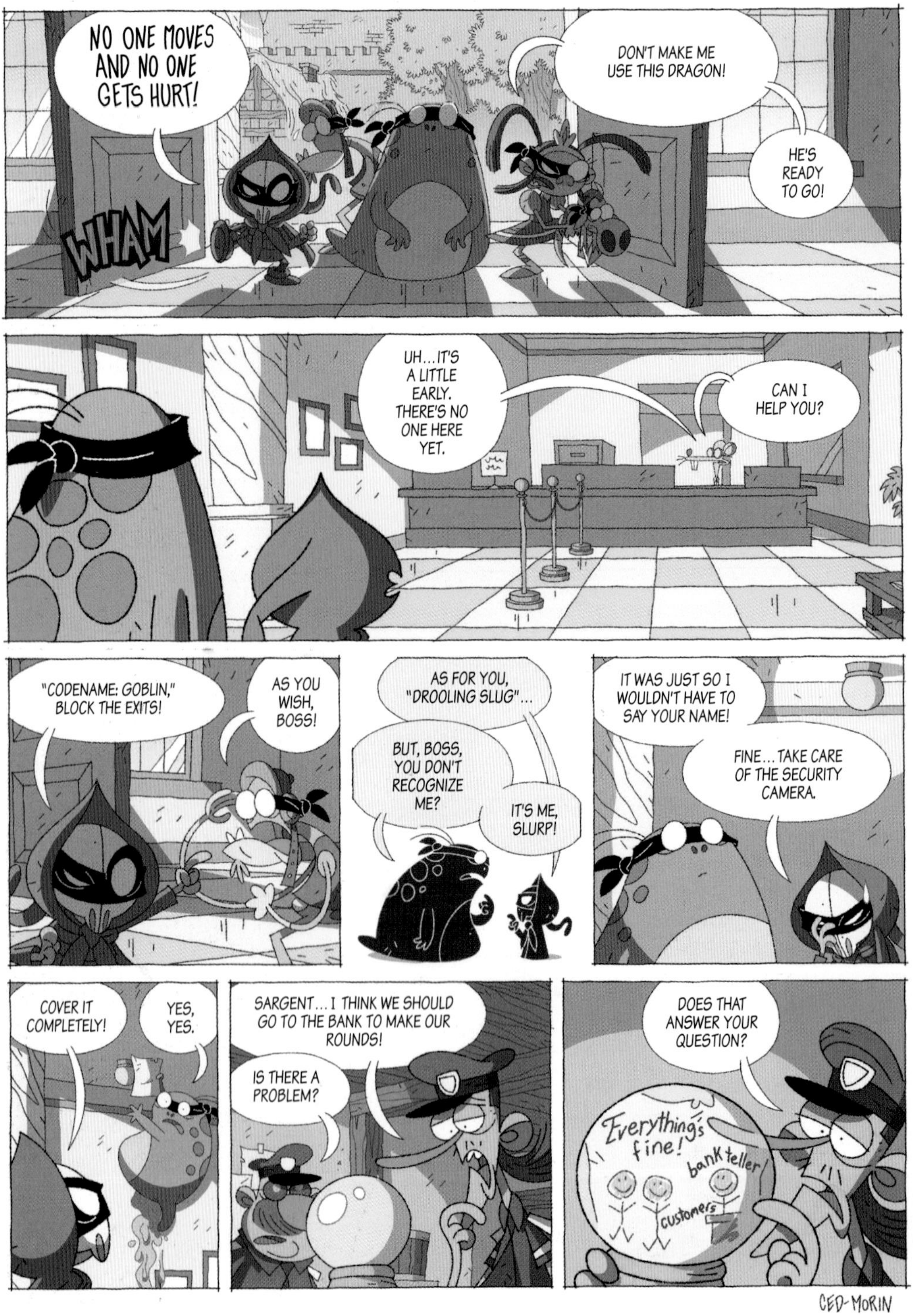
NO ONE MOVES AND NO ONE GETS HURT!
WHAM
DON'T MAKE ME USE THIS DRAGON!
HE'S READY TO GO!
UH... IT'S A LITTLE EARLY. THERE'S NO ONE HERE YET.
CAN I HELP YOU?
"CODENAME: GOBLIN," BLOCK THE EXITS!
AS YOU WISH, BOSS!
AS FOR YOU, "DROOLING SLUG"...
BUT, BOSS, YOU DON'T RECOGNIZE ME?
IT'S ME, SLURP!
IT WAS JUST SO I WOULDN'T HAVE TO SAY YOUR NAME!
FINE... TAKE CARE OF THE SECURITY CAMERA.
COVER IT COMPLETELY!
YES, YES.
SARGENT... I THINK WE SHOULD GO TO THE BANK TO MAKE OUR ROUNDS!
IS THERE A PROBLEM?
DOES THAT ANSWER YOUR QUESTION?
Everything's fine!
bank teller
customers
CED-MORIN

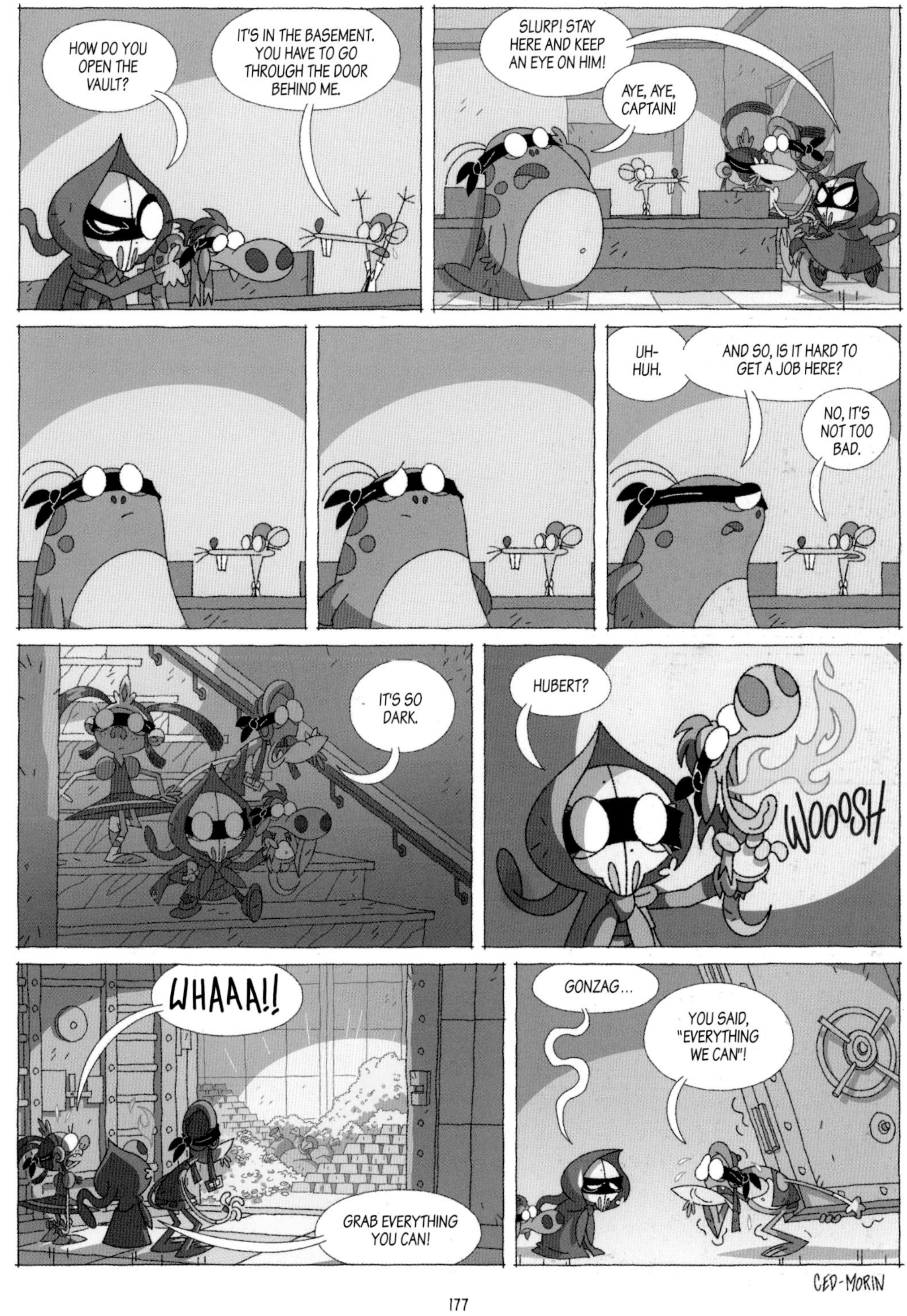
HOW DO YOU OPEN THE VAULT?
IT'S IN THE BASEMENT. YOU HAVE TO GO THROUGH THE DOOR BEHIND ME.
SLURP! STAY HERE AND KEEP AN EYE ON HIM!
AYE, AYE, CAPTAIN!
UH-HUH.
AND SO, IS IT HARD TO GET A JOB HERE?
NO, IT'S NOT TOO BAD.
IT'S SO DARK.
HUBERT?
WOOOSH
WHAAA!!
GRAB EVERYTHING YOU CAN!
GONZAG...
YOU SAID, "EVERYTHING WE CAN"!
CED-MORIN

PHEW! FINALLY, IT'S DONE!

YOU DIDN'T HAVE TO CLEAN UP!

IT'S THE LEAST WE CAN DO!

I'M GOING TO DO THE WINDOWS NOW!

OH!

HEY, DOWNSTAIRS! WE HAVE A PROBLEM!

WHAT'S GOING ON, SLURP?!

THE ARMY IS HERE! THEIR TANK HAS JUST STOPPED IN FRONT OF THE BANK!

OH NO!

WE STILL HAVE A LITTLE TIME TO GET AWAY! IS THE DOOR WELL BARRICADED?

UH... THE DOOR, YES...

BUT I MAY HAVE OPENED THE WINDOWS TO CLEAN THEM!

COME WITH US. WE WILL FIND ANOTHER EXIT!

YES, BUT THEY ARE VERY CLOSE!

HOW CLOSE?

LIKE, VERY, VERY CLOSE!

CED-MORIN

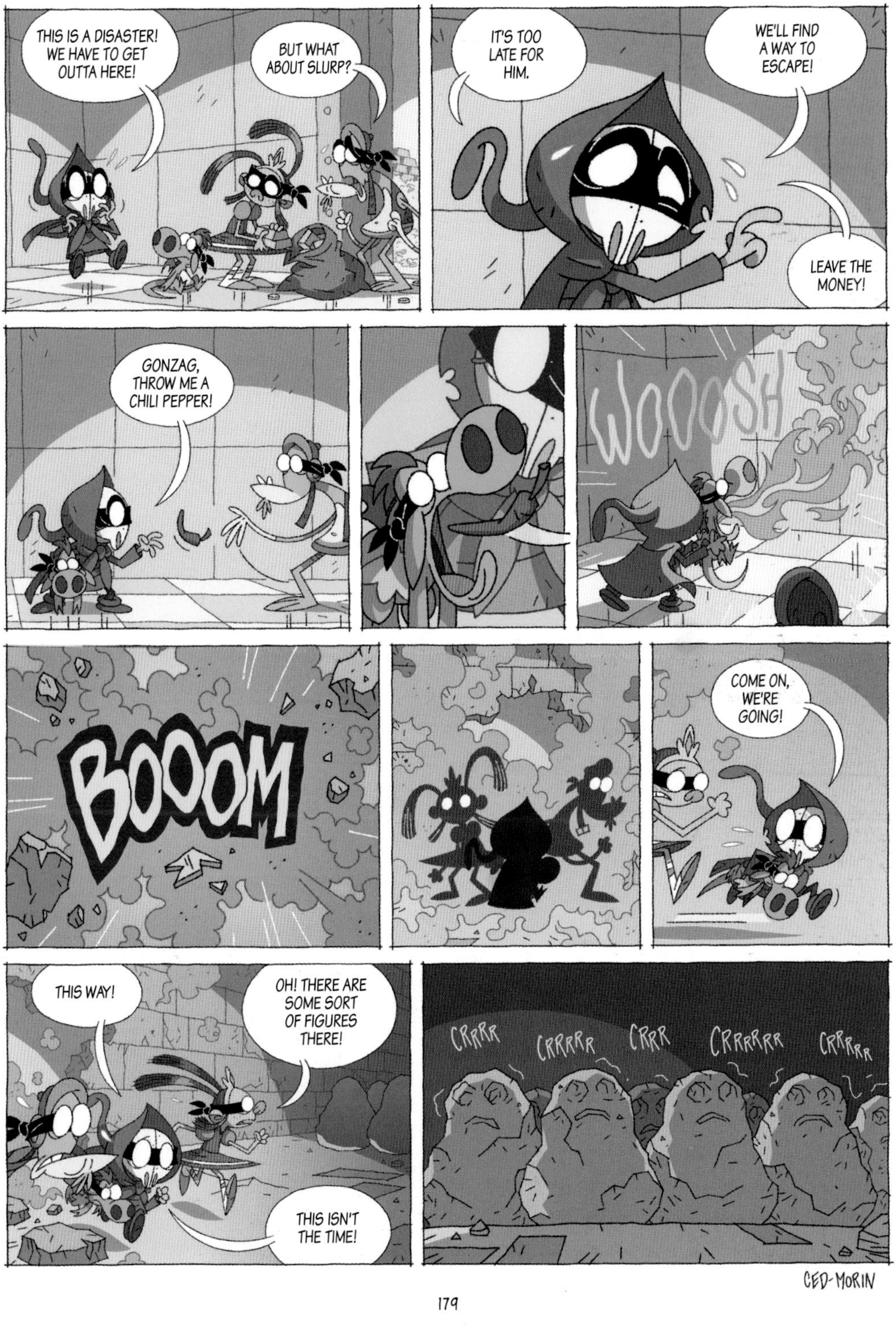
THIS IS A DISASTER! WE HAVE TO GET OUTTA HERE!
BUT WHAT ABOUT SLURP?
IT'S TOO LATE FOR HIM.
WE'LL FIND A WAY TO ESCAPE!
LEAVE THE MONEY!
GONZAG, THROW ME A CHILI PEPPER!
WOOOSH
BOOOM
COME ON, WE'RE GOING!
THIS WAY!
OH! THERE ARE SOME SORT OF FIGURES THERE!
THIS ISN'T THE TIME!
CRRRR
CRRRRR
CRRR
CRRRRRR
CRRRRR
CED-MORIN

THESE CORRIDORS ARE ENDLESS!

OH! WE ARE IN THE BASEMENT OF STEARAS'S CASTLE!

YOU RECOGNIZE THE BUILDING?

NO, I SEE THE LEFTOVERS OF THE GIANT PAELLA WE MADE.

WE SHOULD TOSS IT OUT SOME DAY.

THE HYGIENE CONDITIONS HAVE NOT IMPROVED HERE...

HEY! THE GROUND IS MOVING!

AAAAH! RATS!

BE CAREFUL OF MY TAIL!

EEEK! IT LOOKS LIKE THE SEWERS ARE OVERFLOWING!

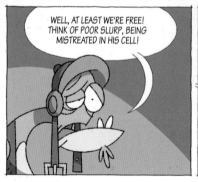

WELL, AT LEAST WE'RE FREE! THINK OF POOR SLURP, BEING MISTREATED IN HIS CELL!

PRISONER, DO YOU WANT ANOTHER MEAL TRAY?

IF IT'S AWRIGHT WICHYOU!

CED-MORIN

WELL, NOW YOU'RE GOING TO ANSWER A FEW QUESTIONS!

WHAT? AGAIN?

DO YOU WANT US TO CALL YOU A LAWYER?

WAIT, I HAVEN'T FINISHED MY WATERMELON.

THEN I HAVE TO FINISH MY AVOCADO!

COME CLEAN!

TELL US WHO YOUR ACCOMPLICES ARE!

DO YOU KNOW WHERE THEY'RE HIDING?

UH... I DO NOT KNOW THE ANSWER.

AND DO YOU KNOW WHY THEY LEFT YOU BEHIND?

UMM... I'M NOT SURE I KNOW.

ARE YOU PLAYING WITH US?

NO... OH, DARN! I LOST!

YOUR TURN! SO, UM... WHAT IS YOUR FAVORITE PET?

HUH? WHAT ARE YOU TALKING ABOUT?

OH, WE WEREN'T PLAYING "TWENTY QUESTIONS"?

WHAT DO YOU THINK?

HE'S TOUGH, VERY TOUGH ...

WELL, SHOULD WE TRY AGAIN WITH "GOOD COP, BAD COP"?

THIS TIME I WILL BE THE BAD COP.

WEREN'T YOU THE BAD COP BEFORE?

NO! I WAS THE GOOD COP. THAT'S WHY I GAVE HIM FOOD!

AAH! BUT I DID, TOO! HA! I THOUGHT I WAS THE GOOD COP!

HA! THAT'S WHY I LOVE WORKING WITH YOU, TERRY!

YES, WE MAKE A GOOD TEAM!

CED-MORIN

HUFF! HUFF!

IT'S GOOD WE WEREN'T FOLLOWED!

SURPRISE!

HAPPY HOLDUP

YOU PLANNED A POST-BURGLARY PARTY?

LOOK! I MADE CHOCOLATE COINS!

AND I MADE A CAKE SHAPED LIKE A SAFE!

SO, HOW DID IT GO?

IT WAS A DISASTER!

WE DIDN'T STEAL ANYTHING, WE ALMOST GOT ARRESTED, AND WE LOST ...

SLURP!

WE WERE SO WORR—

SPLAT

OH YES, AND I MADE A PIÑATA THAT LOOKS LIKE YOUR FRIEND.

182

CED-MORIN

WHAT ARE WE GOING TO DO TO SAVE SLURP?

NOTHING.

NOTHING?

THINK ABOUT IT! WHO PUT US IN THIS SITUATION?

WITH THE GOLEM, THE CRYSTAL BALL, THE OPEN WINDOWS...

EVERYTHING WAS HIS FAULT!

SLURP IS USELESS. THAT'S NOTHING NEW!

YEAH, WELL, THAT WAS TOO MUCH USELESSNESS!

AS A RESULT: WE DON'T HAVE MONEY TO PAY FOR SOLDIERS!

NO ARMY! NO WORLD CONQUEST!

AND IT'S ALL THE FAULT OF THIS...UGH! I DON'T EVEN KNOW WHAT HE IS!

HEY, THERE.

I'M BACK.

SLURP!

WE'RE SO HAPPY YOU'RE BACK!

UMM...HAVE YOU BEEN HERE FOR A LONG TIME?

NO, I JUST GOT HERE.

AH.

CED-MORIN

CRrrr Crrrrr CRrr CRrrrrr CRrrrr

CRACK CRACK CRACK

CRACK

WAKE UP, MY BROTHERS AND SISTERS!

THOSE WHO HAVE AWAKENED CAN HELP OTHERS BREAK OUT OF THEIR SHELLS.

COMMANDER, WE ARE READY. WHAT ARE THE ORDERS?

IT IS OUR MASTER STEARAS WHO WILL GIVE US OUR ORDERS. LET'S JOIN HIM!

WHY WERE WE AWAKENED?

SOMEONE CHANGED THE TEMPERATURE IN THE HIBERNATION CHAMBER.

STEARAS MUST BE SUMMONING US.

NOW WHAT DO WE DO?

WHAT WE WERE CREATED FOR...

...DESTROY THE WORLD!

CED-MORIN

VERY WELL...

STEARAS ISN'T MUCH OF A HOUSEKEEPER.

THAT'S NOT THE PROBLEM...

OUR MASTER IS NOT HERE. THE PLACE HAS BEEN DESERTED FOR A LONG TIME...

WE WERE AWAKENED TOO LATE...

WHAT DO WE DO, THEN?

HMMM... TAKE TWO SOLDIERS WITH YOU AND LOOK AROUND.

THE MORE WE KNOW ABOUT THIS WORLD, THE BETTER WE CAN DESTROY IT.

AS YOU COMMAND!

COMMANDER, HERE IS THE PROTOTYPE ARMOR YOU ASKED US FOR...

PERFECT! IT PROTECTS AND AT THE SAME TIME ALLOWS US TO STICK TO THE WALLS AND...

WAIT... WHAT IS THAT SMELL?

GUYS, STOP USING THE METAL FROM THE PAELLA DISH!

THE COMMANDER THINKS WE WILL BE TRACKED BY THE SMELL OF ROTTEN FISH.

CED-MORIN

SO I THOUGHT, WHAT IF WE WENT THROUGH THE ROOF?

HERE'S THE PLAN...

HELLO, EVERYBODY!

THERE'S SLURP.

BE QUIET!

WHAT ARE YOU DOING?

WE'RE...

MAKING PANCAKES, THAT'S IT!

BUT YOU DON'T HAVE ANY FLOUR.

OR MILK.

BESIDES, YOU'RE NOT EVEN IN THE KITCHEN...

HEY! YOU WOULDN'T BE PUTTING TOGETHER AN EVIL PLAN WITHOUT ME, WOULD YOU?

LISTEN, SLURP. FOR ONCE, WE WOULD LIKE A PLAN TO WORK.

YOU WILL BE INCLUDED WHEN WE PLAN THE NEXT ONE.

OKAY, OKAY ...

HI!

AND WHO IS HE?

THAT'S RICARDO, THE PIZZA DELIVERY MAN, BUT WE LET HIM STAY. HE HAS GOOD IDEAS.

RICARDO, RICARDO... MY REPLACEMENT, NO DOUBT!

THE MESSAGE SEEMS VERY CLEAR...

AAAAAHH

CED-MORIN

COMMANDER, I'VE JUST RETURNED FROM THE RECONNAISSANCE MISSION.

CONCLUSION: WE SLEPT FOR 200 YEARS.

THE KINGDOM HAS ALMOST NO ARMY, NO HEROES, NO WIZARD WORTHY OF THE NAME.

AND OVERALL, THE PEOPLE ARE HORRID.

THEN...

WE ATTACK!

FOLLOW ME, PROUD SLUG SOLDIERS! LET'S REDUCE THIS WORLD TO DUST!

OFFICERS, HERE IS THE DESCRIPTION OF THE SUSPECT.

POLICE STATION

REMEMBER, HE MANAGED TO ESCAPE USING... UH, CUNNING.

ANY QUESTIONS?

WANTED

IS THIS INDIVIDUAL WEARING ARMOR, DESTROYING THE CITY, AND SMELLING LIKE BAD SHRIMP?

ALSO, IS THERE MORE THAN ONE HUNDRED OF HIM?

NEGATIVE. ANYTHING ELSE, OFFICER?

IN THAT CASE, CAN I CLOSE THE CURTAINS?

THANK YOU. THE NOISE OUTSIDE IS DISTRACTING.

LET'S RESUME.

CED-MORIN

AND SO, IF WE FOLLOW OUR PLAN, THE WEATHER IS DRY, AND IT HAPPENS ON A WEDNESDAY...

...WE SHOULD SUCCEED IN BECOMING MASTERS OF THE WORLD!

INDEED, IT CAN'T FAIL!

WE FINALLY HAVE THE PERFECT PLAN!

KNOCK KNOCK

AND NO ONE CAN STOP ME!

THE KING?!

FATHER?

SIRE, HOW CAN I BE AT YOUR SERVICE?

THEY'RE THE ONES I CAME TO SEE!

HOW DID YOU KNOW WHERE TO FIND US?

I ALWAYS KEEP AN EYE ON YOU.

THE CITY IS BESIEGED BY AN ARMY OF SLUG SOLDIERS! WE NEED YOU TO STOP THEM!

YOU...ARE ASKING ME TO ACT AS A HERO?

OF COURSE. YOU HAVE DEFEATED STEARAS AND THE DEMON OF THE FORBIDDEN FOREST.

I...I'M GOING TO BE SICK...

PLUS, WE HAVE OUR OWN SLUG EXPERT, DON'T WE...

...SLURP?

CED-MORIN

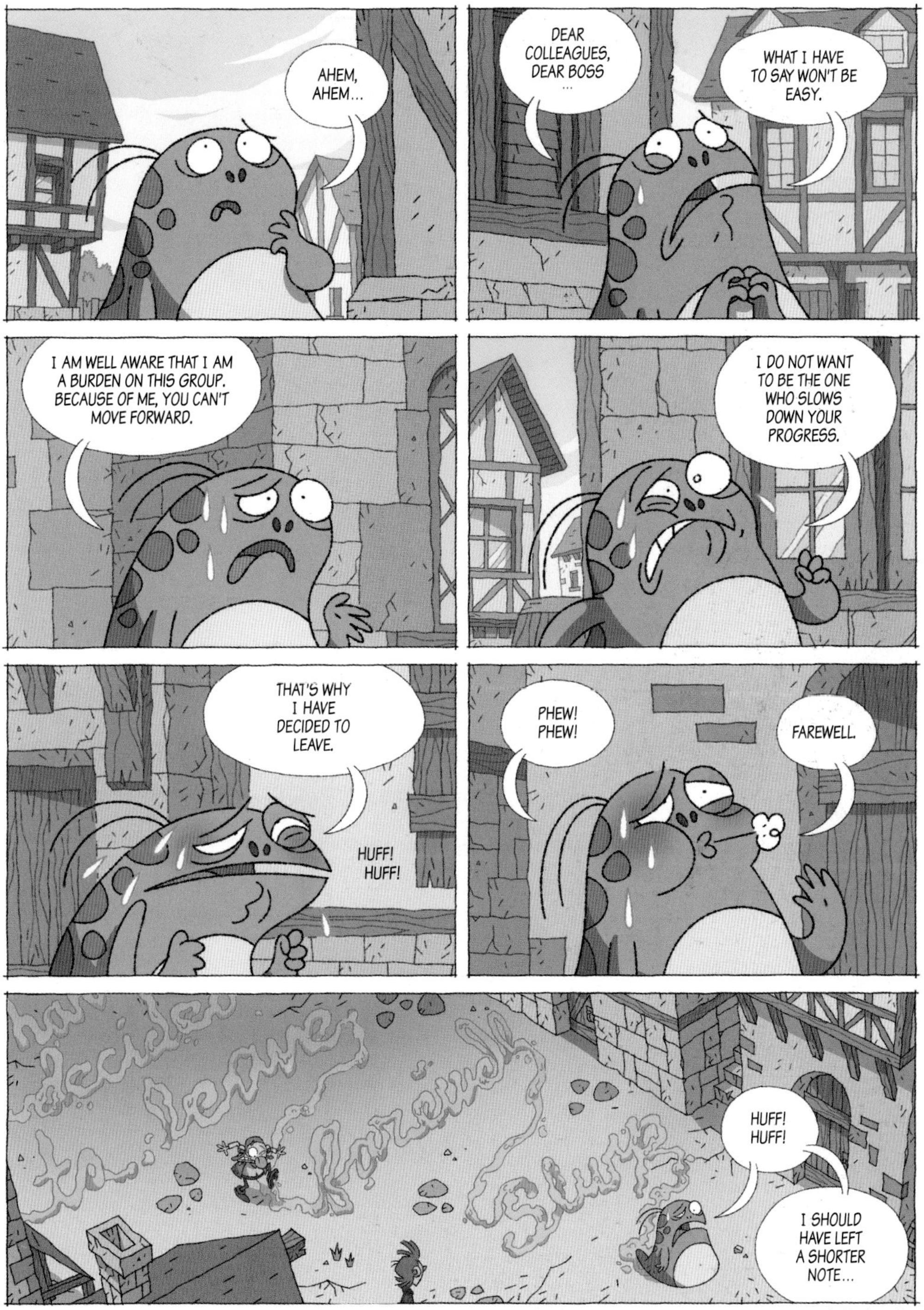
AHEM, AHEM…
DEAR COLLEAGUES, DEAR BOSS …
WHAT I HAVE TO SAY WON'T BE EASY.
I AM WELL AWARE THAT I AM A BURDEN ON THIS GROUP. BECAUSE OF ME, YOU CAN'T MOVE FORWARD.
I DO NOT WANT TO BE THE ONE WHO SLOWS DOWN YOUR PROGRESS.
THAT'S WHY I HAVE DECIDED TO LEAVE.
HUFF! HUFF!
PHEW! PHEW!
FAREWELL.
HUFF! HUFF!
I SHOULD HAVE LEFT A SHORTER NOTE…

CED-MORIN

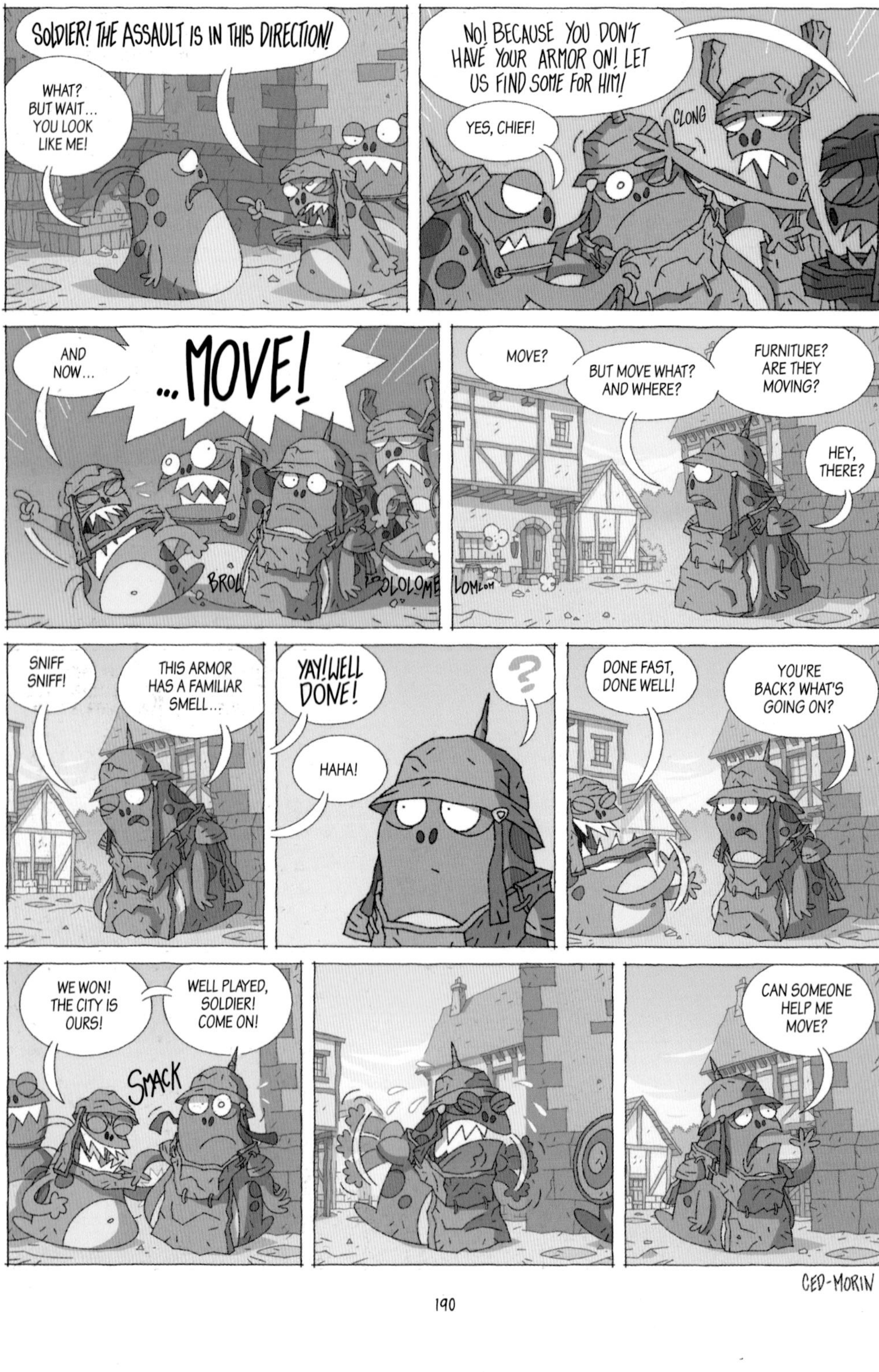
SOLDIER! THE ASSAULT IS IN THIS DIRECTION!
WHAT? BUT WAIT... YOU LOOK LIKE ME!
NO! BECAUSE YOU DON'T HAVE YOUR ARMOR ON! LET US FIND SOME FOR HIM!
YES, CHIEF!
CLONG
AND NOW...
...MOVE!
BROL
BOLOLOMB
LOMLOM
MOVE?
BUT MOVE WHAT? AND WHERE?
FURNITURE? ARE THEY MOVING?
HEY, THERE?
SNIFF SNIFF!
THIS ARMOR HAS A FAMILIAR SMELL...
YAY! WELL DONE!
HAHA!
?
DONE FAST, DONE WELL!
YOU'RE BACK? WHAT'S GOING ON?
WE WON! THE CITY IS OURS!
WELL PLAYED, SOLDIER! COME ON!
SMACK
CAN SOMEONE HELP ME MOVE?
CED-MORIN

DAD, I'M COUNTING ON YOU TO HIDE THE KING.

BE CAREFUL, MY LITTLE ONE.

SO, HERE WE GO TO SAVE THE WORLD!

AGAIN...

LET ME BE CLEAR, I'M ONLY DOING THIS SO THERE WILL STILL BE A WORLD TO CONQUER.

OF COURSE, OF COURSE...

WHERE DID THEY ALL GO?

THE SLUGS ATTACKED THE WHOLE CITY WHEN THEY FOUND THE ROYAL PALACE EMPTY. THEY MUST HAVE THOUGHT THEY WON.

ACCORDING TO YOUR FATHER, THEY WENT INTO THE TERRIBLE TOWER.

AND WE'RE ON OUR WAY...WITH A PLAN?

THESE SOLDIERS MAY BE OF THE SAME KIND AS SLURP. THAT SHOULD HELP US.

I HOPE HE'S OKAY!

LET'S SEE, WHAT ARE SLURP'S WEAKNESSES?

LET'S LIST HIS STRENGTHS. THAT'LL SAVE US TIME...

HE BECOMES LIQUID WHEN HE GETS SCARED!

I DOUBT WE CAN SCARE 300 BLOODTHIRSTY SOLDIERS.

THE COLD SEEMED TO SOLIDIFY HIM, REMEMBER, AT THE SNOWMAN'S HOUSE?

HMMM...AND NOW WE HAVE TO FIGURE OUT HOW TO INFILTRATE THE TOWER...

BY BEING TAKEN PRISONER! THAT'S A GREAT PLAN!

THAT'S IT. EXACTLY AS EXPECTED...

CED-MORIN

THE RENOVATION OF THE TOWER IS PROGRESSING WELL, COMMANDER.

SO MUCH THE BETTER! THE WORLD MUST KNOW THAT THE SLUGS ARE IN CHARGE!

CHIEF! WE DISCOVERED A SOMEWHAT PECULIAR BROTHER.

HIS NAME IS SLURP, AND HE HASN'T SLEPT FOR THE LAST 200 YEARS!

WELL, I SLEPT, BUT LIKE EVERYONE ELSE, BARELY FIFTEEN TO SIXTEEN HOURS A NIGHT...

JUST THINK OF ALL THE INFORMATION HE HAS!

HMMM...

IT WILL BE VERY USEFUL TO CONQUER THE PLANET!

BRING IN THE GROUP OF PRISONERS.

LET GO OF ME, YOU BUNCH OF SLIMY CREATURES!

SLURP!!!

THAT'S WHAT I THOUGHT! WE WERE INFORMED THAT A GROUP OF HEROES HAD BEATEN STEARAS ON HIS RETURN.

AND THAT AMONG THEM THERE WAS A SLUG NAMED SLURP.

THAT'S RIGHT. A GROUP OF HEROES. HMPH!

IT'S TIME TO CHOOSE, SLURP. WHO ARE YOU WITH, THEM OR US?

...

SORRY, BUT SLUGS ARE MY REAL FAMILY.

BUDDY?

IT'S SO DIABOLICAL, I WOULD BE THRILLED BY IT IF IT WEREN'T DIRECTED AT ME...

CED-MORIN

YOU STILL HAVE TO PROVE YOURSELF, SOLDIER SLURP. WHAT CAN YOU TELL US THAT WILL HELP US DOMINATE THE WORLD?

IN ONE OF THE ROOMS OF THIS TOWER, THERE IS A MAGIC PORTAL THAT ALLOWS YOU TO TRAVEL TO ANY PLACE YOU WANT.

SLURP! NO!!!

...

PERFECT! LET'S GO AND FIND THIS PORTAL!

CALL ALL THE TROOPS! WE WILL CONQUER A NEW KINGDOM!!

HERE'S THE PORTAL, COMMANDER!

HOW DOES IT WORK?

JUST THINK OF A DESTINATION AND TOUCH THE PORTAL...

HAVE PITY! DON'T INVADE MIDGARD! IT'S A VERY SMALL COUNTRY THAT I KEPT TO MYSELF!

SO THEN, MIDGARD IT WILL BE!

SOLDIERS! ADVANCE!

SLOOP

WELL DONE, SLURP! I KNEW YOU WOULDN'T LET US DOWN!

IT WAS NOTHING, BOSS!

WHAT?

HE JUST DELIVERED THE WORLD TO THEM ON A PLATTER!

MIDGARD IS THE COLDEST COUNTRY IN THE WORLD, PRINCESS...

THEY'LL BE THERE FOR A LONG, LONG HIBERNATION!

?

CED-MORIN

193

AND YOU WERE ON OUR SIDE SINCE THE BEGINNING?

I TOLD MYSELF THAT FOR ONCE, I WOULD BE USEFUL.

YOU'RE VERY USEFUL, SLURP!

I'VE BEEN CRUEL TO YOU. I APOLOGIZE...

LET'S FORGET IT, BOSS. YOU ARE RIGHT. I AM TERRIBLE AT DOING EVIL.

WE'RE ALL TERRIBLE AT IT! I CAN GUARANTEE YOU THAT!

IN ANY CASE, I'M VERY HAPPY THAT EVERYTHING HAS WORKED OU—

HELP!!!

THAT'S COMING FROM INSIDE!

OUR DADS ARE INSIDE!

AND SO AM I!

WHAT WERE YOU THINKING? I HAD TO STAY BEHIND TO REACTIVATE THE PORTAL!

WHEN I UNDERSTOOD YOUR PLOY, I HID AND FOLLOWED YOU.

NOW YOU WILL GO GET MY SOLDIERS!

CANDY! DON'T DO IT!

WAIT... YOUR FIRST NAME IS "CANDY"?

YES.

AH AH AH AH AH AH AH AH AH AH

CAN WE FOCUS, PLEASE?!

CED-MORIN

SURELY YOU'RE NOT GOING TO SACRIFICE YOUR FATHER OR YOUR KING, CANDY!

DO WHAT I ASK YOU, OR THEY'LL GET IT!

BEFORE I DO, I'D LIKE TO TELL A LITTLE STORY.

SOME TIME AGO, I BOUGHT AN OLD SPELL BOOK AT THE MARKET.

LONG STORY SHORT, WITH THESE TWO, I FOUND A BABY DRAGON TO ENCHANT.

AND WHILE I BLAMED OTHERS FOR MY FAILURES, THE TRUTH IS...

...WE WOULD'VE BEEN UNSTOPPABLE IF I WAS ABLE TO CAST EVEN THE SMALLEST SPELL.

WELL, YOU KNOW WHAT?

I'VE IMPROVED.

195

CED-MORIN

OH.

RWAAAAR

AAAAH!

SPLOSH

HE LIQUEFIED!

YOU WEREN'T AFRAID?

OF OUR HUBERT? NEVER!

POOF

FLAP FLAP

HUBERT BECAME A BABY AGAIN?

I ONLY KNOW HOW TO DO SHORT SPELLS...

BUT THEN AGAIN, WHO WOULD WANT A MONSTROUS DRAGON, WHEN A BABY DRAGON IS SO ADORABLE?

CED·MORIN

CANDY!

MAEVA!

GONZAG!

DAD...

ONCE AGAIN, YOU HAVE SAVED THE KINGDOM.

I KNOW... YOU DON'T HAVE TO REMIND ME...

I CAN'T THANK YOU ENOUGH FOR ALL THE GOOD YOU'VE DONE FOR THIS COUNTRY.

PLEASE STOP!

YOU CAN ACCOMPLISH ANYTHING YOU WANT. YOU HAVE KINDNESS IN YOUR HEART.

ONE DAY WE'LL HAVE TO FIGURE THAT OUT, WON'T WE?

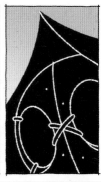

EMPLOY-MENT AGENCY

HUMM HUMM HUMM!

OPEN

DUM DEE DUM!

KRRRR

HELLO!

OH, IT'S YOU!

I ALMOST DIDN'T RECOGNIZE YOU!

LUCKILY I SAW YOUR LOGO THERE.

I HAVE TO FIND YOUR FILE.

HERE IT IS! HMM... YOU KNOW, THERE HAVEN'T BEEN TOO MANY JOB APPLICANTS IN YOUR FIELD...

WHAT WAS IT AGAIN?

OH, YES!

"LORD OF DARKNESS," RIGHT?

NO.

THIS TIME, WE'VE COME TO FIND JOBS AS HEROES!

CLOSED

NEWS

The End

CED-MORIN

CED, Cédric Asna, studied graphic arts in Toulouse, France, before going on to work as a graphic designer. He collaborates as a writer for various comics (*Rikk & Frya, Lolicornes, Marvelouze...*) at the same time continues to lead his own projects (*Un An sans Internet, Wikpanda, Sherlock Holmes*). Since 2015, he has been published monthly in the review *Mordelure* and regularly in the magazine *Spirou*. In February 2021, his first young adult novel *Noé et les animals très dérangés* was published. Currently, he lives in Toulouse and divides his time between his improv theatre troupe (trio-dimpro.fr) and his comic strips.

Jean-Philippe Morin is a Quebec designer and animator, publishing with Vents d'Ouest, Glénat and in the weekly magazine *Spirou*.